Praise for *What She's Hiding*

"If you love a dark, stylish thriller with a wicked sense of humor, *What She's Hiding* by Art Bell is for you. With memorable characters, a noirish New York City setting, and a story that cuts like a knife, this novel will keep you reading until the wee hours. I highly recommend it!"
—DOUGLAS PRESTON, coauthor with Lincoln Child of the famed #1 *New York Times* bestselling Pendergast series

"A rollicking fun thriller, both action-packed and hilarious. A smashing debut that managed to reel me in from the very first page."
—TESS GERRITSEN, *New York Times* bestselling author of The Martini Club series

"Stolen gems, death threats, angry exes with axes to grind, Russian mobsters, and private eyes all come together in Art Bell's terrific *What She's Hiding*, a raucous, twisty, dangerous, and often hilarious trip through NYC's under, and over, world."
—JON LINDSTROM, *USA Today* bestselling author of *w Hustle*

"A darkly funny and twisty thriller that's at once vividly contemporary and reminiscent of hard-boiled Manhattan crime tales of a bygone era. If you're looking for suspense and smarts, you won't regret riding this roller-coaster of a novel.
—KAREN DUKESS, author of *Welcome to Murder Week* and *The Last Book Party*

"Intrigue, deception, and wit sizzle in *What She's Hiding*. With self-deprecating humor and a nod to classic noir style, Art Bell has crafted a thriller perfect for fans of *Suits* and *Moonlighting*."
—SARA DIVELLO, author of *Broadway Butterfly: A Thriller*

"A mysterious ex-wife, a Russian mobster, and a missing ring all add up to a satisfying romp through New York City in Art Bell's *What She's Hiding*. This noir thriller doles out laughs with a hard-boiled edge and keeps you guessing until the very end."
—PAMELA STATZ, author of *Thorn City*

What She's Hiding is an action thriller that will leave any enthusiast panting. This book is for an out-and-out lover of thrillers, especially for those who like it full of twists and turns."
—*SUSPENSE MAGAZINE*

WHAT SHE'S HIDING

A Thriller

Also by Art Bell:

Constant Comedy: How I Started Comedy Central and Lost My Sense of Humor

WHAT SHE'S HIDING

A Thriller

ART BELL

Published by:
ULYSSES PRESS
PO Box 3440
Berkeley, CA 94703
www.ulyssespress.com

ISBN: 978-1-64604-751-2
Library of Congress Control Number: 2024944973

Printed in Canada
10 9 8 7 6 5 4 3 2 1

Project editor: Brian McLendon
Managing editor: Claire Chun
Copy editor: Nina Bodway
Proofreader: Renee Rutledge
Layout: Winnie Liu
Graphics: page 156 emoji © SEJWAL123/shutterstock.com; page 196 hearts © Vectorbro/shutterstock.com

Disclaimer: This novel is a work of fiction. All the characters and events portrayed in this book are fictitious and any resemblance or similarity to any real person, living or deceased, or any real event is purely coincidental.

For Carrie, Thea, and Julia

CHAPTER 1

My cell phone buzzed just as I entered the building where the offices of Loveless, Brown & Cunningham, Attorneys at Law, occupied the thirty-third, thirty-fourth, and thirty-fifth floors. I was sweating through my shirt even though the thermometer hadn't quite reached eighty. By noon it would hit the projected high of ninety-four. New York City heated up fast in August.

"Gary, how are you?" I asked, even though I had a pretty good idea. "And how the hell did you get my cell phone number?"

"I just, I dunno—" he said. Then Gary began crying.

"Gary," I said, "get a hold of yourself and tell me what's wrong."

I hustled to the waiting elevator, phone pressed against my ear, but the doors closed before I could get in. A woman walked past me and pushed the elevator button, saving me the trouble. It would be less than a minute before the next one showed up. Hopefully, the phone call wouldn't take that long.

The sound of snuffling was followed by silence, then more snuffling. "Henry, you gotta keep me out of prison."

I rolled my eyes. "We talked about this, Gary." About a thousand times. "I got you out on bail, didn't I? And seeing as how you stole twenty million dollars from forty unwitting marks, it's a miracle you're not manacled to a dungeon wall at Rikers Island." The woman standing next to me shot me a look. I mouthed, "Sorry," and moved to a corner of the elevator bank.

Gary started yelling. "A million dollars bail, and I put up, what, a couple hundred thousand I'll never see again?" He snorted. "A lawyer with a mail-order degree could've pulled that off. Besides, like I told you, I made a few mistakes, but I was trying to make it good, give back the money. I already made some of the investors whole."

"I know you did." I also knew he made them whole with new investor money. Classic Ponzi scheme. "Doesn't matter. The DA says you stole twenty million dollars from clients. And trying to leave the country before your arrest was not a point in your favor."

"You think I'm guilty?"

I ignored the question. My job was to represent him in court, not worry whether or not he was guilty. Which he was.

"I'm still working on a plea deal. You plead guilty, you do maybe five years, possibility of parole after three."

"Why not community service? Or house arrest? Slap on the wrist stuff like the politicians get?"

"Gary, you're the client, so I'll do it your way. But do you really wanna take your chances with a jury? Three to five years against twenty? I know what I'd do."

"I can't do prison time. If I'm sentenced to prison, I'll kill myself." He choked up again. "I mean it." This wasn't the first time I'd heard that from a client.

"Listen to me," I said in my most soothing voice, "I know guys who did time and got through it just fine. They worked in the prison library, avoided the gangs, and figured out how to get by on the right side of the guards with a little palm grease. You'll be okay. Then you'll get out, put your life back together, maybe get on a dating app for ex-cons."

"Hey!"

"Sorry, that wasn't funny. But seriously, there are consultants who train guys like you for prison time and how to get through it.

Let me introduce you to a good one, see if the law firm will pick up the cost." I knew there was no chance of that, but I needed to toss him a life ring, or in this case, more like a two-by-four with a bent nail sticking out of it, but something. "So, should I keep working on the plea deal?"

Gary grunted. "Okay," he said. "Okay. Fuck, but okay."

I took the next elevator to the thirty-fourth floor and stepped into the lobby. "Morning, Mr. Gladstone," chirped the receptionist with a smile.

"Morning, Maggie," I replied as I glided past her to my office.

***

Nancy, my assistant, welcomed me with a cup of coffee, and I settled in behind my desk. Figuring that Gary's phone call was the big excitement for the day, I started reviewing a legal brief for another client.

An hour later, Nancy buzzed me. "Leslie Dunlop's in the lobby asking to see you. What do you want me to tell her?"

Several things occurred to me, none of them very nice. Instead, I said, "Give me ten minutes, then send her in." I needed to finish the brief I was working on, but that would take only five minutes. The other five minutes were for me to suppress my rage at her showing up out of the blue.

I thought back to that December morning when I'd asked what Leslie Dunlop wanted for our second wedding anniversary. Her answer: "A divorce." It shocked me, but I wasn't surprised. Because after two years of marriage, I'd assumed there was nothing Leslie could do that would surprise me. I witnessed her conversion to Buddhism on our trip to China; I watched from the grandstands the first time she drove a turbocharged Porsche around an oval track at

197 miles an hour; I was there when she punched a cop and then ran, leaving me to do the talking.

A few minutes after she'd asked for a divorce rather than a more conventional gift, Leslie got out of bed, threw on some clothes, stuffed her pocketbook with a change of underwear, and walked out the front door. "Don't try to find me."

I called her name as she walked out. She didn't turn around. She didn't even close the door when she left.

That was three years earlier, and I hadn't heard from her since.

My office door was closed, but the floor-to-ceiling glass wall gave me a chance to catch a glimpse of her in a summer skirt with pink flowers, a white blouse with an oversized collar, and an unbuttoned purple sweater with the sleeves pulled up. Still beautiful, I thought. My mouth was dry. I reached for the plastic bottle of water on my desk and continued looking at her while I drank. She didn't look at me. Whatever was on her cell phone must have been far more interesting. She shoved the phone into her pocketbook and walked into my office without knocking.

"Leslie," I said. "How distressing to see you." I stayed seated safely behind my desk, watching as she closed the door and, uninvited, settled into the chair in the corner of my office. She stared down at her purse and started latching and unlatching it, a nervous habit she'd developed right after we got married. The clicking of the latch always bothered me. Ordinarily, I would ask her to stop, but this time I had no intention of opening the conversation. She finally put her purse to the side, and the office was quiet except for the ticking of my desk clock.

"Henry, I don't know how else to say this, so I'll just say it. I need money. A lot of money, and if I don't get it …" She hesitated, looked down, and pushed a few stray strands of hair behind her right ear before looking up. "You'll help me, won't you?"

I thought back on the phone calls from my divorce lawyer telling me that Leslie had rejected our latest offer, that she wouldn't be satisfied until she took me for everything I owned. In the end, she'd gotten what she deserved, which was not much, but more than I cared to shell out given that our marriage didn't even make it past year two.

"You've got a lot of balls coming to me for help," I answered. "The answer's no. So, unless there's anything else …" I stood up, walked around my desk, and put my hand on the door handle.

"Please hear me out," she said. "After we separated—"

I interrupted. "You mean after you walked out."

"Yes. Okay. After I walked out, I—"

"Stop," I said. "I'm sure this is a terrific story but find someone else to tell it to. Great seeing you, Leslie. Let's not do it again soon, okay?" I opened the door.

"Henry, they threatened me. If I don't lay my hands on two hundred and fifty thousand dollars before next week, they said they'd kill me."

I stuck my head outside my office door and checked if anyone was near enough to hear what she'd said. I couldn't afford to feed this to the gossip machine and have it printed, bound, and distributed to the firm's partners. Bad for my career.

"Okay, Leslie, that's plenty." I cocked my thumb toward the hall. "Leave."

"Wait. You gotta listen to me," she pleaded. Then she let me have it. "They said they'd kill you, too."

I looked down both sides of the hallway. Mercifully, there was nobody close enough to hear what Leslie had just said. I closed the door and glared at her. "Two hundred fifty thousand dollars in a week, or we're both dead. Have I got this right?"

By saying it out loud, I expected Leslie to realize how ludicrous this little fable of hers sounded. Then she'd admit trying to scam me out of whatever money I had left after the divorce settlement. We'd share a laugh, and she'd leave my office and tell me I'd never see her again, just like the last time when she'd walked out saying she'd never see me again. Instead, she blew her nose with a tissue, then looked up at me, her magnificent eyes streaked with mascara, her eyebrows pleading, her face lovely enough to make it all work.

"Henry, you've got to believe me," she said through tears. "I've lied to you before, but this is true."

Her supplicating gaze followed me like a spotlight as I walked back to my desk and sat down.

"As much as I've enjoyed this, I think your visit is over," I said, gesturing toward the door.

"Henry, wait," she said. "I can prove it."

I looked at my watch. "I've got a meeting in ten minutes, and I need to hit the men's room first." I knew I would regret what I was about to say, but I said it anyway: "So you've got five minutes to prove it. This better be good." I leaned back in my chair and waited for the bullshit to start. She hesitated. I made a show of checking my watch. "Four minutes, thirty seconds," I said.

"Fuck you," she said. "You'll believe me when you're staring down the barrel of a gun wondering if you'll hear the shot that kills you."

I laughed. "Why, that's almost poetic. At least your grifter's patter is improving."

She stood up and walked out. This time she slammed the door.

CHAPTER 2

I was sure she was lying. From the day we first met, Leslie had excelled at deception. You wouldn't know by the looks of her—I certainly didn't—but she had the heart and soul of a high-end con artist. She was at her best playing the aggrieved party, the one the whole world has slighted, so you'd want to fold her in your arms, place her head on your shoulder, and whisper into her ear, "Don't worry, I'll protect you." Which is how she'd suckered me in shortly after we first met.

I'd been in my fifth year practicing law at Loveless, Brown & Cunningham, a distinguished white-shoe law firm in New York City. The hours had been crushing. Office politics hung in the air like the fog they used to spray from trucks in the summer to kill mosquitos. My social life was restricted to gazing longingly at one of the paralegals who inspired schoolboy crushes in all the male lawyers (and probably in some of the women lawyers, too). But based on the size of the engagement ring on her finger, someone would have to steal not only her heart but show up with a house in the Hamptons, a yacht, and enough money to bankroll the upkeep for both. She was engaged to a foreign-born financier twenty years her senior. Her name was Leslie Dunlop, and she'd started six months earlier. How did I know all this? My assistant. If you want to know anything about what goes on in a big law firm, check with the assistant network. It's like the internet, only with more information.

Since we'd never worked together on a case, the only times I'd see Leslie was when we happened to pass each other in the halls. A glimpse of her would linger in my mind for the rest of the day. Sometimes she piled her dark brown hair on top of her head, but usually she wore it down, past her shoulders, brushing the hollows above her collarbones. Her eyes, set wide on her face above cheekbones you could slice a finger on, were an alarming blue, but with a sadness about them capable of overruling her smile, should she choose to smile. And just below her lips was a cleft chin so subtle it looked as if someone had started to chisel the indentation only to abandon the project before it was complete.

For me, Leslie Dunlop was more than a crush.

All my life I'd had a knack for getting attractive women to fall for me. Not that I was particularly tall, or even considered classically good-looking. But I'd grown up on Long Island and had spent summers from the time I was thirteen working at the local yacht club. There was a guy there, Tony Metrano, who took me under his wing. Tony was seventeen, a ladies' man who'd decided he needed a boy Friday to help him work his way through the roster of wealthy, bored women in search of short-term companionship. He trusted me to deliver notes to his marks: the women who sat by the pool in their undersized two-piece bathing suits, sipping oversized frozen daiquiris that anesthetized them into forgetting about their kids, husbands, dogs, maids and Mercedes. They'd read the notes, smile, and slip me a buck or two as they whispered, "Tell Tony I'll be there in a few minutes," or something similar. "There" was a 28-foot sailboat with four berths below deck that was owned by the yacht club. It was Tony's responsibility to keep the boat clean and operational and to endlessly polish the hardware. The job came with a key so Tony could air out the cabin. The key was, well, the key.

Watching Tony operate, along with hearing his detailed stories of seduction and conquest, had been the education of a lifetime, and it served me well. I never hesitated to approach a woman I was interested in, and up until then, I never flinched if it didn't go my way. So, several years ago, when I found myself alone in the elevator with that lovely paralegal named Leslie, the one we all had crushes on, I said, "I've heard that Chinese place on Thirty-Ninth has the best fried pork dumplings this side of Hong Kong."

She smiled demurely, then used the next thirty seconds (the time it took the elevator to transport us thirty-seven floors to the lobby) to tell me all about her fiancé and why she wasn't interested in joining me for lunch. "But thanks for the tip," she said as the elevator doors opened. "I love a good dumpling."

As I watched her glide into the lobby, I found myself mesmerized by those lovely hips swaying lazily amidst the hubbub of the lunchtime throng. I wanted to call out to her. The elevator doors started to close, but before they did, I saw her turn and toss me a wink and a smile. She may have meant it as a consolation prize, but I took it as encouragement.

I shot my hand in front of the elevator door and followed her. My hope was that she'd enjoyed our conversation enough to have lunch with me despite her quick exit. Just as I was about to tap her on the shoulder, someone called my name. It was one of the senior partners, John Miller, who had a reputation for torturing the more junior lawyers at every opportunity. "Hey, Gladstone, hold up a second." He smiled at me as I turned to face him. "Plans this weekend?"

"Heading out to the Hamptons," I said, knowing that my weekend plans were about to be obliterated. "I have a share in a summer house, and it's …"

"Don't tell me," John said, cutting me off. "It's your weekend. Well I hope you can switch it with one of your housemates."

I spent the weekend in the office working on a nuisance lawsuit involving an off-brand toothpaste someone claimed caused cavities. There were plenty of other junior lawyers there that weekend but not many senior partners. I noticed a few paralegals roaming the halls and wondered if Leslie was in the office. Every time someone walked by my door, I looked up, hoping it was her, but no dice. She was in my head like an infectious tune I couldn't stop humming. Between that and checking out the hall traffic every thirty seconds, I wasn't getting much done, so I called a paralegal I sometimes worked with and asked if she'd seen Leslie.

"No," she replied. "Come to think of it, I don't think I've ever seen Leslie work a weekend. Lucky girl." Unlucky me—I'd have to wait until Monday to see her.

Since I promised John Miller that his "extremely time-sensitive" brief would be on his desk Monday morning, I resigned myself to missing out on Saturday night and maybe Sunday night, too.

CHAPTER 3

I'd turned in the brief Monday morning and gotten a pat on the head from the senior partner for doing a good job. I'd expected him to thank me for giving up my weekend, thanks I felt I deserved, but no such luck. So I asked him, choking back any hint of irony in my voice, if he enjoyed his weekend. "Very relaxing, thank you," he said, and that was that.

Despite being exhausted from working the weekend and despite the chip on my shoulder the size of a copy machine, I walked down the hall with what I hoped was an air of confidence, the glossy brochure version of a young attorney on his way up, who got things done and couldn't wait to get more things done. But when I got to my office, I slumped down in my chair and eyeballed the stacks of files filled with legal documents that could put me to sleep faster than my go-to insomnia cocktail of Ambien and NyQuil.

I'd grown up surrounded by attorneys. My father was a lawyer who ran a successful boutique firm specializing in family law with his brother and my mother, also attorneys. My grandfather on my mother's side had been a US attorney. Everybody went to Yale and Yale Law School. One Thanksgiving dinner when I was twelve, my grandfather leaned close to my ear as if about to speak to me in confidence. Then he said in a voice loud enough for the entire table to hear, "Henry, it's been remarked that with our family history, we could get a cocker spaniel into Yale as long as it didn't have rabies." Everyone at the table laughed. Five years later I got into every college

I applied to except Yale. When I told my grandfather, he looked at me with horror as if, well, as if I had rabies.

After that, I made sure I followed my own path, majored in film studies, and spent a year at NYU grad film school before facing the inevitable: law school, followed by a job with my present firm. I had no intention of joining my father's family law practice even if he asked, which he didn't.

Six months into the job, I learned three things. One, I was a very good lawyer. Two, I hated being a lawyer. And three, I had regrets: Seeing the name of one of my film school friends in the credits of a movie was like acid thrown in my face—it surprised me, and it burned.

I sat up in my chair and took a fresh look at the work piled in front of me. There were five nearly identical stacks of files lined up at the edge of the desk because Nancy preferred order to chaos. So I was surprised to see a small white envelope between piles one and two. I glanced at my "in" box, the place Nancy invariably and reliably put all my correspondence. Empty. I opened the envelope. In it was a handwritten note. It said, "Hi there, Dumpling. Meet me in the lobby. Today, one o'clock." Leslie had left it unsigned.

At five minutes to one, I stood in a corner of the lobby, away from the doors but with a view of the elevators. After waiting for twenty-five minutes, I pulled out my phone, dialed my assistant, and asked her to check my messages. There weren't any. Apparently, I'd been played, but I decided not to let some paralegal I didn't know, regardless of how beautiful she might be, keep me from lunch—I'd been thinking of those pork dumplings all morning. I shoved my phone into my pocket and pushed myself away from the wall. That's when I saw Leslie step out of the elevator.

She was wearing a white silk, chiffon blouse, a navy-blue pencil skirt, and black heels. A couple of young guys walking by turned to let their gazes linger on her as long as they could. After checking her watch, she looked around, slowly scanning the lobby as I watched her without making a move or a sound. She spotted me. Her eyes narrowed for a split second. Then she started across the lobby, slowly and deliberately, like a cat stalking its prey. I leaned against the wall and put my hand in my pocket, hoping to project an air of nonchalance.

"You're late," I said.

She gave me a smile and a girlish shrug that I took to mean "What of it?" before stepping toward the nearest revolving door. Without looking back, she said, "Come along now."

I followed her out, and when she stopped on the sidewalk, I stopped. She sidled up close to me. I could smell her perfume through the stink of the city.

"Take me to your dumpling," she said as she put her hand in mine.

The restaurant was packed, but there was a small bar with a couple of open stools, so I grabbed them. Leslie climbed onto the stool next to me, and I watched her wrestle with her blue pencil skirt as she made herself comfortable. She put her elbow on the counter and faced me. I didn't have to look down to know that our knees were almost touching. The bartender happened by, and I ordered two glasses of white wine and dumplings for both of us. Leslie raised no objection.

"So," she said when the wine arrived, "tell me about yourself."

"Not before you tell me why you changed your mind about having lunch with me." I glanced at her hand. "That size large sparkler on your ring finger reminds me you're engaged."

She lifted her hand and admired her ring. "That's true. I am engaged. To a very rich man with a big house on Long Island. He's an investor. Russian oil, mostly."

"Sounds like you hit the lottery."

She laughed, then tilted her head and looked right at me, like she was trying to figure me out. When she was done looking, she picked up her wine glass and clinked mine. "Yeah, I hit the lottery all right."

"But you agreed to have lunch. Why?"

She reached for my tie, lifted it away from my shirt, examined it, then tossed it over my shoulder. "You're cute," she said. "I like cute."

I pulled the tie off my shoulder and put it back where it belonged. "What would your fiancé say if he walked in here right now?"

"He'd probably say he was sorry."

"Yeah? Sorry for what?"

"Sorry for throwing a punch at you before asking me who you were." She took a sip of wine without taking her eyes off me.

"What is he, some kind of mob guy?"

"Some kind."

"And crazy about you?"

"I work extra hard to keep him that way."

That made me smile. Leslie shifted on her stool, and this time her knees brushed mine. Sitting next to Leslie at the counter instead of waiting for a table was paying unexpected dividends.

An old Chinese waiter arrived with our dumplings. He put them on the counter between Leslie and me along with some linen napkins, chopsticks, and a couple of those little red-striped white teacups, the kind without handles that you only see in Chinese restaurants. He gave us a deferential nod, then poured the tea. I thanked him, and he nodded again and placed the teapot on the counter. The aroma of pork dumplings was almost strong enough to overpower the allure of Leslie's perfume. Almost. That, and the sound of clinking plates, the din of the diners, the occasional snippets of Mandarin as waiters passed each other, reminded me I was hungry.

I picked up my chopsticks and attempted to grab a dumpling, but I fumbled it. When it hit the plate, soy sauce splattered polka dots all over my white shirt. Leslie laughed and said "Oh, no!" blotting at me with her napkin. Then she slipped her hand behind my neck and kissed me. At first it was hard, like she was kissing me as punishment, but then her lips softened, and the vice-like grip on the back of my neck relaxed. She ended the kiss, picked up her chopsticks, and deftly maneuvered a dumpling to the dumpling sauce before taking a bite.

"Delicious."

***

That night, as I lay on my bed watching the news while shoving most of a microwaved hot dog into my mouth, my cell phone buzzed. An unknown phone number flashed on the screen. I answered with my mouth full of hot dog. "Hewo?" Silence. I swallowed and tried again, louder. "Hello!" Again nobody answered, so I hung up and went back to my hot dog. The phone buzzed again. "Who is this?" I barked.

"It's me," she said. "Can I come over?"

I sat up so fast I got dizzy. I stammered, "What—now?"

"Why? Is now a bad time?"

After explaining to Leslie that now was a good time, a great time, in fact a perfect time, I gave her the address and rubbed my eyes to make sure I hadn't dozed off into some strange and wonderful dream. I must have rubbed some mustard into my eye because it stung like hell; this was no dream.

I glanced at the clock. I assumed she was coming from her fiancé's mansion on Long Island and that the trip would take at least an hour, but in twenty minutes she was in the lobby. I instructed the doorman to send her up, then opened my apartment door, leaned against the door jamb, and kept my eyes glued to the elevator across the hall.

With a whoosh, the elevator arrived, the doors parted, and Leslie stepped into the hallway, sparkling in contrast to the surrounding shabbiness of faded wallpaper and dingy carpet. She was dressed in jeans that were so artfully weathered and so carefully ripped at the knees they probably cost more than one of my suits. She wore a white T-shirt with a portrait of Andy Warhol in glitter and spangles on it, and carried a light blue blazer over her shoulder, holding it by one finger.

"Hi," I said. "Whadja do, hail a helicopter? It's forty minutes by train from where you live." Without answering she walked past me and dropped the blazer on my couch.

"This the bedroom?" she asked, peeking in.

"I guess the bed's a dead giveaway."

"Yeah, that and the mess." She ducked into the bathroom saying she'd be out in a minute. That was the minute I needed to stuff the bedroom mess into a closet and shove the door closed.

When I turned around, there she was. No light blue blazer, no Warhol spangled T-shirt. She wore only the soft, warm light from the living room torch lamp and the hint of a smile.

CHAPTER 4

So began our affair.

Leslie was the kind of package I sought out, someone who took life by the balls and lived dangerously. I was never like that, so even as a kid I'd sought out a more adventurous crowd, thinking it would help me avoid becoming a complete nerd. Maybe that explains why I chose to defend white-collar criminals. While most of my clients worked for a living, they were somehow comfortable with deluding, defrauding, lying, cheating, and stealing, as if all those things were written into their job description. They did it mostly for money, sometimes for revenge, but I think more often than not, they did it for the adventure of getting away with something. None of my clients were ever happy about having been caught, but they shared one sentiment: It was a helluva ride while it lasted.

The next night, Leslie came back without phoning first. Both nights were short on talk and long on sex. And both nights, before my heart rate and blood pressure started heading back to normal, she was dressed and gone. It was her party, so I didn't want to ask too many questions, lest she take me off the invite list.

But I got curious. On night five, she walked in and, as usual, dropped her coat on my couch on her way to the bathroom. As she passed me, I grabbed her arm and held on.

"What?" she asked with a look that almost made me let her go without saying a word.

"Where's your fiancé?"

"Away on business. In Moscow. He'll be away for a long time." She freed her arm from my grip and disappeared into the bathroom.

Back in the office it was as if I didn't exist. No notes, phone calls, or lunch dates. She would pass me in the hallways without a word, her eyes straight ahead, her face blank. Okay, I thought, I get it. I'm just a piece on the side, a diversion, a plaything. But realizing that didn't put me off. Not one bit.

Sometimes when we were together, I got the feeling Leslie not only cared for me, she needed me, or maybe even loved me. Other times she said or did things that reinforced her indifference. And the worst? The worst was when she ignored me after sex.

Three months after our lunch date the nighttime visits stopped without warning or explanation. I assumed this break in the action was because her fiancé was back from Moscow. But after a month went by without hearing anything from Leslie, I realized our relationship, if in fact what we'd had could be called a relationship, was done. I was plenty busted up about it, but all I could do was focus on my work and try to forget her. The downside of office romances is that when they're over, every day is another chance for an awkward, and often heartbreaking, encounter. But I thought it strange that we never ran into each other in the hall like we used to. What were the chances?

One day I decided I'd spend my lunch break looking for her. I started with the law library. No sign of her, so I asked if anyone knew where she was. One of the other paralegals looked up. "Leslie? She left the firm a few weeks ago. I heard she got another job."

"You know where?" I asked.

"No idea. Sorry," she said and went back to her work.

I stood up and walked back to my office, thinking about our short affair and telling myself that if it meant nothing to her it should mean nothing to me. But by the time I reached my office, I felt sick to my stomach. Because I knew there was absolutely nothing I could do.

She was gone.

CHAPTER 5

After Leslie's abrupt departure from the firm I'd assumed I'd never see or hear from her again, but six weeks later she phoned. "My fiancé called off our engagement," she said, whispering, possibly because Boris was nearby. "He wants me out tonight. Says he's fallen in love with our so-called houseguest."

She went on to explain that Boris had returned from a recent business trip to Moscow with some nineteen-year-old Russian model he claimed was the daughter of a friend. She'd always wanted to see New York City, and she was just staying for a few weeks. "Now he's planning to marry the tramp. I told him I didn't give a damn what he did because I'd found someone new, too. Then I told him all about you."

"About me?" I grunted. "That's a hoot. All you know about me is that I'm a lawyer, and I'm great in the sack."

"I made a big deal out of that second part, giving him plenty of details. He didn't much like it."

"And you're telling me this why?"

"I need a place to stay," she'd replied without hesitating. "Just for a few days until I get a place of my own."

"Try someone else," I said and hung up.

She immediately called back saying she was desperate and had nowhere else to go. "You wouldn't want me to sleep on the street, would you?" By then she was crying, and despite myself, I felt a little bit sorry for her. An hour later, she was at my door, her hair dripping wet, her trench coat soaked through, holding two mud-splattered suitcases. Rainwater was puddling at her feet.

I planned to say something biting and mean, but she looked so pathetic I held my tongue. Her watery eyes made me think of a lost puppy long past any hope of finding its way home. I threw a kitchen towel to her across the living room. She used it to wipe her face and dry her hair before draping her wet trench coat over the upholstered silk chair I'd inherited from my favorite aunt, instantly transforming it from valuable antique to worthless piece of junk. She sat down at one end of my couch. I seated myself at the opposite end and turned to look at her. Even with her hair wet, makeup smeared, and clothes disheveled, Leslie looked as gorgeous as ever, and she knew it. She slid across the couch and sat next to me. Very next to me. With her head nestled on my shoulder, she whispered, "I knew I could count on you."

This was going in the wrong direction, and I was in no mood to be played for a sap. When she reached up to put her hand on my face, I grabbed her wrist. "Knock it off," I said through clenched teeth. That's when I noticed her engagement ring wasn't on her finger. "Don't tell me he made you give the ring back?"

"Not exactly. I took it off and threw it at him." She snorted. "Hit him in the face."

"Too bad," I said, letting go of her wrist. "If you'd hocked it, you could have stayed at the Waldorf for six months." I peeled myself away from her, but as I stood up, she caught my hand in hers and started massaging it with her thumb.

"Don't go," she said. "Not yet. Hold me for a minute, won't you?" She looked up at me, and her eyes appeared twice as big as they were five seconds earlier. I averted my gaze and pulled myself free. She leaned back, draping herself over the arm of the couch with a half-smile. She was an eyeful in her white angora sweater.

Something about that sweater, the way it flowed around her curves from her waist to her neck, the way the short sleeves, cut almost to her shoulders, showed off her slender arms and delicate hands. That angora sweater … something about it. Leslie sure knew how to gift wrap herself.

"Henry," she purred. I felt sweat on the back of my neck. I didn't know whether to accept her invitation or take a cold shower. Whichever I chose would leave me naked and in shock, but only one would rob me of my self-respect.

I walked to the closet where I kept sheets and a blanket. The blanket was clean, but I wasn't sure about the sheets. "You can sleep in my room. I'll take the couch."

"You can't sleep on the couch," Leslie said, batting her eyes. The breeze from her eyelashes rustled my hair. "That wouldn't be fair. To you. Or to me. Or to us."

"Okay, you win," I said. "I'll take the bed."

With that, Leslie sat up. I handed her the bedding, mumbled a goodnight, and retreated to my bedroom.

At around three, she climbed into bed with me, claiming she was cold.

The next morning we were officially living together.

***

After Leslie moved in, I considered us a couple, but our relationship in those first few months mostly felt like a boulder on the edge of a cliff during an earthquake. Sometimes Leslie would text me ten times in one day, telling me ten different ways she missed me. Other days I wouldn't hear from her at all. Once, while I was making dinner and Leslie was lying on the couch leafing through a catalog, I asked why she hadn't answered my texts. "I didn't feel that close to you today," she explained.

Like the addicted gambler, I only needed the occasional win to keep me at the crap table. She might be surly and remote for days, but then she'd pull me close and kiss me and say something like, "I love being with you. You know that, don't you?" I lived for those moments.

But the thing that really got me? Leslie was mysterious in a world where mysterious women were all but extinct, or maybe just out of style. The first time I asked a question about her childhood, she told me it was none of my business. "Here's the deal," she said, glaring at me. "You don't ask about my past, I won't ask about yours." I responded that I had nothing to hide. And doesn't getting to know each other require swapping life stories? Not for Leslie. She made it clear that her background was whatever I could see behind her that wasn't blocked by her beautiful body.

But she did talk to me about her future.

A few weeks after she moved in, we were sitting at a bar having a couple of martinis. I asked her why she'd quit the law firm.

"Because, when you come right down to it, my job sucked," she explained. "Being a paralegal was like having to do all the crappy parts of lawyering without any of the fun stuff."

"What fun stuff?" I took a sip of my martini.

She chuckled. "Yeah, you got that right." She began stirring her martini with her finger, gazing at the glass like there were tropical fish swirling around instead of green olives filled with pimentos. She pulled her finger out, licked it, and dried it with a cocktail napkin. "I've wanted to be an actor since I graduated college. I've been taking acting classes on and off since then, but working full time made it harder for me to audition." She paused long enough to remove an olive from the martini. "My acting coach says I should audition for television commercials. And if I can get some commercials, maybe

I can start paying my share of the rent." She popped the olive into her mouth.

"You don't have to worry about the rent," I said with a dismissive wave of my hand. "Makes me feel like a patron of the arts. And I bet you're a terrific actress."

"Actor."

"Actor."

She cocked her head and smiled. "Really?" She pulled another olive from her drink. "Boris never took my acting seriously. He thought acting classes were a complete waste of time and money."

"Sounds like Boris didn't believe in you the way I do." Even though I had no idea if her acting was good, great, or terrible, I was happy to be her supportive new boyfriend.

***

After living together for only five months, I decided we should get married. One Saturday night, at a little Italian restaurant in Greenwich Village, I got down on one knee and proposed. My eyes were wet with tears, but hers were dry. "You can't be serious," she said. I assured her I was. She looked around. People were watching. "Sure I'll marry you," she said quietly. "Now, for chrissake, stand up and get a hold of yourself. You look like an idiot."

Maybe I did, but never before had I loved anyone as intensely as I loved Leslie.

CHAPTER 6

Leslie had suckered me into marriage, but I wasn't about to fall for her latest scam. Her office visit rattled me but not because I believed her story about needing my money to keep us both from getting killed. That was pure Leslie bullshit. What rattled me was her sudden reappearance after all this time. I opened the desk drawer where I kept a bottle of scotch for the occasional office celebration or one-man pity party. After eyeing the bottle of Johnny Walker Red for a few seconds, I slammed the drawer shut. The hell with Leslie. Time to forget her and get back to my job.

The rest of the day was filled with meetings and phone calls, all of which helped distract me from Leslie's visit. By the end of the day, I was beat. All I wanted was to get to my apartment, pour myself a scotch, and collapse into my soft leather chair.

My apartment's on the Upper East Side in a modern high-rise building with lots of balconies. Everyone in New York City has a story about how they got their apartment, fabulous or not, and I'm no exception.

When I started working in the city, all I could afford was a breathtakingly tiny studio apartment above an Indian Restaurant. The apartment smelled of curry, and not in a good way. One day, my friend Aiden knocked on my door. He looked terrible, as if he hadn't slept or smiled in weeks. Collapsing on my couch, Aiden told me his six-month-old marriage was falling apart, and since he'd just walked out on his wife, he needed a place to stay. "My couch is your couch,"

I said. "Stay as long as you want." Between the toxic curry odor and the cramped space, I figured he'd be gone after one or two nights. He stayed a week.

Aiden Jackson and I had been friends ever since the first day of law school nine years earlier. He always said he was good-looking enough to marry rich and that was his goal. While it was true his boyish smile, easy manner, and abundance of shaggy dirty-blond hair made him attractive to women, I'd assumed he was joking about marrying rich. So when Aiden became engaged to Emma Honeywell, he broke the news to me by saying he was marrying a three-bedroom apartment and couldn't wait to move in. A three-bedroom apartment on the Upper East Side of Manhattan doesn't necessarily qualify as "rich," but I acknowledged it as a step in the right direction. It turned out to be more than just a step, because Emma's father not only owned said three-bedroom apartment, he also owned the entire building and seventeen others like it in Manhattan. None of this had anything to do with why I didn't care for Emma, unless being stuck up, self-centered, and snooty automatically came with wealth. Since I knew rich people who weren't jerks, I attributed Emma's undesirable traits to bad genes and private schools.

Aiden spent the entire week on my couch looking miserable, and that was when he was asleep. While awake, he drank my scotch and shared the most intimate details of his failed marriage. He said horrible things about Emma and called her names that would make a longshoreman blush. I let him rant, aware that my taking cheap shots at her and saying "I told you so" could backfire if they got back together, and then I'd be the jerk. Aiden was my best friend, and I intended to keep it that way, Emma or no Emma.

It turned out to be the smart play. At the end of the week, Aiden went back to Emma and her three-bedroom apartment. A few days later, Emma surprised me with a call, thanking me for rescuing her marriage. Before hanging up, she told me there was an apartment available in her building, and it was mine if I wanted it.

That's how I landed an apartment on the Upper East Side.

On my way home from the office that Friday night, despite Leslie dropping the bombshell that her life was in danger, I didn't think of her at all. Not on the subway, or on the walk from the subway station to my building, or in the elevator up to my apartment. I was on a roll. But my streak ended when I opened my apartment door and stepped inside. I froze. What I saw made no sense. For a few seconds I thought I'd walked into the wrong apartment. I glanced at the number on the door. It was mine alright, but nothing in the apartment was where I'd left it that morning. My leather chair was turned upside down, its little wooden legs flailing skyward. My liquor bottles were all over the floor, some broken and lying in their own puddles. Drawers and cabinets were open, their contents scattered. I stood there, hoping the scene in my apartment was a mirage that would shimmer and disappear if I stared long enough.

My first thought was that Leslie tossed my apartment, or maybe she had someone else toss it. But if she was looking for money, she knew she wouldn't find much. Or maybe it was the thugs who were after Leslie. But why would they toss my place? Did they think Leslie had left something with me? Or were the bad guys trying to send me a message?

Of course, I had to consider that it was just a robbery, and Leslie had nothing to do with it.

I picked my way through the living room, navigating carefully to avoid broken glass, overturned lamps, and books knocked off the shelves and scattered around the floor like random stepping stones in a stream. The kitchen was similarly busted up—plates, glasses, and what little food I had swept onto the counter and the floor. The freezer door stood open, and water was dripping onto the linoleum.

Whoever did this must have made quite a racket, but I guess nobody heard anything, or they would have called the doorman. I remember when I first moved in, Emma claimed this was the quietest building in New York City. "Seriously," she said, "you could detonate a grenade in here and the guy next door wouldn't hear a thing." Turned out she was right.

Before cleaning up, I checked to see if anything valuable had been stolen. I kept fifteen hundred dollars in C-notes in the freezer hidden in a box of peas: still there. I had a small collection of first editions, some of which were inscribed by the author: I located all of them. My old Cartier watch was still in my sock drawer, although my socks weren't. In less than an hour, I'd inventoried the place, and while everything was there, some of it was in pieces. Nothing that couldn't be replaced except a Chinese, amber-colored glass vase my grandmother left me when she died. I didn't care that it was worth a few thousand dollars. I cared because it was one of the few things I had of my grandmother's. Her grandfather, who was in the import-export business, brought it from Peking in the 1930s. She saw me examining it during one of my visits when I was a boy, and she told me the story of her grandfather's daring escape when the Japanese invaded in 1937. Other than his clothes, the vase was the only thing he took with him. That vase made me smile whenever I happened to glance at it.

I called the cops, but after the desk sergeant asked me if anything was missing ("No, officer …"), or if anyone was hurt ("Thankfully, I wasn't home but—"), he cut me off. "Consider yourself lucky, sir," he said before hanging up. "And have a nice night."

I spent the next few hours cleaning up. The big chunks of the Chinese glass vase went into a cardboard box in the hope that someone could piece it back together. As for the rest of the broken glassware, I managed to save only a couple of cheap place settings and a few mugs.

It was nearly four in the morning when, exhausted, I passed out on my bed. At 6:30 a.m., the phone rang. I fumbled for the receiver next to my bed. "Hello, who is this?" I asked, alert despite the time and my lack of sleep.

A guy with a Russian accent said, "Let's just say I'm a friend of your wife's."

"She's my ex-wife, and she's not here."

"I know she's not," the guy said. "I was just checking to see if you were."

I dropped the phone, jumped out of bed, and got the hell out as fast as I could.

In the elevator, I called Aiden even though he was probably still asleep. I told him I needed to talk without saying why. He must have read the panic in my voice because he agreed to meet me at the diner across from his apartment building in Chelsea. He'd moved there when he and Emma got divorced.

CHAPTER 7

I ran out of my building and hadn't even reached the street with my arm fully extended when a cab screeched to a stop. The cabby asked if I was okay. "Why wouldn't I be?" We looked at each other, his eyes fixed on me in his rearview mirror.

He hesitated. "None of my business, right?" Instead of answering, I turned away, looked out the window, and watched Manhattan waking up on a Saturday morning, getting ready for the tourists and ticket holders that would soon flood the city.

I knew the cabbie was right—I wasn't okay. I was scared. Scared because I didn't know what the hell was going on. Scared that Leslie might get hurt. And scared that I was still in love with her, which might make me do something stupid. Or get me killed.

Leslie had made a mess of something and wanted my help. I could have asked her questions in my office—like who was threatening her, what they wanted, whether she'd called the cops—but I didn't give her a chance. Now that I believed she was really in trouble, I needed her to tell me what was going on. But first I had to find her.

After leaving me, Leslie had changed her mobile number and email address. I had no idea where she lived or worked. My only contact with her since she'd walked out was through our divorce lawyers, and I didn't recall her lawyer's name. But Aiden, my best friend and confidante, would know. Because Aiden was also my divorce lawyer.

I paid the cabby, over-tipping because he'd told me I looked scared, and that was something I needed to know. He smiled when I told him to keep the change from a twenty, and I managed a grateful nod back. He made me think about how perfect strangers can sometimes size you up in an instant, while people you've known for months or years, people you've lived with or worked with, have no idea who you really are. It's as if you hide your real self from others, doing everything you can to look the part, dress the part, act the part, whatever the part happens to be—the tough guy, the smart guy, the tender guy—whatever works for you in the moment. But when all is said and done, nobody knows the real you. Nobody, except for the guy who shows up in the bathroom mirror every morning looking back at you with a mouth full of toothpaste. Shakespeare said it right—about all the world being a stage. And Shakespeare knew what I know. Sometimes the players get played.

The Malibu Diner was empty except for a young guy sitting in one of the booths next to the window, slumped over a cup of coffee, looking crumpled and tired, both the victim and the perpetrator of an all-night drinking binge that somehow ended here. The waiter was leaning against the counter talking Greek to the grill man. He eyed me when I hesitated at the door looking for Aiden. "Sit anywhere, my friend," he said, sweeping his hand around the restaurant in case I wasn't sure what "anywhere" meant. I headed for the corner booth.

Diners in New York are all the same—from the way the coffee tastes, to the oval breakfast plates, to the oversized blueberry muffins in the plastic display case next to the register—and that's one of the best things about them. Tourists might be drawn to one diner or another by a unique name, thinking it might offer a clue about the cuisine, but they'd be disappointed. The Malibu Diner menu didn't even hint at Southern California, nor did the décor deviate from the norm. If you lived here, you could walk into any diner in the city and feel that it was a place you knew and where they knew you. Because it was.

The waiter came over with a full carafe of coffee and poured me a cup without asking. "You need a menu, or you know what you want already?" I explained that I was waiting for a friend, but in the meantime, I'd have a toasted blueberry muffin. The waiter turned his head and yelled, "Toasted blue!" and the grill man yelled back, "Toasted blue," a routine I'd witnessed a thousand times before at diners just like this one.

Aiden arrived and sat down across from me at the same time the waiter delivered my toasted blue. Aiden was usually very particular about his appearance, but when he sat down, I noticed his white T-shirt was on inside out, and his dirty blond hair stood in unevenly spaced tufts that pointed in various directions. He looked like a stray collie. "Coffee," he said to the waiter without looking at him, then he reached across the table and tore off a piece of my muffin. "I had company last night, and the company is still there this morning. If you get my drift." He took a bite of the muffin and grinned as he swallowed.

I nodded, confirming I got his drift. He liked talking about his sexual conquests, and sometimes I liked listening. But not today.

"Aiden, I'm in trouble. I think. Probably."

His grin vanished. "What kind of trouble?"

"Someone may be trying to kill me. I need to find Leslie."

"Your ex-wife Leslie?"

I nodded.

"Are you telling me Leslie's trying to kill you?"

Shit—I hadn't thought of that. I hesitated, wondering if I'd missed something. "Of course not," I said. "But I need to find her."

"What's going on, Henry?"

"Last night my place got tossed, and then right before I called you, I got a phone call. From a guy."

"What guy? The guy who tossed your place?"

"I'm not sure. Maybe." Aiden drank some coffee, put the cup down, and sat back in the booth, his red-rimmed eyes on me the whole time. "Hank," he said, using my nickname from our law school days, "I got a warm bed to go back to. So tell me what's going on, starting with a headline and moving quickly to who, what, why, where, and when, instead of making me cross-examine you."

When I didn't answer right away, he slid across the seat like he was about to leave, so I started talking, telling it from the beginning. How my ex-wife paid a surprise visit to my office. How she told me she needed money, a lot of it, fast or both of us would be killed. How I dismissed her story as hooey, and she left my office in tears, capping a performance Streep would envy. And how when I came home and saw my apartment violently rearranged, I figured it had something to do with Leslie.

"That it?" Aiden asked.

"And the phone call I just got. It was a nasty Russian-sounding guy who said he was making sure I was home. Scared the shit out of me."

"Jesus, Hank." Aiden took the remaining gulp of his coffee and held the cup aloft in the direction of the waiter. Apparently satisfied that the waiter had gotten the message, Aiden put the cup down. "I assume you called the cops?"

"Yeah, a lot of good that did me." I thought back to my conversation with the local precinct. "Apparently, unless you're bleeding to death, or better yet, completely dead, the cops have better things to do."

Aiden nodded. "Victim triage. New York City cops have their hands full."

"Aiden, you've gotta help me find her."

"How?" he asked. "She dropped out of sight years ago, no forwarding address. I always assumed she left the city." The waiter came and filled both of our cups. Aiden took a sip of his coffee. "Shit—this stuff's hot," he said, wiping his mouth with the back of his hand. Forewarned, I added some lukewarm half-and-half from a metal creamer that looked like it hadn't been washed since I was in diapers.

For a minute Aiden was hunched over his coffee, lost in thought, but then he looked up at me. "When Leslie was in your office, did she mention anything about where she lived, what she's been doing?"

"No, nothing like that."

Aiden rolled his eyes. "For chrissake, Hank, ever heard of small talk? 'How ya been, Leslie, haven't seen you in a while, you still living in the city?' Something like that?"

"Not my style," I said. "The last thing I thought I'd be doing is trying to get in touch. Mostly I wanted her out of my office. It was painful—ya know, seeing her."

Aiden's tone softened. "Yeah, I get that. Sorry." He stared into his coffee as if it were his magic eight ball and answers were swirling around in the blackness before floating to the surface. He looked up. "She have any places she liked to hang out? Maybe a gym or, I don't know, a favorite bar or restaurant?"

I shook my head.

Aiden lightly drummed his fingers on the table as he concentrated. "Wait a second." He stopped drumming, and his eyes brightened. "I just remembered something, something her lawyer mentioned to me over the phone during your divorce. I forgot about it until just now." He sat back with a satisfied smile.

"You gonna tell me what it is?"

Aiden looked around the diner. "Not here," he said. "Let's go to my apartment. Maybe we can figure some things out."

"Your bed warmer won't mind me crashing the party?"

"This takes precedence," he said. "Besides, it's time you two met."

CHAPTER 8

I requested the check by making a checkmark in the air in the direction of the waiter. Our bill came to twelve bucks, but I put a ten and a five on the table and shot a thank you to the guy at the cash register. He smiled, told me to have a nice day. With that, Aiden and I stood up to leave. As I followed Aiden to the door, I was starting to feel a little better than when I'd first walked in. I'd been panicky and in need of help. The diner, the coffee, the muffin, and most of all, Aiden, calmed me and gave me hope. Aiden seemed confident. Maybe together we'd be able to find Leslie and figure out how to get these bad guys off her back. Maybe I'd be saving her life. Maybe I'd be saving mine.

I couldn't help wondering if I was dragging my best friend into this ice-cold bucket of borscht with Leslie and me, but if he knew something that could lead me to Leslie, I had to take that chance. On the other hand, I knew how dangerous this was in a way that Aiden didn't. I'd seen Leslie scared to death. I'd had my apartment trashed. I'd taken a threatening phone call from a Russian thug. I was the one with a knot in my stomach. So far it was me, not Aiden, who was in danger. I owed it to him to try to keep it that way.

As we left the diner, I stopped outside the door to look around, because I was afraid. I'd always loved the city, but now it seemed as warm and welcoming as a crowded prison yard in January. Aiden was well ahead of me, but he doubled back, grabbed my arm, and we began running to make the light. It turned red before we reached the corner, but Aiden charged ahead with me in tow. Cars and trucks bolted into the intersection, bearing down on us from both directions, drivers hitting their horns rather than their brakes, ready to abandon their humanity and run us over to teach us a lesson. I heard a cabby yell, "You guys crazy or something? Go back to Jersey!" but, somehow, we made it safely to the other side.

Aiden led me into his building, an art deco job that was built in the thirties. The entrance looked like a miniature version of the lobby at the Empire State Building, where I'd worked one summer taking tickets at the elevator from tourists on their way to the observation deck. The black and gray inlaid stone floor, the onyx black and steel elevator doors, the sharp-edged design on one wall adorned with aluminum leaf—it all took me back to the New York of the thirties when some of the most iconic architecture was built by Depression-era construction crews. These were guys who walked around on girders hundreds of feet in the air like they were walking from their front door to the mailbox, even though the threat of death by gravity was everywhere.

As the elevator doors closed, I turned to my friend. "Listen to me, Aiden. This could be a shit show, one where people get hurt or worse. I didn't come here to drag you into anything nasty. I just need your advice."

Aiden smiled. "I'm a big boy, and I've been threatened by lawyers, judges, and clients a helluva lot scarier than your Russian guy on the phone. I can take care of myself."

I hoped he could take care of me, too.

Aiden unlocked the door, and as we walked in, I heard a woman's voice, husky from cigarettes or a rough night, or both. "Hey, Aiden," she said. "Where'd you go? Come back to bed. I wasn't finished with you."

Aiden answered, "Coming, precious." Then he turned to me and winked. "Be right back, Hank."

"Wait," I said, "you're not going to …" Aiden laughed. "Relax. I'm taking care of you now. Precious will have to wait." He disappeared down the hall into the bedroom and closed the door. I heard him talking to his lady friend, but I had no interest in eavesdropping, so I retreated to the seating area in the living room.

Aiden's place looked like it had been decorated by a college kid with unlimited funds: a television as big as a billboard hanging on the wall opposite a black leather couch, a couple of matching leather chairs, a marble and steel coffee table, and in the corner of the room a Gibson electric guitar propped up next to a Ludwig drum kit. On the wall behind the couch was a large vintage poster of the Rolling Stones from their Sticky Fingers Tour, signed by Mick Jagger and his mates, that Aiden proudly paid twenty-two hundred for. No sign of a woman's touch anywhere.

I sat down on the couch and reached for the only thing on the coffee table, a Rubik's Cube, and started wrestling with it. Ten minutes passed. I hadn't made much headway with the puzzle and had just put it down when I heard the bedroom door open and close again. I looked up to see Aiden walking into the living room, buttoning the cuffs on a freshly ironed white shirt. A red necktie was draped over one shoulder.

"I'm dressing for work—a rare Saturday morning client meeting," he explained. "Before I leave, we can have a word with Leslie's lawyer."

"Sounds good, but you haven't told me what he said that makes you think he can help."

"She. Leslie's lawyer's a woman. Name's Debbie Maxwell, remember?"

"I never met her. You sure she'll talk to us?"

"Positive."

Just then a woman in a white terrycloth robe stepped into the hall and walked toward us. "Hi," she said. "I'm Debbie Maxwell." She was barefoot and her short brown hair was tousled, but she didn't seem embarrassed or uncomfortable as she reached over the coffee table and shook my hand. "And yes, I was Leslie's divorce lawyer." She must have read the look on my face. "Oh for god's sake, get over it. It's not like we're committing a capital crime here. We're consenting adults."

"Sorry, no. I'm just surprised that you and Aiden ..." But then why wouldn't Aiden be sleeping with the opposing divorce lawyer?

She looked me up and down. "I like your friend, Aiden. He's ..."

"In trouble," I said, finishing her sentence. "I need to find Leslie and figure out who's threatening her. And get them to stop. Aiden said Leslie's lawyer might be able to help, but ..."

"... but you didn't expect he was sleeping with Leslie's lawyer," she said, grinning. "Coffee anyone?" She walked into the kitchen.

She was right. Why should I care if she and Aiden had a relationship that went beyond the professional? Except that I thought Aiden was going to tell me something he heard that might help. With Debbie here, I wasn't sure we could even discuss it because of attorney-client privilege. Depending on the information, it would be unethical. Whatever a lawyer discusses with her client is privileged, and the lawyer is obligated to keep it a secret. I glanced at Aiden. He knew the attorney-client privilege rule as well as I did.

"If you're worried about privilege," Debbie said, "you should be." She sat down next to me. My eyes automatically went to the top of her robe, and she pulled it closed before continuing. "However," she continued, "what I'm about to tell you makes use of an exception to the rules." Then she began a lecture on the exception. The long and short of it was that someone else had been in the office with them when Leslie gave her the information she later mentioned to Aiden.

"Okay," I said, putting my hand up and stopping her mid-lecture. "Whatever. Now, what can you tell me?"

Debbie, looking slightly miffed that I'd stopped her from showing off her legal chops, said, "I don't know if this will help you find Leslie, but it might be a clue to why someone's chasing her." Debbie paused to recheck the top of her robe before continuing. I rechecked it as well.

"At our first meeting, Leslie and I talked almost entirely about your marriage and why she wanted the divorce."

"What did she say?"

"That's privileged," Debbie deadpanned, then laughed. "Sorry, I couldn't resist." When I didn't crack a smile, Debbie dropped the comedy and continued. "I asked Leslie if she was married before you, and she said no, although she'd been engaged to a wealthy guy named Boris something-or-other, who she suspected was in the Russian mob. She said she broke off the engagement when she caught him fooling around with some nineteen-year-old Russian model he brought back from Moscow after a business trip. Tanya, I think her name was."

I nodded. "Yeah, I heard all about Tanya, although Leslie told me it was Boris who broke their engagement after announcing he was marrying Tanya."

"Well, looks like she lied about the particulars. Maybe to me, maybe to you. Does that surprise you?"

"Not even a little bit," I answered.

"Didn't think so," she said. "Anyway, here's what I let slip to Aiden during the divorce." Debbie hesitated. "I'm not sure I'm comfortable telling you this."

"C'mon, Debbie," Aiden said. "Out with it."

"Okay," Debbie said. "When Leslie first phoned me, I told her about my retainer, payable at our first meeting. When I told her how much, I thought that would end the call. Nine out of ten people can't raise that much, and I thought Leslie was in the majority. But she said fine, and we made an appointment to meet."

"What's your retainer?" I asked.

"Fifty thousand dollars."

I whistled. "That ought to ensure a better-quality clientele." I knew Leslie didn't have that kind of money. "What did you do when she didn't pay the retainer?"

"She did pay," Debbie said.

I looked at Debbie blankly. "I thought I heard you say Leslie paid you." Debbie nodded. I was waiting for the punchline, but it didn't come. So I supplied one. "And, of course, the check bounced."

"No, the check didn't bounce. There was no check."

"No check? I'm not following …"

Then Debbie landed the punchline I hadn't seen coming. "Leslie paid cash."

"What? How is that even possible?"

"She walked in with a briefcase full of it, like in the movies," Debbie said. "I had to deposit it in chunks so it wouldn't get flagged by the Feds."

"What'd she do, rob a bank?" I asked, hoping the answer was no, but bracing myself in case it was yes.

"Don't be silly. She told me she'd sold some jewelry."

Aiden, who'd just finished knotting his tie, sat down in the chair across from us. "Yeah, Debbie let that slip right before we signed the papers," he said. "I told you about it, said we should investigate, because it sounded like she had more money than we thought, but you said the jewelry you gave her wasn't worth much and to let it go."

I winced, recalling how I'd been sick of all the back and forth and had just wanted to sign the papers and be done with it. Besides, all she had was a cheap watch and some costume jewelry, plus what I'd given her: a few pairs of earrings, a bracelet, a couple other small things that couldn't have fetched much. The engagement ring I gave her was pricey. After all, I was smitten, and, like every other American, brainwashed by the diamond industry into spending two month's salary on the ring because "a diamond is forever." That last part was true. Leslie slid the ring off her finger and dropped it on the hall table the morning she left me. I still had it in my night table drawer. Her little show of defiance reminded me that she'd nailed her last fiancé in the face with his ring when she walked out on him. Maybe she loved me more than him. Or hated me less. "The only other jewelry I ever saw her wear was that ring that she got from her ex."

"Was it worth anything?"

"I'll say. Diamonds, emeralds, and rubies packed onto a fat platinum band, and I'm pretty sure it was an antique. But Leslie gave it back to him when she left—she told me she was so mad she threw it at the guy."

"What, the ring?" She chuckled. "Did it hit him?"

"Uh-huh. Hit him in the face."

Debbie looked away and rubbed her lower lip. "But … what if she didn't throw the ring at Boris?" She looked back at me. "What if she kept it?"

That stopped me. "Hold on. You're saying …"

"I'm saying that maybe she kept the ring, and now Boris wants it back."

I thought about it, then shook my head. "Here's why that doesn't work for me. If this is about Boris wanting his ring back, why would

Leslie show up in my office yesterday asking for money? Why not just return the ring and be done with it?"

Debbie's eyes rolled. "Because she doesn't have the ring! That's the jewelry she sold that got her all that cash!" Debbie slapped her thigh and smiled, obviously jazzed by her new theory. "The ring's history! So now all she can do is pay Boris off and hope he's satisfied."

I nodded. Maybe she was on to something.

And," she added, "if she's already gone through a chunk of her stash from the ring and the divorce settlement, that would explain why she came to you asking for money."

"Right," I said. "Except why would Boris come looking for the ring after waiting, what, six years? Makes no sense."

Debbie said, "I know, that is strange." She looked over at Aiden, but he just shrugged and shook his head.

"I don't know, Debbie," I said. "Maybe she got herself in trouble with someone else who's shaking her down."

Debbie scoffed. "Aiden said somebody tossed your room but didn't take anything. Sounds to me like they were searching for the ring."

Aiden jumped in. "And this morning, Henry got a threatening phone call from a Russian thug."

"True?" Debbie asked. I nodded. "Well," she said, "there's your connection to Boris." With that, she sat back in her chair, flipped her left leg over her right, and crossed her arms.

So that was it. Leslie didn't have the ring, and she didn't have the money to pay Boris off. That was why she was scared for her life. I jumped up. "I have to find Leslie before Boris does. You were her lawyer. Don't you have an address, a phone number, something?"

She shook her head. "I have no idea where Leslie is," she said. "But I do know where you might find Boris."

CHAPTER 9

Aiden finished dressing and headed for his office, leaving me with Debbie. She'd told me that Leslie's ex's last name was Smirnoff, like the vodka. I remembered a frat brother holding a half-empty bottle of the stuff, telling me that Smirnoff meant "peaceful and gentle" before he unpeacefully and urgently threw up all over me. From what I knew about Boris Smirnoff, his last name was equally ironic.

It took a couple of minutes for Debbie to find Boris's address on her phone. I took a hundred-dollar bill from my wallet, wrote the address on it, then put it back in my wallet. "That your way of safeguarding important information?" she asked.

"It works in a pinch," I said. "How do you safeguard yours?"

"It wouldn't be nearly as safe if I told you, now would it?" she said with a coy smile. I smiled back. I was beginning to see why Aiden liked her.

I thanked her for her help and made my way to the door. As I was closing it behind me, she said, "Henry? You be careful." I turned and nodded to her. But as I headed to the elevator, I realized I'd left careful behind the day Leslie kissed me after I fumbled that pork dumpling.

Outside, I squinted into the morning sun. The city was already uncomfortably hot and headed for stifling. Leslie was out there somewhere, but where? And how would I find her? Sure, Debbie gave me Boris's address, but what was I supposed to do, show up at his place and accuse him of threatening Leslie? If some random guy did that, I'd tell him to mind his own business and slam the door in his face. And from what Leslie had told me about him, I pictured Boris as the type who would ask the man in, beat him to a bloody pulp, wipe the blood off his floor with the poor guy's shirt while he was still wearing it, and throw him out head-first before telling him to mind his own business. At least that was the impression I got from Leslie. She didn't tell me much about Boris, but it was a helluva lot more than she'd told me about herself.

***

One Saturday morning right after we married, I found Leslie at the kitchen table poring over the *New York Post*. "G'morning," I said. She paid no attention to me, as if I wasn't even there. "Anything interesting in the paper?" I asked, putting some bite into it. Crickets.

I grabbed some Wheaties from the cupboard, poured them into a bowl, put the cereal box away, got the milk from the fridge, poured it over the cereal, and put a spoonful in my mouth, all before Leslie said, "What? In this paper?" She looked at me as if to make sure we were talking about the newspaper she was holding. She flipped it so I could read the headline. "ASST ATTY GENERAL TO RUSSIAN MOB: DASVIDANIYA." Having brought the hammer down on the Italian Mafia over the last several years, the Southern District was staging a repeat performance, this time in Russian.

Leslie chuckled and said mostly to herself, "Amazing." She chuckled again.

Still standing, I swallowed another spoonful of cereal. "What's amazing? That they're going after Russian mobsters?"

"No," she said, closing the paper and tossing it on the table. "What's amazing is that Boris, my ex, kept his name out of the paper. Out of the investigation, too, I bet."

I wanted to know more, but Leslie had always resisted my questions about her past. And she never talked about Boris. I put my cereal bowl on the table and sat down. Maybe this was my chance to seduce Leslie into talking about him. And like any successful seduction, I began by looking her right in the eye. "So Boris was in the Russian mob?"

"I'm not sure," she said. "I never asked, because I didn't want to know."

"But you suspected he might have mob ties?"

Instead of answering, she picked up the newspaper again. I changed it up with a longshot question. "How'd you meet?"

"Oh, come on, you really want to hear how I met my ex?" she asked.

I nodded.

"Most guys don't want to know about their girlfriends' exes. Why is that?"

"Ego," I suggested. "The lingering fear that they're not the all-time favorite."

"Listen, honey, you got Boris beat in some ways, not in others," she said.

Not only was that not the answer I was looking for, but my ego was beginning to sport a shiner, like it had been roundhouse punched in the eye. Without knowing whether alligators lurked in this swamp, rather than wading in, I cannonballed. "Let's start with how I got him beat."

She looked at me for a few seconds so intensely it made me think she was trying to see past my eyes. "You aren't like the rest of them, are you?"

"The rest of what?"

"Men."

She started to get up, but I stopped her by saying I really wanted to know how I stacked up against Boris.

"You're honest for starters," she said. "And when we have sex, I get the impression you really love me. With Boris, I never knew. And you're proud of being with me, I can tell, like when we're walking down the street and guys check me out."

So far, it sounded like I was way out in front. "What else?" I asked, counting on my luck to hold.

"Nothing else." Then she started in on Boris's advantages. "Unpredictable, and in a good way." Her eyes drifted up and to the left, as if she was thinking about that. "Yeah, unpredictable. And strong, you know, so I always felt safe around him, like he would protect me no matter what. And ..."

"So I'm predictable and weak?"

She sat back in her chair and turned her head slightly but kept looking at me, skeptical-like. "I was wrong," she sighed. "You are like other men. You still interested in hearing how we met?"

"Tell me."

"Okay." She paused, maybe weighing where to start. "Eight years ago, after graduating from Long Island College, I came to the city to take acting lessons. People had always told me I was beautiful enough to be a model or an actress."

"People were right," I said. A smile crept onto her face, but she doused it.

"Anyway, I was taking acting classes, so I had to waitress to make ends meet. One night the hostess quits, and the manager makes me hostess. In walks this guy, a regular, slight Russian accent, like a more sophisticated Boris Badenov, you know? Boris and Natasha in the cartoon? Not too tall, dark eyes with a hardness to them, very well dressed in a blue sharkskin suit and tie, thick black hair slicked back like an old-time gangster. And very good-looking, like a movie star. I show him and his date to their seat, and he slips me a hundred bucks. I'm so naïve, I go back to his table and tell him he must have given it to me by accident, but he says, 'No, darlink, you keep it.' So I smile and thank him for the tip, and when I'm walking away his date gives him the evil eye and says something like, 'Jesus, Boris, can you just keep it in your pants until dessert?' When I hear her say his name's Boris I almost fall over laughing."

"Because he talked like Boris Badenov?"

She nodded. "Anyway, next night, he's back, this time alone. I take him to his deuce—you know, table for two?—and he slips me another hundred. I see he's alone, so I start to clear away the second setup when he says he's expecting someone, so I leave it. An hour later I see he's still by himself. Next time I pass by his table, he says, 'Excuse me.' So I stop, and he says, 'I think you're very beautiful.' Then he asks me to sit with him, says it's me he's been waiting for. I smile and say thanks, but I can't sit with customers while I'm working and start to move away. Then he says, 'You look like you could be Russian.' That got me. I never thought about whether I looked Russian, but maybe I did. It was the first time in a long time I thought about my real parents." She took a breath. "Anyway, he asks what time I get off and offers to buy me a drink. And that's how it started."

"And just because to you he looked like a mobster you thought he was Mafia?"

"No. Not then. I just knew he was cute enough to date, and since I wasn't going out with anyone else, I figured what the hell, have a drink with the guy. After work, he picks me up in a limo and takes me to his place on Long Island—a mansion with servants and a circular driveway and a pool and guest house—you know, standard rich guy stuff."

"That's why you moved in with him? Because he was rich?"

She glared at me. "Don't do that, okay? It's not cute, and I don't like it." I cursed myself—I didn't want to blow my chance to hear more, and she seemed to take that personally, maybe because it had the ring of truth. She looked away, pouting, and I wasn't sure what to do to get her talking again. I tried putting my hand on hers.

She looked down at my hand and pulled hers away. "I moved in with him," she said, "because he asked me to. And even though I didn't know him that well, I liked him, so I figured, why not?"

"Did Boris have a job?

"Yeah. He did. At least he said he did, but he didn't keep banker's hours. I never knew where he was or when he'd be home, except for the times he had guys over for a meeting or something.

"He ever tell you what he did for a living?"

"Yeah. He told me he exported oil. To Russia. I remember asking, 'Didn't Russia have plenty of oil,' and he said, 'It's complicated.' So I said, 'I'm pretty smart, explain it to me.' That's when his eyes went stone cold, shark eyes, you know? For a second I thought he might hit me, but he just told me to knock off the third degree."

"He ever get violent?"

"Not with me. But, once …" she hesitated. "Once I saw him get really angry." I waited for her to tell me what happened, but she stood up and started walking into the bedroom.

I abandoned what was left of my cereal and followed her in. When I got there, she was naked from the waist up, shimmying into an exercise top, and I lost the thread of the conversation. But when she was covered up, I started in again. "So you saw Boris lose it?"

"Yeah," she said, grabbing her cross-trainers and sitting down on the bed. "He had a big meeting at the house, and he ended up throwing one of the guys out. The guy was bigger than him, but Boris was like a professional wrestler the way he manhandled him through the door. Next thing I know, the guy's lying face up on the driveway with blood coming out of his nose and his ears, not moving at all. When I started to run out and help the guy, Boris grabbed my arm, told me to leave him alone. Said the asshole was lucky he didn't kill him. At first, I thought he was just being a tough guy. But when I saw the look in his eyes, the way he was holding on to my arm, I realized Boris was actually capable of killing someone."

"Jesus."

When she finished tying her shoes, she looked up at me. "I'd seen more than my fair share of violence as a kid, so it wasn't that I was scared," she explained. "More surprised. But I started wondering about Boris and this job he claimed to have, so I went snooping in his office one day. There were no files in the filing cabinet, no papers on his desk, nothing to see. But I did find an automatic pistol in one of the desk drawers. That's when I started thinking maybe I was involved with a guy who was mobbed up."

"What do you mean, you saw plenty of violence as a kid?" I asked.

Leslie said nothing, just walked by me, putting her hand on my face as she passed. When it slid off, she made her way to the door, said, "I'm going to the gym. Be back later." And that was that.

***

To find Leslie I'd need to contact Boris. Approaching him would be dangerous. I had to have a plan.

Ordinarily on a sunny day like this, I'd make the trip from Aiden's back to my place on foot. The long walk would have taken the better part of an hour, time I could use to think, but the sidewalk was already so hot it shimmered, so I thought better of it. My first choice was a cab, and just imagining the cab's blasting air-conditioning was almost enough to cool me off. I pushed through the crowd waiting for the light on the corner and tried flagging a cab, but after five minutes I gave up. The subway entrance was right behind me, so I trotted down the steps and through the turnstile and grabbed a train that was just pulling in. I stepped into a nearly empty car—just a mom with a stroller full of toddler sleeping through the chill of the air-conditioning—and stood clinging to the pole near the door. A minute later, the brakes screeched as the car came to a stop at the Eighth Avenue station. The toddler woke up and went squeal for squeal with the subway brakes. The mom jumped up and, paying the screaming kid no mind, hurried out the opened doors. Then the platform full of people pushed their way into my car. I scrambled to a seat rather than let myself get wedged into a crowd of sweaty citizens all trying to keep from falling as the train pulled out of the station. Twenty minutes later, I was taking the stairs two at a time out of the Seventy-Ninth Street station.

I had almost reached my block when I realized that whoever had threatened me could be waiting at my apartment. Up ahead was a Starbucks, and there was probably one behind me and one across the street, too. They were everywhere in the city, like toadstools after a rainstorm. For a couple of bucks, I could sit there all morning, nurse the most expensive bad cup of coffee money could buy, and plan the best way to confront Boris.

Before I reached the Starbucks I was jolted by the sound of a car horn. It was a blue Chevy Tahoe, parked illegally next to a hydrant. A young blonde woman in the passenger seat caught my eye and gestured to an unfolded map, indicating she needed help. Her window slid down, and I approached the car. She looked up at me, and as she did, I noticed there was something in the curve of the nose and the wide-set blue eyes that reminded me of Leslie. Or maybe it was the cleft chin. Or maybe I just had Leslie on the brain.

The woman in the car held the map out, and I bent down to speak to her. "Lost?" She nodded and pointed to the map. It was a map of Italy, and she was pointing to Rome. "Lady," I said, "either that's the wrong map, or I'm the wrong guy to ask directions."

A voice behind me said, "No, you're the right guy." The accent was Russian. I felt a sudden jab in my ribs. I glanced down long enough to see the gun. "Get in the car, mister." He opened the back door and gave me a head-banging shove that put me into the middle of the seat.

"Hey, what the fuck!" I said, rubbing my forehead.

"Boss wants to see you."

The blonde got out of the car, walked around to the driver's side, and opened the rear door. She was skinny and slightly built, someone you might mistake for a tall twelve-year-old if you didn't know better. She put on an additional ten years as she got closer. A black T-shirt and black jeans slimmed her further but didn't mask her curves. There were four Cyrillic letters tattooed on her left forearm, and the whole package made her look like a fashion model turned motorcycle moll. "Put hands out now. Back behind." It took me a second to understand that she wanted me to turn around and put my hands behind my back. I shifted on my seat to comply, but I must not have moved quickly enough because she shoved my head down toward the guy with the gun, then got a nylon zip tie around my wrist. I grunted when she yanked it tight. She said something in Russian and the guy, still holding the gun, nodded. He grabbed my throat and shoved me back into the seat. I didn't struggle. There were two of them, and even though one was a woman I outweighed by at least fifty pounds, I didn't know what she was capable of. The pressure on my neck increased, and I started to panic. When she covered my face with a cloth, or maybe a handkerchief, I tried twisting away, causing something, her nail or maybe a ring, to cut into my cheek. When I started choking, the hand around my throat loosened, opening the airway. The handkerchief, tight against my nose and mouth, smelled like alcohol. I took a gulp of the noxious air through my mouth. The light behind the girl went fuzzy. She and her crooked smile started to darken. My eyes moved from her to the guy. He, too, was getting darker. My second to last thought before everything went black was that things couldn't have worked out better, because I was about to meet Boris. My last thought—I hope I didn't die first.

CHAPTER 10

I came to. People were speaking, but I couldn't make out what they were saying. Fear kept me from opening my eyes. There was a steady pounding that made me think I might be at a disco before I realized it was inside my head. I wiggled my fingers and toes, just to make sure I wasn't paralyzed or drugged so badly that my nervous system stopped trafficking signals to my limbs. Whatever they used to knock me out worked as advertised. At least the thug who'd kidnapped me hadn't bashed me on the head with his gun. While not yet gripped by Stockholm syndrome, I was still grateful they hadn't cracked my skull.

I lay still and listened. A man and a woman were arguing, but I couldn't make out what they were saying. Then I realized they were speaking Russian. The guy who'd thrown me in the car had a relatively high, hoarse voice. This man's voice was deep. The woman sounded like the one who'd drugged me. As my brain fog lifted, the man shifted to English and said, "Okay, Tanya, that's enough." Tanya didn't agree and kept hectoring. The argument continued, rising to a crescendo until the man told Tanya to be careful or she'd end up like her sister. The woman shouted, slowly and in her Russian-accented English, "Fuck-it you, Boris." The man laughed and said with almost no accent, "And fuck-it you, Tanya." The next thing I heard was a door slamming. My eyes popped open.

I was in what looked like a den or a library, lying on a couch face up with a pillow under my head. The room was darkly paneled with a vaulted ceiling and built-in bookcases. The books were all leatherbound and arranged neatly enough to make me think they might be fakes. The windows were full of daylight, so I assumed I hadn't been unconscious for more than a couple of hours.

The man with the deep voice walked over to me. He looked to be in his forties and was dressed in gray slacks and a white golf shirt, unbuttoned. He wasn't tall, but he had wide shoulders over a broad chest with a tangle of chest hair that reached almost to his neck, all of which painted a picture of a man you couldn't knock over with a bulldozer. His hair, black and heavily pomaded, looked like an oil slick on an asphalt road at midnight, with a white line of a side part. Although clean-shaven, he was one of those guys who could never shave close enough to avoid a face perpetually darkened by a five o'clock shadow. Ruggedly handsome in a threatening sort of way. I could see Leslie throwing in with a guy like him.

It seemed Boris hadn't noticed me yet, and I debated whether to play possum or sit up. My fingers were numb. I clenched my fists and found that my hands were still bound by zip ties, and while I couldn't see them, my ankles seemed to be zip-tied as well. I decided to stay put rather than risk falling off the couch by trying to sit. "You must be Boris," I said.

He smiled. "Boris Smirnoff," he said with a slight bow I'd last seen in a Dracula movie, "at your service."

"Service—great. Why don't you start by servicing these zip ties? They're digging into my wrists, and I'm worried they might leave a mark."

Boris laughed and, as he walked over to the door, asked, "Do you find this amusing, Henry? May I call you Henry?" I made his accent as minted in Russia but groomed in London rather than New York. Leslie had exaggerated—he didn't sound like Boris Badenov at all.

"Yeah, call me Henry. And no, I don't find this amusing. I just like to keep it light during my kidnappings." In fact, I was scared to death.

Boris went to the door, opened it, and gestured to someone in the hall. "Leo, please come in and relieve our guest of his restraints." Leo came in but didn't seem to know what to do until Boris dumbed it down. "Leo, cut off the zip ties," he commanded, then turned to me, smiling. "Leo learned English by watching American gangster movies on television, so I have to remember to keep it simple. Isn't that right, Leo?"

Leo replied, "Right, boss." As he walked toward me, I couldn't help wondering what else he'd learned from gangster movies.

You might expect a guy in Leo's line of work to be a big muscular guy, but that wasn't Leo. He was small, maybe five-six or five-seven, and wore a gray suit, white shirt, and a thin black tie carefully knotted below a prominent Adam's apple. His small eyes were set wide above hollow cheeks. A prominent nose hooked over lips so thin and pale they almost disappeared into his face.

Leo pulled a long knife from his waistband, bent over me, and used it so quickly and artfully that the zip ties seemed to fall away of their own accord, as if the blade had nothing to do with it.

I sat up and rubbed my wrists together while keeping track of Leo's knife. When he saw me eying it, he flipped it in the air a couple of times and winked before leaving the room. Boris closed the door behind him and turned to me. "That's more comfortable, isn't it? Now we can have a civilized conversation."

"I prefer my conversations civilized. Cuts down on my dry-cleaning costs."

"Ha! Very amusing, Henry." Boris wandered over to a table in the corner. On it was a tray with a couple of crystal rocks glasses, a stainless-steel ice bucket, and an open bottle of vodka. He dropped some ice into the glass and poured vodka nearly to the top, then picked the glass up and walked over to a green leather wing chair across from the couch and sat down. He seemed relaxed as he rested his drink on the arm of the chair, crossed his legs, and smiled as he looked at me with eyes as black and forbidding as intergalactic space. "I don't intend for you to be my guest for very long, Henry. I just wanted to make sure that you understand our arrangement, and I like doing business face to face."

"You're saying we have an arrangement? We just met—how can we have an arrangement?"

Boris glared at me. "Didn't your ex-wife go to your office yesterday?"

"Leslie? Yeah, she was there. She said she was in trouble, her life was in danger, and she needed my help." I paused as if remembering. "Oh yeah, and that if I didn't help her my life was in danger, too."

Boris raised his eyebrows. "And …?"

"I didn't believe her."

"I thought that might be the case. Which is exactly why I had you brought here, Henry," he said. "You see, Leslie was telling you the truth. She's in trouble. With me. Because when that bitch walked out on me six years ago, she neglected to return the ring I gave her. I want it back."

"What's that have to do with me? I don't even know where Leslie is right now, let alone where the engagement ring is."

"To be clear, Henry, it wasn't an engagement ring. I never proposed, and we were never engaged. If Leslie told you otherwise, she was lying."

I thought back to my first conversation with Leslie. "She told me the ring on her finger meant she was spoken for. Maybe she didn't say she was engaged. But that's a distinction without a difference."

Boris smiled. "Didn't stop you from seducing her."

"Or of her seducing me."

"A distinction without a difference, Henry."

"Touché." If I didn't fear for my life I might have enjoyed our banter, cheap as it was.

Boris took a sip and crossed his legs in the other direction. "I didn't give her the ring. As I told her at the time, the ring was my mother's, and I was letting her wear it. She asked me if I was proposing or just letting her wear it to keep Tom, Dick, and Henry from hitting on her, like, what did she call it …?" Boris put his hand to his forehead as if trying to remember. "Oh yes … like a chastity belt."

"Well whatever it was, when she showed up at my apartment that night soaking wet, she wasn't wearing a ring."

"She was soaking wet?" Boris asked.

"It was raining that night."

"Funny," he said, "I'm certain she left on the Fourth of July. I remember hearing fireworks when she walked out the door. Later, I went out on my deck, had a cigar, and looked at the stars. It was a crystal clear night."

A crystal clear July 4th evening filled with fireworks? I wasn't even home that July 4th—I was at a friend's place in East Hampton celebrating his thirty-fifth birthday, and I recall sitting on a beach while a fireworks show lit the cloudless sky over a nearby country club. I stayed the whole week. Leslie showed up a few days after I got back to the city. By then it was mid-July, or later.

Neither of us spoke for a few seconds. "Well, doing the math, it looks like Leslie didn't come straight to me. She spent a week somewhere else."

Boris frowned. "All the more reason to assume she was up to no good."

"Yeah, well, the no good could have been she was sleeping with somebody else for a week before she picked on me. Probably had nothing to do with the ring," I said, wondering if it did. I didn't want to telegraph that to Boris. "All I know is what she told me, that you broke off the engagement, and she was so mad she threw the ring at you before she left. And now you're telling me it's missing? Maybe the ring's been around here all the time, hidden under a radiator or something."

He laughed. "Hidden under a radiator ... why didn't I think of that?" He laughed some more. "That's probably it! If only I'd looked harder, emptied the vacuum cleaner bags, undid all the plumbing in case it fell down a drain." He leaned forward. "Do you think I'm some kind of idiot?" he asked through clenched teeth.

The look on his face scared the shit out of me.

"I have no doubt," Boris continued with the same menace in his voice, "that she took the ring with her." He paused, leaned back into the chair, and returned to his original mock-friendly demeanor. "A few weeks ago I was reminded of how special that ring is to me."

"Reminded by what?" I asked, genuinely curious about the delay.

Boris returned to snarling. "None of your fucking business." He took a large gulp of vodka. "I sent Leo to get the ring back. Leslie told him she didn't have it, that she wasn't sure where it was, told him to ask you."

"Me! How the fuck would I know where the stupid ring is?"

"And yet," Boris said, standing up and jiggling the ice in his glass, "And yet, after Leslie told Leo she didn't have it, I had him follow her, just in case she did anything ... of interest." He shrugged. "And sure enough, a few days later she went to your office." He crossed the room, picked up the vodka bottle and refilled his glass, then stirred it with his index finger. "I think you know more about the ring than you're telling me." He wiped his swizzle finger on his pants before downing the entire glass of vodka in one gulp. "Here's the arrangement, Henry. I don't care who has the ring or who doesn't have the ring. All I know is when Leslie left me, she was wearing it, and not long after that, you two got married. So I hope you can see how I have to consider you both responsible."

"At the risk of repeating myself, I don't even know where to find Leslie."

"You'll find her, or maybe she'll find you," Boris said. "And if, three days from now, I don't have my ring back, well, I'm afraid I'll have to send Leo to find you both. And I'm not sure he'll be as gentle as he was today."

"Thanks for the warning," I said.

"Oh, and one more thing." Boris put the empty glass on the tray. "I've got a little carrot and stick thing here, too."

"What do you mean?"

Boris started in on a smile but stopped halfway. He folded his arms over his chest. "I'm sure you understand how I can make things difficult if you don't bring me the ring."

"You just told me. Leo, the homicidal maniac. I take it he's the stick. And the carrot?"

"Well, you understand that I can't have you going to the police," Boris explained. "If you do, I'll be forced to reveal certain incriminating information, secrets that would have an impact on your career. And not in a good way." He smiled. "But, if you keep your mouth shut, now and forever, your secrets are safe with me."

It took me less than a second to figure out what he was talking about. It wasn't a carrot. It was blackmail. And blackmail belonged in the "Stick" column along with Leo. The only way Boris would know about my early indiscretion was if Leslie found the evidence before we were married and somehow Boris got hold of it. Maybe Leslie gave it to him, but I preferred to think he found it after she'd left him. Either way, Boris could use it to get me fired, maybe even disbarred. Suddenly, getting beaten up by Leo for failing to do Boris's bidding didn't seem bad compared to losing my livelihood.

I glared at Boris, and he stared back with a half-smile on his face and eyes that were black and cold. He called Leo into the room and told him that I was leaving, and he should return me to wherever it was he found me.

"Should I knock him out first?" Leo asked.

Boris looked at me. "That won't be necessary. I'm sure Mr. Gladstone will be the perfect gentleman on the ride back." As I walked out the door with Leo behind me, Boris called out, "Henry— keep in touch."

CHAPTER 11

I sat in the back seat during the hour it took Leo to drive me home. When I put on my seat belt, I realized my cell phone wasn't in my pocket—it must have fallen out during the scuffle. Rather than just sit there, I thought I'd try and engage Leo in conversation, hoping to get some clue as to why Boris had waited six years to recover the engagement ring, because to me that made no sense. But Leo wasn't much for small talk and, after ignoring my questions for a few minutes, told me to shut the fuck up unless I wanted another nose full of narcotic. I didn't, so I shut the fuck up. Leo probably had no idea what the newfound urgency was all about anyway.

I leaned my head back on the seat and thought about the incident Boris was threatening to reveal if I didn't play ball. It could end my career at Loveless, Brown, and possibly my career as a lawyer.

My eyes closed as I recalled my youthful transgression.

***

It had been twelve years earlier. I'd been working as a summer associate at Loveless, Brown when my phone rang. I picked it up. "This is Henry Gladstone."

"Gladstone! It's me, Metrano. From the yacht club? How the hell are ya?"

"Tony Metrano, long time no hear from," I said, wondering how my teenage mentor had gotten my number. "What are you up to?"

"Working my way through community college. The yacht club gave me a scholarship."

"Good for you, Tony."

"Yeah, and now you're a big-shot lawyer."

I laughed. "I'm a big-shot first-year law student working as a summer associate."

"Well, that's close enough for me. I need help."

"What, legal help? You in trouble?"

"Stupid trouble, not legal trouble." I listened to Tony's stupid trouble story for ten minutes. I should have guessed that sleeping his way through the yacht club's ladies' auxiliary roster would finally catch up with him.

"Just because she fell in love with you doesn't mean you have to take her calls," I offered. "Tell her it's over."

"I tried. I broke it off weeks ago, but she's not taking no for an answer. She's threatening to rat me out to the general manager if we don't go back to our regular rendezvous schedule."

"… putting your scholarship in jeopardy?"

"That, and also putting my balls in jeopardy. Losing a scholarship is one thing, but my balls? It would be like losing my two best friends."

I laughed again. "How you gonna lose your balls?"

"Her husband's got a reputation around the yacht club as kind of a rough guy—I think he's an ex-boxer or something. If he finds out …"

That's when he outlined his scheme. He wanted me to write a letter threatening to sue her for stalking. "See? If she gets her husband involved in a court thing, he'll kill her twice, once for sleeping with me and once for dragging him into court. She gets a letter from a lawyer, she gets scared and walks away."

"Nice," I said, thinking his scheme might just work. "There's just one thing. Can this wait three years? I'm not a lawyer, remember?

"Oh for chrissake, type up a nasty-sounding letter and pretend you're a lawyer."

If I did, was there any chance someone at the firm would know? Not if I was careful, but if I got caught there would be life-changing consequences. I'd be dismissed from the summer associate program, and they'd probably inform my law school. The dean could decide to suspend or expel me. Getting caught could end my career.

The next morning I arrived at the office early enough that I had the place to myself for at least an hour. After drafting a threatening letter to Tony's stalker, I printed it out on Loveless, Brown letterhead and addressed the envelope. But just before dropping it in the mail slot, I hesitated. Was Tony's problem worth risking my future as a lawyer? I weighed that against my chances of getting caught, decided they were slim to none, and pushed the envelope through the slot.

Five weeks later, I was back at school. Nobody'd blown the whistle, so I stopped thinking about it. I never heard whether the letter worked, but I assumed the husband didn't find out, didn't kill his wife twice, and didn't cut Tony's balls off. That would have made the news for sure.

***

At around ten that night, Leo announced, "We're here, asshole," and pulled up to my apartment building. As I unbuckled my seat belt, Leo turned and handed me my cell phone, which he must have taken after they drugged me, and with it a folded piece of manila paper wrapped in cellophane tape. "Boss told me to give you this," he said. I undid my seat belt, shoved the phone and the package in my pocket, and climbed out onto the sidewalk. Without a word, I closed the door of the car I'd been kidnapped in, driven by the guy who'd kidnapped me. Somehow, I couldn't bring myself to thank Leo for the ride, a breach of etiquette that I felt entitled to under the circumstances. The tires squealed as he pulled away from the curb and found a place in the summer Saturday night traffic.

Back in my apartment, I fell into my favorite chair, exhausted. I pulled the manila paper out of my pocket and ripped off the tape. The handwritten note said, "Here's Leslie's address. Find the ring. You have three days. Boris." Taped to the note below her address were two keys, presumably to her apartment.

Boris and I were now partners. I'd just been officially enlisted by a Russian mobster in a hunt for stolen jewelry. In order to find that ring, he'd kidnapped me, intimidated me with bodily harm, and threatened blackmail. He'd also handed me Leslie, all tied up with a ribbon and a bow. Maybe he thought keeping track of the two of us would be easier if we were together. Boris assumed she cared about me. The truth was, she didn't. I thought I'd forgotten about her. When I threw her out of my office a few days earlier, I fooled myself into thinking I'd washed my hands of her. It would have been easier to wash off a tattoo.

I had to hand it to Leslie, Boris was quite a guy. Of all the mopes who'd probably tried to pick her up when she was a hostess in that classy restaurant, she'd chosen Boris, an older, charming, and dangerous character, who checked off all the textbook boxes for sociopath and then added a few of his own. I could only imagine what she'd been thinking. Maybe she'd been low on adventure in her life at that moment and hoped Boris could supply some. In the brief time I'd known her before we'd gotten married, she'd had a fetish for excitement that put her in harm's way plenty. Like driving fast and walking through dangerous neighborhoods at two in the morning daring someone to mess with her. One day, after we were married, she suggested parachuting. "C'mon," she said, "you don't even have to do anything except fall down." When I declined, she called me a pussy and went by herself. I worried her adrenaline addiction would get her killed someday, but every time I mentioned it she just laughed.

I'd been staring at the note and keys in my hand for what seemed like an hour but was more likely twenty seconds when my cell phone rang. I pulled it out of my pocket and answered on the fourth ring. "Hank!" Aiden barked. "Jesus H. Christ, Hank, I've been calling you all day, why didn't you answer?" Exhausted, I didn't reply and even thought about just hanging up. The last thing I wanted was more interrogation, especially by my best friend.

"Hank, are you there?"

"I'm here, Aiden."

"Oh, man, you scared the shit out of me. I thought maybe … well I thought something bad happened to you. You okay?"

"Why shouldn't I be? My kidnappers were nice enough to release me and drive me home—that would send anyone's spirits soaring, wouldn't it?"

Aiden was quiet for a few seconds. "Are you gonna tell me what in fucknation you're talking about?"

"Not now," I said. "I'm too tired, but I promise to tell you the whole story tomorrow. Speaking of tomorrow, I'm holding a piece of paper with an address on it—Leslie's address. Can you drive me to Brooklyn in the morning so I can check it out?"

"Wow, I guess finding her is going to be a lot easier than you thought," he said. "Where'd you get her address?"

"I'll fill you in tomorrow. Promise."

Aiden agreed to pick me up the next morning at ten and drive to the address. "See you tomorrow, pal," he said. "And get some rest. You sound beat."

As soon as he hung up, I started shaking. When I tried to put my phone on the table my hands were shaking so hard I dropped it. The shaking spread from my hands to my arms and down my legs, until eventually my whole body was overcome, shivering like it was minus ten degrees, and the wind was howling, and I was naked and exposed and afraid of dying.

Which I was.

On the drive home, I'd focused on Boris's threat of career-ending blackmail, possibly to distract myself from the less explicit but implied threat of violence.

I'd been in scary situations before: fist fights, brawls, muggings, even a hotel fire once that landed me unconscious in the hospital. I'd gotten my share of nasty threats in the mail, even death threats on a few occasions, mostly from imprisoned clients who thought I'd done a lousy job of defending them. But Boris and his thug Leo? They were the stuff of nightmares. The kind that involves being chased into dark alleys that dead-ended, forcing you to turn and face the guy trying to kill you; the kind where you wake up breathless and sweating; where you need a minute to convince yourself it was only a dream because your pulse is racing, and you're staring into the dark at the lingering face of death.

I'd never dealt with the likes of Boris and Leo; never thought I would.

Blackmail and the threat of a beating, or worse, were very motivating. I'd do as Boris had asked.

After a few minutes, I got a hold of myself somehow, and the shaking subsided. My phone lay at my feet, but instead of retrieving it and inspecting the screen for signs of cracks, I forced myself into a standing position, zombie-walked to my bed, dropped the note and keys on my night table, collapsed face first onto my pillow, and immediately fell into a dreamless sleep.

CHAPTER 12

Nine hours later, I was awakened by the thin shaft of sunlight that somehow jinked around neighborhood buildings and found my window for a few minutes each morning. Not quite awake, I squinted at the alarm clock on my nightstand and made the time as 7:40 a.m. before the events of the previous day found me and pounced like a hungry panther.

I rubbed my eyes in a further attempt to leave sleep behind, then reached for the keys on my nightstand. One was brass, one silver, but both shone like newly minted coins. Running my finger over the teeth of the brass one, I could feel the metal shavings that came with a key fresh from the duplicating machine. I wondered how Boris managed to get Leslie's keys long enough to make copies. Then I remembered—Boris had sent Leo to find Leslie and get the ring back. If Leo had grabbed and knocked her out with a narcotic-soaked handkerchief like he did me, he'd have plenty of time to go through her bag, find her keys, and duplicate them before she came to. For all I knew, he'd made copies of my keys, driver's license, social security card, and the slip of paper I kept in my wallet with all my password recovery codes. By now Leo could have stolen my identity, drained my bank accounts, and remotely accessed my computer. I shook my head, annoyed that the dark place I was in could get darker, like a mole on your arm you don't notice until it darkens, turns purple, and becomes a skin cancer that ruins your life for a while before killing you.

I put the keys back on the nightstand and pushed myself up from the mattress before realizing I was still wearing yesterday's clothes. Out of habit, I raised my arm and took a whiff. It wasn't pretty, another reminder of the rough day I'd had, courtesy of Boris the Russian mobster, his gunsel Leo, and Tanya, the slight, hot-tempered blonde with the Russian tattoo. I decided a shower and a cup of strong coffee would help put me right.

I turned on the shower and while waiting for it to get hot, I ran my hand over my face, causing my right cheek to sting. I turned to the mirror. There was a four-inch scratch below my right eye, a souvenir from yesterday's struggle with the Russian girl. Maybe the scar would make me more attractive I thought, as I considered my reflection in the mirror, or at least more memorable. I'd always thought of my face as forgettable, occupying the zone halfway between homely and handsome. My teeth were straight thanks to the braces I'd worn as a kid. I had lots of thick, wavy brown hair and hoped it stayed that way. My nose was bigger than necessary, but Vinnie, my barber, showed me how combing my hair so that it hung shelf-like above my forehead made my nose recede into my face. "… like Lenny Bernstein, the conductor," he'd said. "Great conductor, great hair. Lucky for him, because his honker was gigantic." My eyes were mahogany brown, according to my mother, but just plain brown on my driver's license. Even though I'd gotten a few hours of shuteye, there were bags under my eyes begging me to sleep.

But I had work to do.

I got into the shower. The water pressure in the building turned my shower into something like a high-pressure car wash and left my skin tingling. Before getting out of the shower, I twisted the handle so it ran cold for the last twenty seconds, imagining the shock of the icy water forging me into a tempered-steel version of myself. I toweled off and felt fresh and ready. After throwing on a clean pair of jeans and a black T-shirt, I grabbed the two keys, tossed them a few inches from my palm, and caught them in my fist, a small gesture of self-confidence. The keys went into my pocket, along with the note that I no longer needed, since the address was now lodged in my brain like a small caliber bullet: 797 Sixth Avenue, Apartment B, Park Slope, Brooklyn, NY. On a sleepy summer Sunday, with half the Upper East Side still in bed and the other half in the Hamptons, it wouldn't take more than thirty minutes to get there.

Aiden was waiting in front of my building in his silver Porsche 911 convertible. He'd bought it as soon as he got divorced, along with some new clothes and a state-of-the-art sound system for his apartment. My divorce from Leslie had the opposite effect on me. I didn't want shiny new stuff, or a new girlfriend, or a new life. All I wanted when she'd left me was for her to come back. For months, I couldn't stop thinking about her, and I ignored everything else but my job. It was ridiculous, of course, to hope Leslie and I would get back together. I fought the feeling for a year, then gave up fighting and just tucked the dull ache into my soul for safekeeping.

As I opened the car door and fell into the bucket seat, it occurred to me I'd gotten what I wanted—Leslie was back in my life. Not the way I pictured it, and probably not for long, but Boris and death threats aside, we'd been thrown together for one last dance.

"Hey," I said to Aiden while I looked for a place in the cockpit to park my coffee cup. "Where's the cup holders?"

"Does this look like a minivan to you?" Aiden shoved the car into first gear and released the brake. "It's a Porsche. It looks great and goes fast. The engineers hated the idea of cup holders."

I spotted one hiding near the door. "Found it."

"I'm happy for you," he said. "Now let's go find your crazy ex-wife."

As we tore away from the curb, I watched my coffee spill out of the small hole in the plastic lid and onto the black leather seat next to my leg. I wished I'd finished the damn thing before getting in the car.

Aiden zipped down Second Avenue, deftly maneuvering around slower cars to make every green light on our way to the entrance to the FDR Drive. We floated onto the highway and hit seventy miles an hour on our way to the left lane. Wind in my hair, heart in my throat, seat belt compressing my chest, I found the ride soothing rather than thrilling after all I'd been through.

Aiden had to shout for me to hear him above the roar of traffic. "You want to tell me what happened yesterday?"

I gave Aiden the highlights at the top of my lungs while Aiden yelled an occasional "Jesus" or "Oh my god" back at me to let me know he was getting it all.

It wasn't a long story, especially since I skipped the part about Boris's threatening me with blackmail. Aiden had known me for so long that he assumed he knew everything about me, and he pretty much did, except for that one thing Boris knew. I wasn't about to tell Aiden about it now. I thought the whole episode was behind me, that I'd successfully tied a cinder block to it and dropped it in the East River. Boris had somehow found out and was threatening to expose me. I could sense the rope around the cinder block fraying. I had to get that ring back to him.

Before long we were on the Brooklyn Bridge with Manhattan at our backs; fifteen minutes later, we were on Sixth Avenue. Aiden had stopped talking after I'd told him my story, and I found his silence unusual and unsettling. No questions, no comments, no nothing, just hands on the wheel and eyes straight ahead. I glanced at him several times, but he didn't glance back.

Aiden slowed down to neighborhood speed, which allowed me to track the numbers on the townhouses. "There it is. 797." Aiden pulled to the curb next to a fire hydrant near the corner of Fourth Street.

"You can't park here," I said, stating the obvious.

"I'm not parking. I'm stopping to ask what you plan to do."

"Improvise."

"Well, I've got a couple of questions. Like what if she's not home?"

"We go in."

"Breaking and entering?" Aiden shook his head. "Not for me. Even you can't get me to commit a felony."

"Well," I said, pulling the keys from my pocket, "How about just entering?"

"Holy shit, are those the keys to Leslie's apartment?"

I nodded, and Aiden reached for them. "I'm not going in, and neither are you."

I pulled my hand back before he could snatch the keys. "Hey, she might be home. Then we go in and offer to help. If she's not there, well, we take a look around. Maybe we find something useful."

"Like what?"

"Like clues to where she is and what happened to the ring."

Aiden considered that for a few seconds. "How about this? You knock on the door while I wait here, watching. If Leslie answers, I'll join you. If nobody's home, and you use the keys to get in, then I'll wait in the car."

"That still makes you an accessory."

"Not if I take off at the first sign of trouble."

"You wouldn't."

Instead of answering, Aiden just glared at me for a few seconds, then looked away. I started to get out, and he grabbed my arm. "Wait," he said. "I don't know how to say this, so I'll just say it. When I picked you up this morning, I felt good about helping you find Leslie. I thought, yeah, this Boris character wants his ring back, and Leslie, being the lying piece of shit she is, either has it or knows where it is, so let's find Leslie and end this. I'm your best friend, and you're in a jam. But ..." He shifted in his seat and put his hands over his face, then raked his fingers through his windblown mop of hair.

"But what?"

He turned off the car and leaned his head back against the headrest. "But," he said, turning toward me, "now you tell me he's kidnapped you, threatened you—god only knows what's coming. You could have been hurt yesterday. I understand you feel obligated to help Leslie because you were once married, but I always thought she was crazy, and frankly when she left you, I breathed a sigh of relief. For you, not for me. There was something about her that made me uneasy, like the way she didn't talk about her past, and how she acted around you."

"How do you mean?"

"She seemed, I don't know, separate from you. Indifferent? Like you were there, but you didn't matter. And I just kept thinking that someday Leslie would drag you into something ... nasty. And here we are."

A large red dump truck made too much noise as it lumbered past us, interrupting Aiden's tirade. I shifted in my seat and wanted to get out, but something told me Aiden wasn't finished, so I stayed put and listened.

"Boris is a really bad guy," he said. "Worse than I imagined. You're in this, Leslie's in this, but so far, I'm not. The last thing I need is to show up on Boris's radar. Because if I do, then I'm a potential target, and I don't think I can go that far. Even for you." He turned away and looked at the street for a few seconds, even though there was nothing to see.

The thing of it was, he was right. It was unfair of me to put Aiden in danger.

I put my hand on his shoulder, and he turned to look at me. "You should go," I said. "Get some bagels and lox, call your girlfriend, and enjoy your Sunday. I'll be fine. I can take the subway home."

Aiden shook his head. "I drove you here, and I'll drive you back. But Hank, be careful, for chrissake. If Leslie's there, you don't know what she might do. You're not a team. She's in this for herself. She's fucking dangerous."

I hated hearing it but didn't argue. As a lawyer, I made a living arguing with people I knew were right, and for the worst reason in the world—money. But no one was paying me to object to what Aiden said, so I let him have the last word.

I climbed out of the car.

I had no idea if Leslie would be there to answer the door, but my bet was no Leslie. Better if she wasn't there. That way I could nose around for a few minutes, and then, before rejoining my fair-weather friend Aiden, I'd slip a note under the door. The note, already written and folded in my pocket, said "Leslie—Please don't make this difficult. Call me so we can both get out of this jam. Henry."

I walked down the street with my eye on the house numbers. Good thing they were numbered because from the outside they all looked the same, with three floors, three rectangular windows side by side, and a variety of air conditioners dangling above the sidewalk. Most of the row houses were painted the original brown. Only their doors were painted different colors.

When I came to number 797 my heart started to beat a little faster. I opened the waist-high, wrought iron gate and walked slowly down the steps to apartment B, the garden apartment. Before I knocked, someone said, "Hi there." I looked up. A middle-aged woman wearing jeans and a flowered short-sleeved top stood at the railing of the stoop next door. She wore her dark hair pulled taut into a ponytail that wagged behind her, like a friendly puppy's, as she moved. The large pink watering can in her right hand must have been full because she held the bottom with her left hand. "Beautiful morning," she said, then tilted the watering can toward one of the potted plants surrounding her on the stoop. Some water splashed off the plant leaves and landed on my shoulder. I wiped it off with my hand.

"Yes it is." I rang Leslie's doorbell and waited. Then I knocked.

"She's not home," the woman said. Her smug smile was an advertisement for the "knowledge is power" school of social grace. "I know because she asked me to water her plants." She pointed to the plants next to me just in case I'd never seen one before and didn't understand what she was talking about. "Those plants," she said, "not the ones inside, if she has any. I wouldn't know because I've never been invited in." I listened passively, not wanting to appear rude but hoping the lack of nodding and smiling on my part would deter her. She moved to another plant and poured, and again some water splashed around me. "Said she'd be gone a few days."

"That's okay," I said, "I have keys." I held up the keys in the same way as she pointed to the plants, in case she didn't know what I meant by keys. We were both speaking unaccented English, but for some reason, maybe because we were strangers, we took pains to make sure we were understanding each other.

I jiggled the keys. "She called and said something about a stain on the ceiling in her bathroom and wanted me to see it." The woman stared at me like she wasn't buying any of this. My mind bounced around to some possibilities, including the truth (ex-husband nosing around), a half-truth (a friend or family member, which somehow seemed insufficient), or a complete lie. "I'm the landlord," I said, before realizing how ludicrous a lie that was. This lady might know the landlord—she could be the landlord for all I knew—but it was too late.

The woman looked at me and squinted a little. "You're not the landlord. The landlord's an older woman. Marion I think her name is."

I stiffened, and my mind raced to find a comeback. "Oh, that's my mom," I replied as casually as I could. My neck was starting to ache from looking up at her. "She rents out the place. I'm looking after it for her. She's not well."

"Really? The last time I saw your mom I thought she looked great."

"I'll tell her you said that. I'm sure it will make her feel better." For a moment I thought she would challenge me further, but when she didn't, I slipped the brass key into the top lock. It slid in, and I turned the deadbolt, settling the question of whether these were the keys to the apartment.

As I turned the handle and stepped in, the woman said, "Please say hi for me. I'm Nola, by the way. Tell her Nola from Apartment A said hi, and I hope she feels bet—"

I slammed the door on Nola's last word and listened instead for any sounds coming from inside the house. I had to make sure the place was empty before I started poking around. Other than a leaky faucet dripping and my heart pounding, the place was quiet. "Hello," I said quietly, and then, a little louder, "Anybody home?"

Satisfied that Leslie wasn't there, I got down to business.

After a quick glance at the kitchen straight ahead of me, I scanned the living room to the left. A couch, a couple of throw pillows tucked neatly into the corners, and a television across from the seating area, but no signs of life. The room didn't look like it was used much. Leslie was never big on watching television—she always considered television a waste of her time, calling it "a propaganda machine masquerading as entertainment."

I moved to the kitchen. On the counter was a yellow legal pad with some names and numbers on it and notes scribbled on the top and the sides. I took a picture with my phone before continuing my search. There was a closed door at the back of the kitchen that probably led to a bedroom. I walked over to the door and knocked lightly before walking in, just in case Nola was wrong and Leslie had come back unannounced. Then it occurred to me that Leslie could be in there sleeping. Or dead.

I opened the bedroom door slowly and walked into an empty room. The bed was unmade. She'd never made the bed when we lived together either, so that became my job. I resisted the urge to make the bed (for old time's sake) and walked over to the night table. Nothing on it but a couple of *Cosmopolitan* magazines, this month's and last month's. Next, I opened the night table drawer. It was full of junk. Floating on top was what looked like a copy of a photo from a newspaper. I took a picture. Peeking out from under the newspaper photo was a pack of birth control pills. I closed the drawer and checked out the bathroom.

It was an undistinguished space, small, clean, and tiled in white. There was a single toothbrush lying on the small Formica countertop next to the sink, suggesting Leslie lived alone. The bathroom smelled like Leslie—I guess she was still using the same soap or shampoo. Lavender. Until I met her, I'd disliked lavender, but I'd gotten used to it, just as I'd adapted myself in a hundred different ways for Leslie. After the divorce, I wanted the scent of her out of the bathroom, so I scrubbed the walls, the bathtub, and the sink until the bathroom smelled like bleach and vinegar, which was, in a way, Leslie all over again.

I popped open the mirrored medicine cabinet above the sink and gave her medication the once-over. It was the usual assortment of over-the-counter pain relievers, cough and cold medicines, and sleeping pills. There were also several vials of prescription pills, some of which I assumed were the sort of pain, sleep, and anxiety pills that can become a habit. One bottle was almost full, and I could see the prescription on the label had been written a couple of days earlier by a Dr. Phenergan. Leslie's name was typed on all the labels, further evidence that she didn't have a roommate or a live-in boyfriend. I took a picture of the meds without disturbing them. When I shut the cabinet, the mirror swung my reflection at me. For a split second I thought there was someone else there, and I stupidly whipped around to face the imagined intruder. When I realized what had happened, I chuckled to myself, but just as the adrenaline jolt began to fade, I got a text. It was Aiden.

That lady you were talking to just made a phone call. I'd leave now

I glanced around the bathroom to make sure I hadn't disturbed anything, then hurried through the bedroom, down the hall, and out the front door.

Nola was still standing on the porch fussing with her plants. "Hey, did you find it?"

"Um, find what?" Was she talking about the ring? How could she know about that? I fumbled with the keys as I tried to relock the door.

"The stain," she said. "Did you find the stain?"

"Oh … right." Of course. I'd told her I was there about a stain. "Yeah, I found it." The first key slipped into the lock, and I flicked my wrist to lock it. "I'll have the plumber come by and check it out." I turned the second key and felt the deadbolt slide into place. Time to get the hell out of there. I trotted up the stairs and said, "The stain was right where Leslie said it would be."

I hustled off, but as I did, the woman shouted. "Leslie … who's Leslie? She told me her name was Robin!"

That was when I started running.

"Hey," Nola yelled, "Did you hear me? That's Robin's apartment! Hey … I know what you look like, mister, so you'd better hope—"

Her words faded, replaced by the pounding in my head as I ran. All I could think about was getting out of there. Aiden, true to his word, was waiting for me on the corner of Garfield Place, near where I'd left him. He must have seen me running because as soon as I jumped in the car, he tore out of the parking space, and within thirty seconds, we were out of the neighborhood and racing toward the Brooklyn Bridge. I took a deep breath and dropped my head back against the headrest in an attempt to calm down. My fist was still clenched around the keys and for a second, I thought it was stuck closed, but slowly, I opened my fingers and felt the blood percolate back into place. I shoved the keys into my pocket, and when I pulled my hand out, a folded piece of paper came out with it. It was my note to Leslie, the one I'd intended to slip under her door.

Aiden was driving fast, but when the soft wail of a faraway police siren hit us, he slowed down considerably.

"Shit, you don't think she actually called the cops?" I asked, my voice shaking.

"Maybe she did, maybe she didn't. Either way I don't want to be doing sixty in a twenty-five-mile zone if there's a cop around."

The siren was getting closer.

"She got a good look at me, but she doesn't know my name," I said. "And she couldn't have seen me get into the car, right?

A flashing red light was coming toward us, fast.

"Yeah, but what if she did," Aiden said. "A silver convertible Porsche is kinda conspicuous. The cops could be looking for us."

The cop car, siren blaring, flew past us. I watched it in my sideview mirror and saw it come to a screeching stop near Leslie's apartment.

Neither of us said a word until we were across the bridge and back on the FDR Drive. I looked over at Aiden. "That was close," I said.

Aiden was as rattled as I was. "Tell me what the fuck you said to her."

"I told her my mother was the landlord, and I was there to check for a leak."

"How the hell did you come up with that?"

"Why? What should I have said?"

"Nothing, just nothing. You could have just ignored her, like you were rude or deaf or something."

"Somebody says good morning to me, I say good morning back. Maybe that was my mistake, but that's just me."

"Which is why you needed a plan, like, 'if there's a neighbor asking questions, I pretend not to hear.' But what was your plan? Let me think … Oh yeah, you planned to IMPROVISE." Aiden was screaming at me now. "How'd that work out for you, Hank?"

I didn't answer his question. Instead, I said, "Thanks."

He looked over. "Is that supposed to be sarcastic?"

I smiled. "Nope. Just thanks."

"You don't think I'm some kind of jerk for not wanting to get mixed up in this?"

"I wouldn't if I had a choice, but I don't. You do. You're right to steer clear of this mess. I'll handle it … somehow."

But even though I pretended everything was fine, I was disappointed.

Aiden was quiet for the rest of the FDR. When we got off the highway, he said, "Do me a favor, will you? This isn't fun and games anymore. You're a lawyer, not a superhero—you need help here, and for a while, I thought my help would be sufficient." He glanced over at me. "It's not, and I'm scared for you. Can you just go to the fucking police and tell them about the ring, the kidnapping, and all the other shit you're rolling around in thanks to Leslie?"

"And tell them what? That I was drugged and kidnapped by a Russian mobster? That he let me go without laying a hand on me? That he demanded we return a ring he says was stolen from him or else he'd kill us?" I laughed at the absurdity of my predicament, and I thought of the last time I'd gone to the police and how bored they'd seemed. "I can picture the cops at Boris's door. 'I'd like to help, officer, but I have no idea what you're talking about. I haven't seen my ex-girlfriend in years. And the guy she divorced? I didn't even remember his name until you mentioned it just now.' C'mon, Aiden, this isn't some network crime show where the cops get the bad guy before the end credits."

"Well, I just don't want to see you get hurt."

We drove in silence for a few more blocks.

Aiden was afraid of Boris, afraid of getting involved, and probably as rattled as I was after nearly getting caught breaking into Leslie's apartment. I didn't blame him for not wanting to be involved. But I was scared, too, and now that he said he wanted no part of this, I couldn't help feeling abandoned, even though I knew he was just being sensible.

I looked over at him. At that moment, he was my lift home and nothing more. Not my best friend, not my wingman, just a driver with a familiar face and a helluva nice ride. I crossed my arms and slumped down in my seat.

Aiden put his hand on my shoulder. "Please don't be angry with me."

"I'm not angry at you," I said. "I'm angry at the situation."

After a few more minutes of silence, Aiden said, "I got an idea." I turned to look at him as he went on. "There's a private detective I use when I need to track down someone who's gone missing or get photos of a cheating spouse in action. Whaddya say? Can I introduce you?"

I'd encountered my share of private dicks working at the law firm and didn't like them, didn't trust them, and generally regretted any interaction with them. Most struck me as just this side of crooked, with their shabby suits, stained ties, and tough-guy attitudes. The ones I knew were mostly ex-cops with a pension that didn't cover their living expenses, alimony, and gambling debts, so they needed a second career like a rummy needs rum. They still figured they had the juice, and while some of their buddies went into personal protection services or security gigs, the ones with the big egos hung out a shingle with a come-on that matched the one on their cheaply printed business cards. "Private Investigator—No Job Too Small."

"Thanks Aiden, but I don't think so." Even as I said it, I wondered whether I was making a mistake turning him down.

"Really? C'mon, Hank, you need help." He turned the corner onto my street and pulled to the curb. "You can't do this by yourself." When I didn't answer, he said, "Just tell me you'll think about it," so I did. I popped open the car door and swung one foot onto the sidewalk when Aiden stopped me. "Hey, I forgot to ask. Did you find anything in Leslie's apartment?"

"Not much," I conceded. "But according to the nosy neighbor, the woman who lives in the apartment is named Robin. Looks like Leslie's using an alias."

"Anything else?"

Sadly, my morning with Aiden, for all the emotional sturm and drang, probably hadn't netted much information. The phone numbers and scribbles on the yellow legal pad were Leslie's handwriting all right, but I had no idea if they would prove useful. The picture from the newspaper would probably turn out to be a waste of my phone's digital memory. "No. Nothing else," I said and resumed my climb onto sidewalk, "but thanks again for your help."

As I closed the car door, Aiden said, "Do me a favor, Hank. Send me a text or something once a day. So I know you're not dead." Before I could object, he took off, leaving me standing outside my building alone, with the photo of the notepad my only hope.

Time was running out. Boris had said three days. That made the deadline Tuesday. As I thought of that, I realized that Boris and I hadn't synchronized calendars, so maybe he wasn't counting kidnapping day as one of the days, meaning the deadline was Wednesday. If he meant Monday, that was tomorrow, and I was fucked.

CHAPTER 13

Fernando, the weekend doorman, swung open the door and put a finger to his cap to say hello. I nodded at him and then went straight for the elevator without stopping to pick up my mail. I hadn't cracked my mailbox for several days, but I had more pressing problems than unpaid bills. If anyone urgently needed me, they'd phone or knock on my door.

I hit the elevator button and waited. After a minute the doors slid open and there, facing me, was Emma, Aiden's ex-wife. She was dressed in tennis whites, her hair was pulled back and secured with a white scrunchy, and she was holding a tennis racket in one hand and a bottle of designer water in the other. The sleeves of her shirt were cut high, and so were her shorts. Her face, arms, and legs were smooth, and the Hamptons' sunshine had favored her with a glowing tan the color of light honey.

"Henry," she said, "I was just thinking about you."

I smiled despite my troubles. "I can't imagine why," I answered as I sidestepped her and stepped into the elevator.

"I've got someone I want to fix you up with," she said. Then she put her hand to her face with the thumb and pinkie mimicking a phone. "Call me!"

"I will—nice to see you, Emma, you look good." The elevator doors closed, rescuing me from further chitchat.

Despite my initial impression of Emma as a rich, unapproachable, stuck-up East-Sider, my opinion of her had softened in the three years since she and Aiden divorced, especially after she called me one afternoon to help her reposition her piano. I felt I couldn't refuse, what with her getting me my apartment and all. After we moved the piano, she offered coffee and, having nothing better to do, I stayed. We talked for over an hour, and while I still found her kind of upper-crusty, I got a glimmer of why Aiden fell for her. She was a petite strawberry blonde with an upturned nose that may or may not have been her original equipment. Either way, her lollipop green eyes and the spray of freckles across her nose reminded me of my Irish sweetheart, the one I'd dreamed of but never met. Her sharp humor clashed with the innocence of her pretty face, and I found myself enjoying my cup of coffee with her.

"Emma," I said as she poured me a second cup of coffee, "I think I had the wrong impression of you."

"Really?" She put the empty coffee pot on the counter and sat back down. "And what impression was that?"

"That you were an insufferable brat who lived off her family's money."

Her mouth dropped open. "What? Where'd you get that idea?"

I shrugged. "From Aiden. I mean, I knew you were from a wealthy family when I met you, but Aiden made that your best feature. I never bothered to look beyond Aiden's description."

That made her laugh. "Yeah, I could see how Aiden skipped over my more redeeming qualities while he was staying on your couch. And during our not-so-friendly divorce."

"He didn't paint the nicest picture of you," I said. "And on top of that, you pissed me off by stealing my best friend. Aiden and I had been hanging out since college. After he married you, I hardly ever saw him."

"Well, that wasn't my fault." She paused. "Or maybe it was. After we got married, our social life revolved around my friends, not his.

But Aiden didn't seem to mind, or so I thought. Turned out he did mind. Just one of the many things that bothered him while we were married. Anyway, I admit I never made the effort to get to know you, even though you seemed nice."

As we sat there chatting, it occurred to me that Emma was completely different from Leslie and the other women I'd been with before. She seemed, somehow, incredibly normal.

Of course, I could never date Emma. Even though she was no longer married to Aiden, my code of ethics concerning my friends' significant others still applied, rendering her radioactive. A few small doses might be tolerated, but no way would I risk radiation poisoning by becoming romantically involved. Most of the time, I avoided her, which I thought was for the best. But since that afternoon in her apartment, every time I saw her, she lingered in my consciousness, causing me to pause and consider revising my code of ethics. Or ignoring it.

With Emma's scent still tickling my nose, I opened my apartment door. My cell phone buzzed. It was a New York City phone number, but not one I'd seen before. I answered it anyway.

"Henry Gladstone? My name is Gabriella Lopez and …"

"Not interested," I barked and hung up. My phone immediately rang again. I answered it with a snarl. "Listen lady …"

"Don't hang up. I'm a private investigator, and I work with Aiden Jackson. He said you could use some help."

I'd told Aiden I wasn't interested in having his PI sticking their nose into this, but he apparently overrode me. "Lopez … it's Lopez, right?

"Gabriella Lopez, yes. I'm a licensed private investigator. How can I help?"

"Listen, Gabriella Lopez, I appreciate my friend's concern, but the last thing I need is to start paying …"

"Mr. Jackson's got me on retainer," Lopez said. "Costs you nothing. I understand you need help finding your ex-wife. That's my specialty—finding missing persons."

"I'm not looking for help, free or otherwise."

"Well, it's your funeral," she said. "You've got my number, mister. Who knows—maybe you'll change your mind."

"Maybe I won't," I barked. "Thanks loads for the call."

She snorted. "Calls. I had to call twice, remember?"

I hung up the phone before she did and tossed it on the coffee table on my way to the bathroom, where I threw up. There's nothing like kneeling in front of your toilet and staring down at your latest uncontrolled panic response to remind you what a mess your life has become. I stayed like that, knees on the floor, hands on either side of the toilet bowl, waiting for more panic puke, but none came. I pushed against the porcelain and slowly stood up, not knowing what other surprises my body had in store—like vertigo, fainting, or maybe a massive cerebral hemorrhage. I stood at the sink and slapped some cold water on my face, then brushed my teeth so hard my gums bled. I tossed my ruined toothbrush in the trash, then paused to address myself in the mirror. "You fucking idiot. You just turned down your last possible offer of help. Good job."

CHAPTER 14

All I wanted was sleep. The adrenaline-inducing events of the morning coupled with the vomiting left me wrung out. Coffee might have helped, but I couldn't trust it to stay down. My bedroom seemed far away, so I collapsed on the couch and closed my eyes, but when sleep didn't come, I reached for my cell phone to have a look at the pictures I'd taken at Leslie's apartment. They were hard to see on my phone's small screen, so I printed out the two best photos, placed them side by side on the kitchen table, and turned on all the kitchen lights to facilitate a close examination.

The newspaper picture I'd found in Leslie's night table drawer showed a glass display case with maybe nine or ten shelves packed with every kind of jewelry and bejeweled object imaginable. There was also an insert highlighting some Fabergé eggs, a set of nested Russian dolls decorated with tiny diamonds, and a collection of rings. The larger items included several tiaras laced with diamonds, elaborate pendants, and a scepter richly decorated in sapphires. There were a couple of shelves with smaller items and lots of them. If not for the Russian flag above the display case, I would have assumed all that booty belonged to the Brits, part of the collection of Royal Crown Jewels in the Tower of London.

Was Leslie's ring in that display case?

With a magnifying glass, I examined every ring I could see. None of them looked exactly like the one Leslie wore, but I was working from memory. I swiped through the pictures on my phone on the odd chance I had one of Leslie wearing the ring. No dice. Still, I wondered if her ring was somewhere in that picture.

In the middle of the ring shelf was a printed card with a legend written in Cyrillic, the only one of its kind in the display case. The print was small. Maybe it said something useless, like, "If you can read this, you're too close," but I had a feeling it conveyed something important about those rings.

My attention shifted to the bottom edge and what might have been the first line of the photo caption. Only the tops of the Cyrillic letters were visible and difficult to read, which would make translating it a challenge. At the left edge of the photograph was a woman standing near the display case with her back to the photographer. She must have been standing close to the camera because she was out of focus and only partly visible. Judging by her uniform and the gun on her hip, she appeared to be a security guard.

The yellow notepad from the kitchen had lots of scribbles, dots, and tiny drawings around the edges. Leslie doodled a lot, especially when she was nervous, and the handwriting was hers. The only possible lead was the name "Todd," followed by a phone number with a Manhattan area code. The name and number were underlined twice and followed by triple exclamation marks. Nothing easier than dialing the number to see if this Todd person, whoever he was, knew something about Leslie's whereabouts or the ring.

I reached for my phone and started dialing but was interrupted by a knock at the door. Someone must have slipped by the doorman. The last time that happened my apartment was broken into and tossed, and since then I'd learned that the tosser was Lou, Boris's psychopath errand boy.

The idea of violence, real physical violence, with me as the person at risk, made me queasy—again. There was another knock. I considered pretending I wasn't home, but if it was Lou, he'd just pick the lock and walk in. Better to be somewhat prepared. I didn't have a gun, but I still had my trusty Louisville Slugger from a stint at baseball camp when I was twelve. I retrieved it from the coat closet and closed my right fist around the grip of the bat, the part I'd carefully wrapped in black sticky tape. So armed, I crept up to the door, then looked through the peephole.

It was Emma, still in her tennis whites.

I opened the door. She looked down at the bat. "Did I interrupt batting practice, or are you just happy to see me?"

That made me smile.

CHAPTER 15

I stepped to one side to let her in, and she touched my arm as she passed. Most of my physical contact had been unwanted over the last couple of days, making her touch that much more luscious.

She dropped onto my couch, crossed her legs, and flexed her ankle a few times. Her face was damp with perspiration, but the rest of her seemed cool, not a drop of sweat visible on her tennis outfit. "So, seriously," she said, "what's with the bat?"

"Cockroach. I hate the little bastards."

"Did you get him? With the bat?" She looked down at the bat. "I don't see even a hint of smushed cockroach." She looked up at me again. I looked down at the bat and turned it one way and the other, as if searching for any sign of dead cockroach. Emma frowned. "No, really, Henry, what are you doing with the bat?"

I hesitated, wanting to tell her the truth but knowing I couldn't. "Honestly? Just being extra careful," I said, while trying to come up with a lie that didn't stray too far from the truth. "A client of mine is in deep shit. Ponzi scheme. He took money from the wrong people, dangerous mob types, and he's afraid they'll come after him. And what with me being his lawyer and all, I'm playing it safe."

She smiled. "Your cockroach story was better."

"Maybe, but I wasn't expecting anyone, so I thought it coulda been a bad guy that snuck by the doorman. You're the only person I know in the building, but since I saw you leave half an hour ago to play tennis, I assumed it wasn't you. And as I said, my client has enemies."

She raised one eyebrow. "Really? I guess you lead a more exciting life than I thought. Just be careful with that bat. You might hurt someone."

"Hold on, shouldn't you still be playing tennis?"

"My tennis partner didn't show up because her kid got sick. At least that's what she texted me. Everybody lies, right?"

I didn't reply. I just stood there, holding my bat. I glanced over at the kitchen table, at my computer and the printouts, hoping Emma would get the message. She uncrossed her legs and got up from the couch. "Look," she said, frowning, "if this is a bad time … I just thought Sunday morning you'd be hanging out and in the mood for company."

"It's just that my client's in deep shit and I—"

"Yeah, you said that." She picked up her tennis racket and started for the door. I didn't want her to leave pissed. Part of me didn't want her to leave at all.

I blurted out, "Don't go. Please." She looked surprised, and I was a little surprised myself. "Sorry, I just … I'm in the middle of dealing with this client, and as you can imagine, he's scared to death. But I certainly have time for a cup of coffee."

"Thanks," she said returning her racket to the couch, "I'd love a coffee."

I headed to the kitchen but instead of sitting back down, Emma followed me to the kitchen table and picked up the picture of the jewelry. As soon as she started examining it, I panicked. My instinct was to snatch it away from her. For some reason I needed to keep Emma and Leslie separate, as if they were matter and antimatter and would destroy each other if they came close. Of course, that made no sense, so instead of snapping at Emma, I opened the freezer, pulled out a bag of coffee beans, and tossed a handful into the grinder.

"Okay, I give up," she said. "What's so interesting about this picture? The lady security guard or the fortune in jewelry?"

"Both," I said, "or neither. That's what I'm trying to figure out."

"For your case, huh?" She paused when I started the coffee grinder. When it stopped, she said, "The caption's cut off, but I'm sure it's Russian."

I opened the grinder and started to carefully pour the grounds into the filter. "Yeah, that's what I thought," I said, "but I can't even make out enough letters to throw it into Google Translate."

"Hold on. I'm pretty sure this word means 'Museum'.

I whipped around, spilling coffee grounds on the floor. "You can read that?"

Emma looked up, then down at the coffee on the floor, then back at me. "Yeah, I was a Russian Lit major, and so I had to take Russian. I'm pretty rusty, but if you need to know what this says, I'm free this afternoon. Maybe I can help." She held the picture up to the light. "If I were you, I'd try to find out where this was published. Then you'd have the whole article—more to go on."

"Swell idea, but I wouldn't know where to start. Could you find it?"

"Probably. You want me to look? I can't promise, but I can try." She came close, looked up at me with hooded eyes, and smiled. "I'd love to help. Give me a couple hours."

Perfect, I thought. That would give me enough time to track down this Todd character. I stepped away from Emma, pulled out my phone, and searched the papers on the table for Todd's number.

"Hey," Emma said. "Remember me? And my coffee? You planning on giving me a go-cup, or what?"

I looked up. "A go-cup?" For a second I wasn't sure what she meant. Then I saw the coffee beans. "Oh, yeah, the coffee. I almost forgot. Sorry, I'm just a little distracted."

I walked back to the counter and pulled down a couple of mugs.

***

Emma spent the next forty minutes on my couch. She had two cups of coffee, black, all the while wanting to hear more about the case, telling me that she loved nothing better than a good mystery. She read mystery books almost exclusively and always dreamed of getting involved in an investigation. "After graduating from Bryn Mawr, I wanted to work for the CIA or the FBI. I thought having 'fluent in Russian' on my CV would be enough to get me in, but I couldn't even score an interview. So I gave up and took a job at an ad agency that had a Russian client. The client loved me, and the next thing I knew I was managing the account."

"But you left advertising even though you were doing well. What happened?"

"Aiden happened." She smiled. "I took a two-month leave to plan our wedding, and it was such a blast I quit the agency and set myself up as an event planner. Then, when Aiden and I split, well, I just amped up the business. I make my own hours, and I only work with people I like."

"Wish I could say that."

"Yeah, you must deal with some pretty unsavory characters." She leaned forward and widened her eyes. "I'd love to hear about some of your adventures defending scoundrels."

"Not today," I said. "I've gotta get back to work."

"Right." She stood up and looked around for her tennis racket. I'd printed out a copy of the jewelry picture for her, and she held that up. "I'll get on this right away. Should we touch base later?"

"Sure," I replied.

I walked her to the door.

"Thanks for the coffee," she said. "And the assignment." She kissed my cheek, opened the door, and walked into the hall. "And if I find out where this is from," she said, holding up the newspaper picture without turning around, "I expect a big thank you. Like dinner."

I stood at the door watching her walk away. I could tell she felt my eyes on her by the easy way she walked. Confident. Unhurried, like she had all the time in the world to walk down the hall.

"I thought you said you wanted to fix me up with someone. How's that person going to feel? Might send the wrong signal if it looks like we're on a date or something."

She paused and turned her head. "I changed my mind. I'm not fixing you up with her. Wouldn't work."

And with that, she disappeared into the stairwell.

CHAPTER 16

One door closes, another one opens, my grandfather used to say. And that's just what happened. Aiden had slammed the door (well, I slammed his car door), and an hour later Emma walked through my apartment door with her Russian lit degree. The fact that she used to be married to Aiden was a little unsettling, if for no other reason than I liked Emma, and I was starting to like her more. It was a road I didn't want to go down, because that would almost certainly dent my friendship with Aiden, if not T-bone it completely.

So far, I could dismiss the whole thing as a casual flirtation that would probably go no further than Emma's surprise buss to my cheek. But as I stood at my door and gazed at the empty space outside the stairwell, I was reminded of a magician's assistant just before she vanishes, wearing a confident smile that says, "Don't worry, I'll be back soon, looking as gorgeous as ever." And there I stood, the anxious audience, wondering, hoping, puzzling over what would happen next. My fingers involuntarily moved to my face and touched my stubbled cheek where she'd placed her lips before saying goodbye. Where my best friend Aiden's ex-wife had kissed me in a way that left me wondering, hoping, puzzling over what would happen next.

With Emma gone, I returned to the business of finding Todd, whoever he was, hoping he knew something that might help. I dialed the number next to his name. Six rings later, I assumed I wasn't likely to get much more than a voicemail, but a woman answered on the seventh ring. "Tiffany's," she said.

"Sorry, wrong number," I mumbled and hung up. I looked up the phone number of the Tiffany's in Midtown Manhattan. It matched the number on the piece of paper, so I redialed it. The same woman answered.

"Can I please speak to Todd?"

"Todd?" she asked. "Do you have a last name?"

"No, I'm sorry, I don't know his last name."

"I'm not sure there's anyone by that name working here. Is there something I can help you with?" she asked.

"Thank you, but I was hoping for Todd. He helped me a while ago with a gift for my wife, and she loved it. I just thought ..."

"Okay, let me check with my manager."

She put me on hold. I looked at my watch and studied the second hand as it ticked around the dial once, twice, three times. Ordinarily, I would have hung up after being on hold for that long, but if Todd wasn't somehow attached to this phone number, I had nowhere else to go. Finally, a man picked up and introduced himself as the assistant manager. "I understand you're looking for Todd," he said. "We've only had one Todd working here over the last couple of years. Todd Winger. Is that who you mean?"

I wrote down "Todd Winger" in block letters. "That's him," I said. "Todd Winger. Now I remember. Can I speak to him, please?"

"I'm afraid Todd isn't here. But I'm sure someone else—"

I cut him off. "Do you know where he is?"

The assistant manager hesitated before saying, "I'm sorry, sir, but I don't. And even if I did, it's company policy not to give out that kind of information. All I can tell you is that he's not currently in the store. Why don't I transfer you to someone on the second floor where Todd worked? I'm sure one of our salespeople can be equally helpful."

Before I could say no, he'd transferred the call, and the phone was ringing again. A woman picked up. "Antique jewelry, Darlene speaking."

Antique jewelry—did Todd have something to do with the missing engagement ring? Trying to keep the excitement out of my voice, I said, "Hi Darlene, my name's Mike …" I glanced at the yellow pad. "Winger. I hope you can help me. I'm trying to find my cousin. Todd Winger?"

"Todd? He's not working here now."

"Do you know where I can find him? There's been a death in the family, and well, I thought he should know about it."

"Oh, I'm so sorry for your loss."

I responded with a tight smile, despite her not being able to see it. "Thank you."

"Hold on, maybe Missy will know. She and Todd were work pals." She put the phone down on the counter, and I heard her speaking to someone else before getting back on the phone. "Missy's on lunch break," Darlene said. "She should be back in about half an hour."

I said I'd call back, thanked her, and hung up.

I looked at my watch. Too soon to check on Emma's progress with the picture. It had been barely twenty minutes since she left my apartment, and I was starting to miss her. I considered knocking on her door but knew that a better use of my time would be to head over to Tiffany's and find this Missy.

My experience with witnesses taught me that they're more likely to be helpful when questioned in person rather than over the phone. I suspect it has something to do with trust, or maybe just our basic, nearly forgotten need as humans to feel a real connection with other humans through face-to-face contact. Not to mention the smell of perfume, sweat, shampoo, minty-fresh breath, and real facial expressions instead of emoticons. So I grabbed my cell phone and left my apartment to find a salesgirl named Missy, who might know where I could find a former salesman named Todd. On the elevator to the lobby, I thought about how the connection between Todd and Leslie made sense seeing as Todd worked at Tiffany's. He might even be some kind of antique jewelry expert.

I felt the first pieces of the puzzle snap into place.

Tiffany's is located on the corner of Fifth Avenue and Fifty-Seventh Street, and it's considered the ultimate jewelry store. When I was a kid, Tiffany's signature eggshell blue boxes made scheduled appearances around the holidays, as well as unscheduled appearances following parental dustups. Being well-off meant getting the best presents, and for my mother and younger sister that meant a Tiffany's bauble.

I only visited the store once, when a high school girlfriend named Roxanne dragged me in one Christmas to look at some Tiffany's engagement rings, suggesting, as she gazed up at me with love in her pretty blue eyes, that one day I might buy her one. I thought that was kind of ballsy of her since we were sixteen and had only been dating for three weeks. I told her the only way she'd ever get one of those rings from me would be to grab it before I managed to slip it onto my fiancée's ring finger.

She stood there beaming like a love-struck starlet for a second until it dawned on her that maybe I meant someone else. Her smile dissolved, and she slapped me hard across the face, then turned and stomped off. That was the first time a girl had ever slapped me. I stood there rubbing my stinging cheek and thinking of that slap as a rite of passage, something to cherish almost as much as my first kiss.

"Oh, c'mon, Roxanne," I called after her, "it was just a joke."

I'm sure she heard me because she raised her middle finger over her shoulder without bothering to glance back.

The salesman behind the counter tapped my arm and said with a wink, "Don't worry, my friend, she'll come back. They always do. I've seen it a million times."

I smiled and thanked him, but he was wrong. That was the end of Roxanne and me.

I was thinking about Roxanne as the uniformed doorman reached for the handle and swung open the door. "Welcome to Tiffany's, sir."

I stopped just inside the entrance and took in the scene. The clientele, mostly couples, were staring earnestly at jewels artfully laid out on black felt mats and eying them as if they held the secret to eternal youth. Maybe they did. Or maybe they held the secret to eternal love, or some other fantasy I'd long ago outgrown.

I scanned the store from where I stood until I spied the elevators and next to them the stairs. Several people were waiting at the elevator, so I took the stairs. When I reached the second-floor showroom, there were several salespeople, but only one turned and looked me in the eye. "Can I help you?"

"Are you Missy?" I asked.

"No, I'm Darlene. Are you the guy who just called looking for Todd?"

I nodded. "Yep, that was me."

She looked at me up and down. "I thought you said you'd call back."

"Yeah, well, I was in the neighborhood," I explained, "so I thought I'd just pop by. Is Missy back from lunch yet?"

Darlene narrowed her eyes like she was sizing me up, so I smiled. She smiled back and said, "That's her behind the counter."

I turned to see a petite Asian woman in her twenties, with short dark hair, wearing more than her share of red lipstick. Somehow she made it work.

I thanked Darlene and headed for Missy's counter when an older, stern-looking gray-haired woman, conservatively dressed in a white top and green skirt, stormed past me. She began ripping into her even before she reached the counter. Missy leaned forward and looked her superior in the eye. She took the tongue-lashing without a word.

I stopped at the counter several feet away and pretended to browse the collection in the glass case. When the older woman showed no signs of ending her tirade, I interrupted. "Excuse me, can one of you show me this ring?"

That did the trick. The battle-ax turned and forced a smile my way before storming off, high heels clicking like gunshots.

Missy walked over. "May I help you?"

I smiled. "Looks like I just helped you."

She lowered her eyes and blushed. "Sorry you had to see that. Kelly's my manager, and she's a bit cross with me. Nothing a fifty-thousand-dollar sale wouldn't fix. Are you, by chance, looking for something in that price range?"

"No, sorry. I'm actually looking for Todd Winger, and Darlene over there said you might know where he is."

"Figures. Todd's a great salesman, so I'm not surprised you're asking for him. But Todd's not working here right now. The last we heard, he took a leave of absence, but we don't know if he's really coming back." Missy let that sink in, then got back to business. Her business. "How can I help?"

"I'm not here to buy jewelry. I'm sorry to say I have some bad news for Todd—a death in the family—and—"

"Oh, no! That's so sad! But maybe not so sad for Todd."

"Not so sad for Todd?" I repeated, hoping that might help me understand. "Am I missing something?"

"His family kind of dumped him a few years ago. Are you a relative?"

I hesitated. If Todd was estranged from his family, Missy might not be anxious to tell me much about him or where to find him. I decided to hedge my bets.

"Barely. I'm a distant cousin, by marriage, or a former marriage to be precise. I was appalled by the family's behavior toward Todd. It just wasn't fair, was it?"

Missy nodded. "In this day and age? I'll say. I can't understand homophobes, but Todd's father … don't ask. And then when he announced he wanted to become an actor? His parents stopped talking to him altogether. And with him being an only child, you'd think …" She shook her head.

I nodded sympathetically. "Yeah, I know what you mean. I always liked Todd, although I haven't seen him since he was a kid. He really should hear that his, um, relative died. Don't you think?"

"Yeah, I guess. I'd tell him myself, but honestly, we're just work friends, you know?"

I mustered a warm smile. "I'm family, it's my responsibility to tell him. The problem is, I don't know where to find him."

"Yeah, he's in an illegal sublet, so he can't publish his address." She paused to glance at a young woman in jeans and a T-shirt perusing the jewelry case next to us. "Listen, I really should do some actual sales work. I don't need any more grief from you-know-who. Tell you what, write down your name and number, and I'll have him get in touch."

"Missy, I think we both know he won't call me—he still considers me—"

"Oh, right," she said, then began biting her lower lip. "Okay, he's in an off-off-Broadway play. That's why he left. It's called … Oh shoot, what's it called? Something about a fairy tale." A nearby door opened, and I heard the familiar staccato click of her boss's high heels. As soon as Missy saw her, she said, "Gotta go. Say hi to Todd for me," and moved over to the woman shopper. "Good afternoon, madam."

Talking to Missy in person rather than over the phone had paid off in spades. She was easy with the information, and I got some useful details I didn't even know I needed. If I'd had another five minutes with Missy, I might have convinced her to give me more on Todd, like his phone number, but I still got plenty.

I hurried out of the store onto Fifth Avenue. Luckily, there was a newspaper kiosk across the street. I picked up a copy of the Sunday Times, put my six bucks on the counter, and pulled out the theater listings. As I walked away, I dumped the rest of the paper in the trash, where it lasted all of five seconds before being retrieved by a middle-aged man walking his schnauzer. I scanned the listings for anything that sounded like a fairy tale. It only took a minute to find it. There was a matinee at three. I glanced at my watch. Plenty of time to get down to the Lower East Side, so I used my phone to buy a ticket to *That's So Cinderella, Fella* and headed for the subway.

CHAPTER 17

Fifth Avenue was crowded with tourists on that summer Sunday, and most of them were either walking toward me in slow motion or, worse, walking ahead of me, alternately gazing in store windows or craning their necks to spot the tops of tall buildings lining the avenue. But it was the large families holding hands and taking up the entire sidewalk that finally forced me into the street to avoid the pedestrians altogether. When I stepped off the curb, a taxi's side view mirror nearly clipped me before I made it back onto the sidewalk. I finally reached the Fifty-Third Street station and hustled down the steps and through the turnstile to catch an incoming F train. By then I was soaked in sweat and the air-conditioning of the subway car hit me like a frozen side of beef. The car was nearly empty, so I swung around the icy, stainless-steel pole anchored to the floor and ceiling and took a seat.

The subway is my preferred form of navigating Manhattan and the rest of the boroughs. The subway car sways gently. The robo-conductor announces the station and warns you to stay safe, avoid pickpockets, and implores you not to lean against the doors, all in a very upbeat and friendly voice. My fifteen minutes on the subway provided a respite from the hubbub of the city streets, quiet time I could use to come up with a plan. Because chances were good that I'd soon be sitting in the audience—close enough to Todd to scream his name and get him to turn around. That was Plan A. Of course, disrupting the performance would get me kicked out of the theater, so I discarded it and went on to review Plans B through Z. By the time I hit Plan CC, I still didn't have anything I considered workable.

The F train pulled into Delancey Street, the heart of the Lower East Side, and as close as I could get to my destination by subway. The theater was a few blocks away on Clinton Street and unlike midtown, the sidewalks were nearly empty. Todd's theater was located upstairs from a Kosher restaurant, Chaim's Delicatessen, and I walked through a black door next to the deli that led to the stairs. Sitting at the top of the stairs was a young couple dressed in black despite the summer heat. They held hands, and the man's head rested on the woman's shoulder."

"Door's not open yet," the guy said, without moving his head from his girlfriend. "Should be just a few minutes."

Next to me at the bottom of the stairs was a theater poster inside a glass marquis case announcing *That's So Cinderella, Fella*, starring Todd Winger and Tina F. No last name, just an initial for the female lead. The theater was called, appropriately, Deli Stage Two.

I said to the couple at the top of the stairs, "Open seating, right?"

"Yeah," one of them answered. "That's why we're here early. We want to make sure we get a good seat. We've seen the show four times already. In rehearsals. It's unbelievable."

"Well that's good to hear," I said. "I know nothing about it."

"You won't be sorry," the woman said before closing her eyes and snuggling closer to her boyfriend. "Although I find the nudity a little gratuitous. But the playwright's a genius, so I cut her some slack. Plus, she's my kid sister. And she's the co-star."

"Tina F?" I asked. She nodded. "And is your last name F, too?"

She laughed. "No, that's her stage name. Her real name's Tina Farber. I'm Anna Farber. This here's Dustin." She turned to him. "His last name's Farber, too, but we're not related. At least as far as we know. We met at a party last week, and we've been together every minute since."

So much about that was unsettling.

The door opened, and a woman came in, said excuse me, and trotted up the stairs. She wore a black shirt dress and carried one of those huge nylon dancer's bags, also black, over her shoulder. Her short hair was purple. Anna said, "Hi, Zellie." As soon as Zellie unlocked the door, Anna and Dustin stood up and, brushing the dirt off the bottoms of their shorts, prepared to follow Zellie inside.

Zellie said, "Listen, I need a couple of minutes before I let you in." Anna and Dustin sat back down. The street door opened again, and a man and woman came in, took the stairs, and followed Zellie through the door, but before they did, they exchanged muted hellos with the Farbers. The man was short with dark hair and the kind of nondescript black glasses favored by Clark Kent. He wasn't obese but he could stand to lose twenty. With his round face and half smile, he looked like the kind of guy you wouldn't mind having a beer with.

"Break a leg," said Anna before they closed the door. She looked down and smiled at me. "That was them, you know, the stars, Todd and Tina."

"Really? Cool," I replied, although what I was thinking was how easy it would have been to grab Todd by the leg and, before he knew what was happening, pull him out onto the sidewalk and shove him against the wall. Then, with my face close enough to his face that he could feel my stubble against his, I'd whisper through clenched teeth, "Where the fuck is Leslie? And don't lie to me, motherfucker. I know you're in cahoots with her somehow." I would overwhelm him with menace until he started crying like a baby with a full diaper, begging me not to hurt him. Only then would I back off and let him tell me what I came looking for.

It was a nice fantasy, but I knew I'd never be able to push someone around like that. So what I needed was a way to manipulate him into giving up some information. I had the entire play to consider how I might do that.

As more people came in, I moved up the stairs to where Anna and Dustin were standing. A couple dozen people stood in the narrow stairwell, and it was beginning to smell like a junior high school gym in there. Finally, Zellie poked her head through the door. "Have your tickets, or e-tickets, out and ready." She and another ticket taker had barcode readers shaped like guns and were admitting people as fast as they could. I fumbled with my phone and found my ticket in the nick of time.

The theater was cramped, with folding wooden chairs packed in tight to accommodate an audience of fifty or sixty. I took a seat in the front row next to the Farbers. The entire space was painted black, so even with the exit signs on and some overhead lights, it was dark. In front of me was a stage that was only about two feet high. At the rear of the stage was an upright piano in the corner, but no set, no props, and no curtain. Not amateurish but definitely not Broadway.

I studied the playbill to see if I could learn more about Todd. Other than a couple of biographical details (birthplace, acting schools attended), it only listed the handful of off-off-Broadway plays he'd been in, none of which I'd heard of. The last line of his bio touted a recent appearance on *Law and Order*, the television cop show that every actor in New York City claimed as a credit.

Before the performance started, I turned around to check out the house and saw that it was almost full. Zellie had just started to close the theater doors when a young dark-haired woman rushed in and took one of the remaining seats. I did a double take—I was almost positive I'd seen her recently, but when I couldn't put a name to the face, I wondered if I was just being paranoid.

The house lights dimmed, and the audience got quiet. A few seconds later, the piano lamp clicked on, and a man walked across the stage and sat down at the keyboard. He was tall and lanky, dressed in a long-sleeved striped shirt with garters, checkered pants hoisted by suspenders, and a black bowler hat. I couldn't quite see the guy's face, but I wouldn't be surprised if he had a handlebar mustache. He dressed like the piano player in an old west saloon, and sure enough he started in on some upbeat, honky-tonk tune. It hadn't occurred to me before, but maybe *That's So Cinderella, Fella* was a musical.

The music continued for a few minutes and then abruptly stopped. The silence that followed was interrupted by Tina entering from stage left and Todd from stage right. They met in the center and each set up a wooden folding chair they'd brought with them. So far, no dialogue. The moody silence was broken by Anna and Dustin, who applauded as if they were witnessing Richard Burton and Elizabeth Taylor's opening scene from *Who's Afraid of Virginia Woolf*. Nobody else clapped.

Todd planted his chair center stage and Tina sat facing him. They stared at each other without a word for at least thirty seconds when I began to wonder if they'd forgotten their lines. I felt the crowd fidget. After a minute, the crowd began to murmur. Finally, Todd stood up and said directly to the audience, "What are you looking at?"

Tina got up and said, "Yeah, what the hell are you looking at?"

For a few seconds, the theater was uncomfortably quiet. Then the actors started laughing uncontrollably. But then they burst into a song about how much fun they'd just had alienating the audience, and the show, apparently a musical comedy, began in earnest. Two hours and ten minutes later it ended almost as it had started. Todd and Tina walked to the front of the stage and said, "Thanks for looking at us!" and then took their bows to medium applause and no curtain calls. Not much of a matinee in my estimation, but I wasn't there to rate the performance. I was there to brace Todd.

I left the theater as quickly as I could and stood on the sidewalk, waiting for Todd to come out. After fifteen minutes, he and his co-star, Tina F, along with Anna Farber, Dustin Farber, and the piano player, all piled onto the sidewalk. "Hi, Anna, hi Dustin," I called out cheerily.

Anna and Dustin stopped and looked at me. "Oh, you're the guy from the stairs," said Anna. "And you sat next to us." She moved closer to Dustin, and he put a protective arm around her. "What are you still doing here?"

"I started to leave," I explained, "but halfway down the block, I turned around, thinking maybe I'd get a chance to meet the actors. And here you are!"

"Um, yeah, here we are," said Todd.

"And," I said, addressing the Farber couple, "you were right about the play. It was fantastic, especially Tina and Todd." Everyone broke into smiles, and Todd thanked me for coming and asked me to tell my friends about the show. "We're closing in a few weeks, but I'm hoping if we keep selling out, they'll extend the run."

"They'd be crazy not to," I said. "It's such a great show!"

Todd smiled at that. I smiled back. "Todd, can I ask you a question?"

"Sure, ask away."

"When was the last time you saw Leslie Dunlop?"

Todd took a step back. His face dropped. "What?" he asked. "Leslie who? I don't know any Leslie." He turned to his friends and said, "This guy's crazy or something. C'mon, let's get outta here."

I lunged at him and caught his arm just above the elbow. His bicep looked big and fleshy, but I felt plenty of muscle, too. He looked down at my hand and yanked his arm away. The piano player stepped between me and Todd. He had a good four inches on me, but I probably outweighed him. "We don't want trouble. Why don't you just walk that way, and we'll walk this way, and nobody will get hurt."

Then a cop stepped out of the deli, one hand on his gun holster and the other holding a half-eaten sandwich. "What's up folks? Everything okay?"

"Not okay," Todd said. "This guy, this stranger, attacked me for no reason."

"Is that true?" the cop asked. "Did you attack this man?"

I said nothing, so he turned to the others. "Did you see this guy attack your friend?"

Tina said, "Well, he grabbed Todd's arm. In a threatening kind of way." The cop looked back at me. When he put his sandwich on the window ledge of the deli and walked toward me, I felt the threat level go up a notch. The cop kept coming until we were eye to eye and about a foot apart.

Another cop came out of the deli. "What's going on, Frank?" he asked his partner. "Trouble?"

"Yeah, Smitty. Trouble. Apparently, this guy assaulted this other guy."

"Who, the tall guy or the heavy guy?"

"He assaulted me," Todd said, "And I'm not that heavy. In fact, my weight's down in the last ..."

"Skip it," Frank said, without taking his eyes off me. His breath, rancid corned beef on rye with a little mustard, forced me to take a small step back. The cop followed.

Then Anna spoke up. "Officer, nobody got hurt, there's really no harm done here. We just want to be on our way without this guy harassing us."

"You don't want to press charges?" Smitty asked.

Todd, Tina, the piano player, and Dustin Farber all shook their heads.

"Okay, then," Smitty said, "you guys have a nice evening."

They thanked the cops and walked away, although a couple of them looked back before reaching the corner.

Meanwhile, Frank didn't move. I wanted him out of my face but didn't feel I could just walk away. I took another step back. Frank stuck with me. "Smitty," he said, "let's toss this miscreant creep into the back of the squad car and have a talk with him. Give those nice people some time to disappear into the city."

They each took an arm and escorted me to the squad car, where I was shoved, but not too hard, into the back seat.

"Shit," Frank said, "I left my sandwich outside the restaurant. Be right back."

Smitty slammed the car door and got into the passenger seat to wait for his partner. Through the windshield I watched Todd, and my chance to get some answers, walking away. I looked at my watch. It was 5:20 p.m. on Sunday. Two more days until Boris and Leo got nasty. And I was trapped in the back of a cop car.

Frank got into the car, no sandwich in sight. "Fucking pigeons," he muttered as he dropped into the seat behind the wheel. Twenty minutes and a lecture later, the cops let me go if I promised to behave, making me wonder how many other bad guys were released after swearing to abandon their life of crime. I promised, and thanked them, although I wasn't sure why. Could've been worse, I reasoned, but Officers Frank and Smitty effectively kept me from getting any answers from Todd. I had no idea where he was headed. And, as the cop said, they had enough time to disappear into the city. I could start over, and come to another performance, but if Todd or any of his posse saw me at the theater in the next few days, they'd definitely call the cops.

I couldn't believe I was that close and had blown it. Not sure what to do, I checked my phone. No word from Emma. She probably hadn't found anything yet. I considered circling back to Tiffany's and pressing Missy for Todd's address. While I was trying to decide if that was a good idea or not, my phone rang. Unknown number, but what the hell. I felt desperate enough at that moment to talk to just about anyone.

"Yeah, hello."

"Don't hang up," a woman said breathily, almost whispering, making it impossible for me to recognize her voice. If I had to guess at gunpoint, I'd say it was Marilyn Monroe calling from the beyond, but I'd be wrong.

"Why shouldn't I hang up? Sounds like you've got the wrong number, sister."

"This is the right number, Henry."

"Who is this? How did you get this number? And stop whispering, I can hardly hear you. I'm standing on the street in lower Manhattan for chrissake."

The Marilyn Monroe voice continued. "I saw what happened outside the deli. I know you were tracking Todd Winger because you need to talk to him about Leslie Dunlop. And I know you lost him."

"How the fuck?" Then it hit me. "Wait, you're Aiden's PI, right?"

"Shut up and listen to me," she said, the whispering edging up to a growl. "I've got eyes on Todd Winger. He's sitting alone and just ordered dinner, so he should be here for a while."

I pressed the phone hard against my left ear and shoved a finger into the right one. The woman stopped talking, and I could hear the sounds of silverware against plates and the hustle of waiters in the background. "You planning to tell me where he is?"

"Are you planning to come here if I do?"

"What's in it for you?" I asked.

"The joy of helping someone in trouble. And if you do things my way, you just might get an earful from Winger." I thought about it for a few seconds when she said, "He's talking to the waiter. This is a limited time offer, because when he pays his bill and leaves, you may not get another chance. Don't be a sap, Henry. Get up here now." Then everything on her end went quiet. I took a look at my phone and realized what had happened. My phone died.

I stood there holding a dead phone, having no idea where in all of New York City she and Todd were. And a dead phone meant I didn't have her phone number.

I was fucked.

CHAPTER 18

I stood there, stunned, holding the phone in both hands, looking at it and wondering if I was strong enough to rip it to pieces. Probably not, but then I thought of pulverizing it against the sidewalk and what a great feeling of release that would give me. Like drinking a shot of tequila or plunging into a pool on a hot day. I raised my arms, the phone in both hands, so frustrated I could cry. But I stopped myself, certain that smashing my phone was something I'd regret seconds later. A few people walked by and looked at me like I was crazy, but hey, this was New York, so nobody asked what was wrong. A teenager carrying an overstuffed canvas messenger bag stopped to take a good look from about six feet away. He wore a black Foo-Fighters T-shirt, and as an additional tribute, had "Foo" tattooed in black up one arm and "Fighters" down the other. He addressed me loudly but in a calm voice. "Excuse me, mister, if you're planning to smash your phone, let me take it off your hands instead. And in one piece, if that's okay." He extended his hand and held it steady, waiting to see if I'd give him the phone. "My brother and I, we have a business reconditioning phones," he explained as I stood there, half-crazed but listening nonetheless, "and we usually get spare parts from phones we find in trash cans. But sometimes we get 'em from people who, for some reason, smash their phones on the sidewalk. Happens more than you think."

"I wasn't really going to smash it," I said to this complete stranger. Holding my pre-smash, armed-raised position, I reviewed the situation with him, as if he were some guardian angel sent here to save me. "It's just that I feel like smashing it because it died in the middle of an important phone call."

He moved his hand as if to remind me he was still waiting for me to pass the phone over. "What's wrong with it? Screen messed up or something?"

"No," I said, lowering my arms. "The battery's dead, and I don't have a charger."

"The battery's dead?" He muttered something that sounded like "this guy's a lunatic" before reaching into his messenger bag and pulling out a tangle of wires. "Whaddya got there," he asked as he pulled out even more wires, "an eleven or a twelve?" I didn't know, so I handed him the phone "Wow," he said, then whistled. "This thing's a ten, a dinosaur." He handed it back to me, sorted through the wires for a few seconds, then said, "It's your lucky day mister! I got a charger that fits!"

I reached for it, but the kid pulled it away. "Hey, not so fast. This is my business. I deserve to make a buck or two here. What, I'm gonna tell my brother this whole story and at the end say, 'I just gave the guy the charger because I have a big heart?'" I pulled out my wallet and handed him a five-dollar bill. He gestured for more. I rolled my eyes and peeled off another five. "Let's cut to the chase, mister," he said, eyes on my money. "I'll take forty bucks. That work for you?

"Oh, c'mon."

"Up to you, mister," he said and dropped the charger back in his bag. "But where you gonna find a charger at six o'clock on a Sunday?"

I looked up and down the block, then across the street. Except for the deli, none of the stores were open. "Oh for chrissake," I said and forked over the money. He handed me the charger before stuffing the cash in his pocket and turning to leave.

I grabbed the sleeve of his T-shirt. "Hold it, bud," I said. "How's about we go into Chaim's Deli and make sure I didn't just buy a charger good for nothing but practicing the knots I learned as a Boy Scout." I tied a figure-eight knot with the cord and held it up. The kid looked peeved but didn't object, just walked over to the deli, opened the door, and held it for me as I followed him in. An old guy with a white beard, a black yarmulke, and a dirty apron stood majestically behind the counter. "Chaim?" I asked.

"You were expecting maybe Santa Claus?"

"Chaim, listen, I need to charge my phone for a couple minutes. It's an emergency. Can I use your outlet?"

"It's possible, very possible you could use my outlet," Chaim said. He put the tips of his fingers together as if to help him think about the philosophical ramifications of my request. "But," he said raising his index finger for emphasis, "if you order something, maybe a sandwich or a potato latke, you can definitely use my outlet."

I rolled my eyes. This city was full of guys who wanted to shake me down. "You have pastrami?" I asked.

"You know what they call a Jewish Deli with no pastrami?"

"A Jewish health food restaurant?" I wisecracked.

"I was going to say, 'out of business,' but I like yours better," Chaim said, smiling. "So whatever you order, I'm throwing in some kishke for free!"

"Okay," I said, shaking my head. "Pastrami on rye with a little mustard. Now, where do I juice my phone?" He directed me to the side of the counter where an unused outlet hugged the floor. I started to put my knee down but realized a deli floor was no place for my relatively clean knee, so I squatted and plugged it in. The phone hesitated, then came to life.

The kid who ripped me off for the charger was still standing there, watching over my shoulder. "There," he said, grinning, "what I tell you? I only deal in quality merchandise."

"Okay, beat it," I said, "before I ask for a refund."

"You're welcome!" he said as sarcastically as he could and walked out.

I stared at the phone waiting for it to come fully alive.

Chaim called to me from behind the counter. "You want coleslaw or potato salad?" he asked. "Me, I'd take the coleslaw, but it's up to you."

"Look, Chaim, thanks but I don't need the sandwich. Here's …" I reached into my wallet and took out my last bill. "Here's twenty bucks. It's all the cash I have left. Does that cover it?"

"You're giving me money, but you don't want the sandwich?"

I looked around the restaurant. There was a young couple seated near the window. "Wrap it and give it to them to take home," I said, and the couple waved and thanked me. "And don't forget the free kishke."

A minute later my phone was charged enough to beep that I had a new text. I jabbed my finger onto the phone so hard I almost broke a knuckle. It was the address of a restaurant in Chelsea called The Black Cat Bistro. I memorized the address, yanked the phone cord out of the socket, and ran into the street looking for, praying for a cab.

Just before the door closed, I heard the woman say, "Chaim, we'll take the potato salad."

CHAPTER 19

I rushed to the curb with my arm out and an empty cab screeched to a stop. "Eighth Avenue and Twenty-Second Street," I barked, "and I'm in a hurry."

"Mister," the cab driver said as he flipped on the meter and met my eyes in the rearview mirror, "everybody in this city's in a hurry. But we're gonna hit crosstown traffic. Just letting you know."

The cabbie was right about the traffic, but he handled it well enough to get me to the restaurant in under twenty minutes.

I got out of the cab and eyeballed the place. There were a handful of tables on the sidewalk under a red awning with The Black Cat Bistro printed in black lettering on the front of it. A small window next to the door glowed yellow. I scanned the diners at the outdoor tables looking for Todd but didn't spot him, so I sidestepped a waiter taking an order and entered the restaurant.

The joint was narrow, and there was a bar on the left side that extended about twenty feet. On the right, against the wall, were about six or seven deuces filled with youngish couples leaning in and making conversation in the dim light. Beyond the bar, the place opened into a dining area with maybe ten tables. I started to walk past the bar to scout the dining area for Todd, but before I took two steps, I was blocked by the hostess. A petite redhead, she wore a maroon pencil skirt and a white blouse open at the throat. "Hi," she said with a hostess smile that let me know who was in charge. "Do you have a reservation?"

"No," I replied, "I'm meeting someone here. I didn't see him outside and I don't see him at the bar. Can I just have a look?" She said sure and let me by. I walked halfway down the bar when I heard someone behind me call my name. I turned around to see a woman leaning back on her bar stool, looking right at me. Something in the way she looked at me suggested she was the woman on the phone, although she looked nothing like Marilyn Monroe. Her dark hair was tied back in a ponytail, and she wore clingy black jeans and a white T-shirt with the sleeves cut high, almost to her shoulders. She was flanked by two guys, one of whom put his hand on her elbow.

"Thanks for the drink," she told the guy without taking her eyes off me, "but my date's here." The guy was ballsy enough to ask for her number anyway, but she just shot him a look and stood up, carrying a highball glass. I happened to be standing next to two empty bar stools. She grabbed one of them and gestured for me to sit down. When I hesitated, she said, "Yeah, it was me on the phone, Henry."

"And who, exactly, are you?"

"A friend of a friend who has your back."

Before sitting, I took a look into the dining room but couldn't make out too much, other than most of the tables had more than one diner, and she'd said on the phone that Todd was dining alone.

"Where's Todd," I asked, craning my neck. "I don't see him. Don't tell me he left already." I started toward the dining room, but she grabbed my elbow.

"Henry, for chrissakes just sit down. He's still here. But you can't just go barreling in there, turn over his table, and ask where Leslie is, can you? Sit down for a minute, order a drink, and let's me and you come up with a plan that has half a chance."

"What if he leaves?"

"The waiter just brought his entrée. He's not going anywhere until he finishes. A guy that pudgy probably scrapes every morsel off his plate and then orders dessert. My guess, he's here for the duration. Unless you spook him."

The bartender came over. "What'll it be?"

"I'll have whatever she's having," I said, eyeing the amber liquid in her glass. Bourbon, I guessed. Maybe scotch.

"Apple juice it is," said the bartender as he reached under the bar.

"Hold it," I said. "Make mine Jack Daniels, rocks, splash." I turned to my new companion. "Apple juice?"

"I'm AA," she said, sitting down and putting her drink on the bar. "Forty-seven months and twenty-one days sober. So get over it." Now that she was talking without whispering, her voice sounded familiar. Again, she told me to sit. I settled onto my barstool and took a good look at her while I waited for my drink. At the same time, she seemed to be taking a good look at me, like she was daring me to recognize her.

"Where do I know you from?" I asked.

She smiled. "I don't know. Where do you know me from?" She took off her ponytail holder, and her dark hair fell to her shoulders. She wasn't that young, maybe mid-thirties or even fortyish, and something about her smile said she'd seen plenty of what humanity had to offer and didn't care for most of it. It was a smile crossed with a sneer, with a smirk thrown in for good measure. She had a scar, a kind of divot in her cheek below her left eye. When she moved her head, and it caught the light, it looked like a teardrop clinging to her face. That's when I decided she was pretty.

She ran her fingers through her hair and pocketed the ponytail holder in her jeans. Something about the way she did that reminded me where I'd seen her before—at the Tiffany's counter, where she'd pretended to be browsing while Missy told me all about Todd. She'd raked her hand through her hair when Missy went over and asked her if she wanted to see something in the display case. Then I saw her again later, inside the theater when she took a seat in the back row.

Nobody knew I was headed to Tiffany's, so she must've started tailing me when I left my apartment. She saw me get nailed by the cops for manhandling Todd, and while I was sitting in the squad car, she'd followed him to the restaurant. Then she'd called, whispering to keep me from recognizing her phone voice.

My hunch was right. She was Aiden's detective, the one who'd called me that morning.

I'd hung up on her then because I was angry at Aiden. When she phoned again minutes later, I'd told her in no uncertain terms to get lost, that I didn't need her help. So the next time, when she called from the restaurant, she disguised her voice. I figured it was because she couldn't risk me hanging up on her again. She knew I needed to find Todd.

"So you're Aiden's PI?" She didn't answer, just kept looking at me with her piercing black eyes. "Your name's Gabriella, Gabriella something …" I closed my eyes to think. "Lopez. Gabriella Lopez, isn't that it?"

"So, you remembered my name." She half smiled and sat back. "Should I be flattered?"

"Fine, be flattered," I said. "Me? I'm confused. First, I told Aiden I didn't need his PI's help. Then I told you the same thing. Yet here you are. What the fuck?"

The smile disappeared. "Listen, Hank, if it wasn't for me, you'd still be wandering around the Lower East Side wondering how the hell you were going to find Leslie after you let Todd slip through your fingers."

"Don't call me Hank. Only Aiden calls me—"

She ignored me. "Aiden told me what you're up against, *Hank*. Those Russian guys, the mystery ring, your AWOL wife, who, by the way, sounds like a real piece of work, and the cops. That's a shitload of problems if you ask me."

"The cops? What's my problem with the cops?"

"You're kidding, right? You almost got arrested this afternoon for your ham-handed attempt to brace Todd. Only a matter of time before you do something really stupid, dangerous, and possibly illegal. This is New York. Amateurs like you fuck up and get arrested all the time."

I opened my mouth to say something, but my jaw just hung there.

Then she leaned so far forward I thought she was about to head-butt me. "Aiden's worried about you and thinks you need my help. But, hell, if you want to send me packing, I'll just take my apple juice and hang out with that guy at the other end of the bar who appreciates me more than you do. And I'm not even trying to save his bacon."

I was quiet, but she kept talking.

"Look, I don't know a thing about you other than what Aiden told me, and so far, I don't like you. To me, this is just a job. I don't give a shit what you decide. I would've quit by now, except you're not the client, Aiden is. And him, I like." She put her glass down on the bar. "So what's it gonna be?"

I weighed the possibilities. Aiden had told me he couldn't help me himself because he was scared, and while I got it, it pissed me off, too. But after mouthing off to Gabriella, I realized I wasn't pissed anymore. I was desperate. The only other person in my corner was Emma, and I had no intention of putting her in harm's way. Emma deserved better than to get caught up in this tawdry mess.

"Okay, Gabriella, what's our next move?"

"How's about you apologize for being an asshole to me just now."

I nodded. "Okay, I'm sorry for being an asshole. I was just—"

"I don't need an explanation. You're in a tight spot, and you're probably scared. I get it. But don't fuckin' take it out on me. You read me?"

I nodded. "Loud and clear." That ended our little dustup.

"Now can we get down to business?" Again I nodded. "Good. Give me three minutes on who this guy is, how he was involved with Leslie, and why you think he might know where she is. Then we can decide how to approach him."

I told her what I knew, keeping my voice just loud enough for her to hear me over the din of the bar.

"Why didn't Leslie just give this guy Boris his ring back? Everybody's, like, happily ever after?"

"She claims she doesn't have it, although truth telling's not Leslie's best event. Doesn't matter. Boris is convinced she's got the ring, or I do, and, worse, that somehow Leslie and I are in this together." I drummed my fingers on the bar while I tried to make sense of it all. "And why would Leslie ask me for money if she knows Boris wants his actual ring back?"

Gabriella ignored my question. "Okay, what about this Todd guy? How does Leslie know him?"

"No idea," I said. "But I found his name written on a notepad Leslie kept by her phone, so I thought he might know something. Turns out Todd used to work at Tiffany's. So there's that connection to jewelry. Maybe someone gave her Todd's name, said he might be helpful. Maybe Leslie took the ring to Tiffany's to find out what it was worth, or even to sell it to them."

"Maybe."

Gabriella went quiet, as if she were trying to work it all out somehow. Meanwhile, I was getting nervous, thinking Todd might finish dinner and leave before we approached him. When I mentioned that to Gabriella, she said, "Stop worrying. I can see him from here. And if he leaves, he has to walk by us. We got time."

I thought about craning my neck to look, but this was Gabriella's show now, so I just fidgeted on my barstool and assumed she knew what she was doing.

"So," she said, "it's possible Leslie met Todd at Tiffany's or knew him from somewhere else. Or maybe they dated?"

"My understanding is he's gay, so romance is unlikely. She might have met him at Tiffany's, but I'm pretty sure she never worked there, and as far as I know, she didn't even shop there. And Todd's an actor but Leslie's not, so no connection there …" I stopped and bit my lower lip. "Wait a second …"

"What? Did something click?"

"Maybe. Leslie wanted to be an actor, and for a while, she took acting classes. She told me about this one time she had to rehearse a kissing scene with a gay guy. When Boris heard about it, he went ballistic."

Gabriella considered that for a few seconds, then a smile slowly formed, and she looked right at me. "I like it. How's this? Leslie and Todd meet in acting class. Years later, she's got the ring and wants to know if it's real and what it's worth, so knowing that Todd's day job is at Tiffany's, she looks him up. Right?" I didn't answer—I hadn't digested it all yet. Then she repeated, "Yeah, I really like it," and banged her glass down on the bar. "Boris had it wrong. It wasn't you and Leslie working together. It was Todd and Leslie. Did they sell it? Fence it? Take it apart and fence the stones?"

I held up my hand. "Total speculation. We don't know any of this for sure."

"You're talking like a defense lawyer."

"I am a defense—"

She cut me off. "We got nothing else, so for now we go with my theory. Gives us a way to start the conversation with Todd. Even if we're wrong about the whole jewelry angle, Todd definitely knows Leslie. Maybe he even knows where she is. We both saw his reaction outside the theater when you asked if he'd seen Leslie. The guy freaked."

I thought back to that moment and knew she was right.

"And we have leverage," Gabriella said, smiling. She picked up her glass and took a drink.

"What leverage?"

"If we're right, Todd may have been trafficking stolen jewelry." More swirling. Mostly just ice cubes now. "He'll deny it, but when I point out he's better off cooperating with us than getting arrested, he'll come to his senses. Odds are twenty to one Todd couldn't make it through breakfast in the prison mess hall without a beating—and that's just from the guards. Once the other prisoners get a load of him …"

I sat back in my chair and considered my new private eye. "You talk like you've been dealing with bad guys for a long time."

"Three years in Afghanistan with the Marines and six years protecting and serving with New York's finest."

I nodded, impressed but not surprised. Aiden was right about her. She knew what she was doing and then some. I pictured her in uniform, both uniforms, M-16 or Glock at the ready. And that made me wonder. "You carrying?"

"I'm licensed, but at the moment, I'm unarmed. I hope it doesn't get to that. And in this outfit"—she gestured to her T-shirt and tight black jeans—"where the fuck would I hide a gun?"

I checked out her outfit again. Clingy. It showed off her body. Not in a showy way, just enough so anyone could see she was slim, curvy, and fit.

Gabriella looked past me into the dining room. "He's eating dessert. What is that, some kind of cream pie? That's not gonna do him any good."

I turned around to take a look. The diners at the table next to him had been blocking my view, but they'd left. It was Todd alright. I returned my attention to Gabriella. "You have a plan?"

"Yeah. We run our recently concocted theory by Todd."

"Talk to him here? He'll see me coming the second I walk into the dining room. We'll end up making a scene."

She shook her head, dropped her gaze, and muttered something about amateurs. "No, not here in the restaurant, that would be reckless and stupid." She slid off her barstool. "I'm gonna go powder my nose. You get the check, then meet me outside."

"Aren't you gonna tell me the plan?"

"Yes. Outside."

I settled up with the bartender and headed for the door. All the sidewalk tables were still full, and the loud conversations blended with the sound of light Sunday evening car traffic in a city symphony that wasn't all that unpleasant. While the sun was nowhere near done for the day, it was low enough in the sky that the sidewalk was blanketed in shadow.

And it was still hot.

CHAPTER 20

While I'd worked with an assortment of PIs on some cases, I didn't know anything about how Gabriella worked and wondered if her plan was going to involve violence. I hoped not. Violence is nothing but a conversation by other means. I didn't like the idea of getting hurt or watching her get hurt. I suppose it would be my job to protect her if things got rough. Or maybe it was the other way around. Honestly, it wasn't so clear.

From the time I was a kid, I was taught that certain things were expected of me if I hoped to be considered a man one day. Don't cry. Fight back. Don't be a sissy.

My dad taught me how to throw a respectable punch when I was five years old. He wanted me to know how to fight, because that kid I considered my best friend kept pushing me around. Sometimes the kid socked me so hard, I'd run home crying. "Next time Freddy lays a hand on you," my dad said, "you'll know what to do."

I practiced my punches in front of the mirror for a week, so when Freddy showed up at my door, I was ready. We walked to his house. Five minutes after we started playing together in his backyard, Freddy pushed me. I hauled off and socked him good.

Freddy started crying. I ran home to tell my parents. "Good for you," Dad said while my mom smiled proudly. I told them Freddy was crying. "Attaboy!" he said, clapping me on the shoulder. But when I told them Freddy was bleeding, Mom frowned. And when I explained that he was bleeding from his eye, they both ran out of the house to find the kid and, I guess, make sure I hadn't blinded him. They sent me to bed with no supper. So was I supposed to hit him hard or not? I'm still not sure.

But Gabriella? My guess is she would have taken the kid apart. Then she'd have put the pieces on his front stoop, pressed the doorbell button, and amscrayed. She wouldn't have gone home bragging about it either.

Gabriella was tough, tougher than me. Anyone could see that. While she'd been on patrol with her platoon, I'd been studying torts. While she'd been fighting crime in the toughest city in the world, home to gangsters and drug lords, I'd been spending my days defending white-collar criminals who wouldn't know a Glock from a double-barreled shotgun. But I'd been brought up with the notion that a woman needed her husband, boyfriend, or just some nearby joe to step in when violence came a-calling. So as much as I knew Gabriella could take care of herself and probably take care of me, too, deep down I felt uncomfortable stepping aside and letting her handle the bad guys.

The restaurant door opened, and some revelers tumbled out, laughing and shouting. Right behind them was Gabriella.

"Knuckleheads," she said as she watched them head down the street.

"Gabriella," I said sharply enough that she glanced away from them. "What's our play?"

"Right," she said and quickly outlined her strategy.

"Sounds good," I said when she finished. "But what if it starts to go sideways?"

"I'll think of something, and you'll follow my lead. Any other questions?" she asked. I shook my head.

"Feeling good about this?"

I nodded because I wanted to appear confident.

"Okay," she said. "Don't fuck up."

I had to admit, Gabriella impressed me. She'd listened, assessed the situation quickly, and fashioned a neat scheme. I particularly admired how she took control of the investigation. She had confidence and street smarts. Her approach to Todd didn't depend on luck or violence.

We crossed the street and positioned ourselves so that we had a clear view of the restaurant door. It was almost 8:30 and getting darker. I began to worry that if Todd took too long, we might miss him. Luckily for us, the restaurant's outdoor lights blinked on before it got too dark.

I trained my eyes on the door and waited.

Five minutes later, Todd came out of the restaurant and turned left. "He's probably heading for the subway station at Twenty-Third," Gabriella said. "Let's get this done before he gets there." She took off, double-timing it uptown to get well ahead of Todd before crossing, mid-block, to his side of the street. My job was to follow Todd, so I crossed the street at the light and began tailing him, leaving half a block between us. We had five blocks to make this work before he disappeared into the subway station. Todd wasn't walking particularly fast, but when he passed Twentieth Street I started to worry—there was no sign of Gabriella. Finally, as I crossed Twenty-First, I spotted her walking toward Todd. She went a few steps past him, then whipped around and called out. She was facing away from me so I couldn't hear her, but I knew she was saying something like, "Oh my god, you're that actor from *That's So Cinderella, Fella?*"

Todd stopped, smiled, and said something to Gabriella, who was by now gesticulating and gushing. Todd responded with a shy shuffle, obviously flattered at being recognized. At some point I knew Gabriella would say, "I'd love to take a selfie with you, but some asshole stole my purse while I was having a drink with my girlfriend.

I don't even have a phone to call my husband or the cops." Todd would be compelled to feel sorry for his enthusiastic fan and offer to lend Gabriella his phone. We hoped. By then I'd almost caught up with them and was close enough to hear their conversation. I ducked into the doorway of a nearby restaurant.

Todd held his phone out to Gabriella. Before taking it, she asked, "Are you sure?" He nodded and handed her the phone. Then she said, "You are such a sweetheart. Thank you, Mr. Winger." It was a near-perfect line, read dripping with gratitude.

Todd bought the ruse. So far, so good.

Turning away from him, Gabriella dialed, told an imaginary policeman her purse had been stolen, then pretended to make another call. Todd moved closer. "Excuse me, um, I don't mean to be a jerk, but I gotta get going, so could you, like, wrap it up?"

Gabriella turned and held up an index finger indicating she was almost done. Todd retreated but stayed close enough to keep the pressure on. The second she ended her faux phone call, I walked to the curb and hailed a cab. This was the only tricky part, because if we had to wait more than thirty seconds for the cab, Todd might get suspicious. Gabriella kept up the conversation while at the same time inching toward me. He followed because she still had his phone.

A cab pulled up. I opened the front door, leaned in, and asked the cabbie to wait a second for my friends. He said they'd better hurry, so I suggested he start the meter and that seemed to settle him. When I opened the rear door, I heard Gabriella say, "Thanks for letting me use your phone to call my husband and the cops. And don't worry, I didn't tell the cops what I know about you and Leslie Dunlop dealing in stolen jewelry, because hey, that might not be good for your acting career or, come to think of it, your continued employment at Tiffany's. What with prison time and all."

When I turned around, Todd was staring at Gabriella, probably trying to make some sense of what was happening.

Finally he shouted, "Who the fuck are you? Give me my phone!"

Gabriella stepped back, pulled the phone away before he could grab it, and shoved it into the rear pocket of her jeans. Todd started to reach around her.

"Todd," I said calmly as I closed the front door with my hip and gestured toward the back seat. "Get in the cab and we'll give you back your phone. Scout's honor."

Todd turned to look at me. "YOU!" he shrieked. Gabriella gave him a little shove toward the cab and I stepped toward him to make sure he kept moving. I could tell he was physically intimidated because he drew his head down like a turtle retreating into its shell. Todd was shorter than me, overweight, and seemed to have no inclination to fight or make a run for it. So I wasn't ready when he pushed me out of the way and stepped back from the cab. "Get away from me," he said. "Tell that bitch to give me back my phone."

Gabriella was sitting in the back seat of the cab as planned, but she stepped out when she saw Todd resisting. "Todd," she said, "we're not here to rough you up or anything. We just want some answers. And you need your phone, so why not get in the cab?"

"Give me back my phone," he repeated.

The cabbie yelled, "Hey, folks, you wanna go somewhere or should I do the crossword?"

"Give us a second," I replied.

Gabriella closed in on Todd. "There are things we know and things we don't. What we know is that you helped Leslie, who by the way is this gentleman's ex-wife, to sell, hock, fence, or otherwise dispose of a very expensive ring. Which she did not own."

"She never told me it was stolen, not until …"

Gabriella interrupted. "Henry here is a criminal defense attorney," she said without taking her eyes off Todd, "and I have every reason to believe he knows the kind of prison time you'd be looking at for trafficking in stolen jewelry. Did it move across state lines, Todd? If it did, that's bad for you."

"I'm not going to prison for any of this. I didn't know ..."

"Doesn't matter what you knew," I chimed in. "You're looking at ten to twenty, federal, maximum security." I wasn't sure of that, but I was going for impact not accuracy.

"Are you a cop?" he asked Gabriella.

"No, I'm a private investigator. But I used to be a cop, one of New York's finest. And I've got loads of friends on the force who would be rubbing their hands together with glee for an open-and-shut case like this. You're one phone call away from being cuffed, fingerprinted, and booked for an overnight at Rikers which, from what I hear, is nothing like a Marriott. Or even a Holiday Inn."

That seemed to strike a nerve. "What do you want to know?"

"Some details," Gabriella said. "Not a lot. Shouldn't take more than a twenty-minute ride in the cab. Less if you don't try and fuck with us by lying. So, are you coming along? Or do I keep your phone, call the cops, and hand it to them as evidence? Evidence I happened to find when you left it at the restaurant?"

"That's not what happened!" Todd snapped.

Gabriella shrugged. "Who my cop friends gonna believe? Me, their old pal? Or you, a suspected felon?" She started to get into the cab. Before she slid across the seat, she said, "Seems to me you don't have much choice here, my friend."

Todd hesitated. I put one arm behind his back and the other on the cab door. "Get in the cab, Todd."

"Fuck," he said and got in.

"Move over next to Gabriella. You're sitting in the middle."

He did.

"Where to?" the cabbie asked.

"Where to, Todd?" I asked, hoping to hear his address.

He whimpered but said nothing, so I gave the cabbie my address to get us started and told him to go through the park.

"This time a' night, that'll take longer," the cabbie said.

"Perfect," I said. The cab bolted into traffic.

We had Todd right where we wanted him.

CHAPTER 21

I was so happy the plan worked all I wanted to do was high-five Gabriella, maybe celebrate with a drink. It worked because Gabriella was right about Todd—he was Leslie's accomplice in ditching the ring. Without acting on her hunch, we'd never have gotten Todd into the cab. Yeah, it worked, I was elated, but the celebration would have to wait until we finished.

Gabriella made it clear earlier that she would be the one doing the questioning in the cab. I pointed out that as a criminal defense attorney I was a skilled interrogator. "We'll be in the back of a cab," she replied, "not in court. That's my turf, not yours. I ask, Todd answers, you listen and keep your lip buttoned."

We made our way uptown through Sunday evening mid-town traffic. Todd sat quietly, but I could tell he was seething. "Give me my phone," he said without looking at Gabriella.

"Absolutely," she said, "I got it right here in my hip pocket. All you have to do is answer a few questions. Then we'll drop you off, safe and sound, with your phone, anywhere you like. We good?"

"No, we're not good. I have nothing to say to you." He turned to Gabriella. "So just give it. Now." Then he faced front and crossed his arms, scowling. "Cabbie," he said, leaning forward, "I don't know these people. They aren't my friends, they're—"

"Todd, Todd, Todd," Gabriella scolded. "I'll give you back your phone, but ya know, I'm a total klutz. Be a shame if I dropped it."

She put down her window halfway. "Like, out the window." She leaned over and looked at me. "Wouldn't that be a shame, Henry?"

I nodded. "A shame. Tragic even."

Todd looked at me, then at Gabriella. "Alright," he said over the asphalt-scented whoosh of air coming in. "Put the window up and ask your questions." The cab took a hard right into Central Park, and the three of us slid into each other.

"We're looking for Leslie Dunlop," Gabriella said. "Can you tell us where she is?"

"How should I know?"

"Don't fuck with us, Todd." She started lowering the window again.

"Stop with the window!" Todd said. The window slid back up. "Okay, yeah, I know where Leslie's staying." Todd hesitated. "But she said if anybody came looking for her not to tell them."

Gabriella said, "You can tell us, Todd. We know she's in a jam. Some bad people are looking for her. If they find her before we do, that might get ugly." She put her index finger to her lip and paused, like she was deep in thought. "Might even get ugly for you."

Todd stared straight ahead.

"Okay," Gabriella said. "You know where she's holed up, but you can't tell us. Got it."

Looking past Todd, I glared at Gabriella, thinking, we're gonna let him get away with not telling us where Leslie is? Gabriella returned fire with her eyes narrowed, and I sat back in my seat.

"So—how well did you know her?

Todd sighed. "Long story."

Gabriella considered that for a second, then still looking at Todd, raised her voice and said, "Cabbie, would you mind going back to where you picked us up? I lost an earring."

"Sure thing, lady," said the cabbie. He slid into the right lane, then aimed the cab back downtown via Fifth Avenue.

"There you go, Todd," Gabriella said. "Plenty of time for you to tell us the story."

Todd turned to Gabriella. "What the fuck difference does it make?"

"We're just trying to get the whole picture. That's how we work, right, Henry?"

"Yes, right. The whole picture," I said.

Gabriella unleashed a shy grin. "C'mon, Todd, just tell us how you guys met. I bet it's a cute story."

"You think I wanna ride around with you all night telling cute stories? I have to get home—I'm meeting someone there. My mother, if you must know."

Gabriella shrugged. "Up to you Todd, but the sooner you answer my questions, the sooner you'll get a hug from Mom."

Todd sighed. "Leslie and I met in acting class. Happy?"

"When was this?"

"I dunno, five, maybe six years ago? It was before she was married. I'm sure of that because she was still living with her Russian boyfriend." The corners of his lips separated and turned up a fraction of an inch, suggesting a smile. "She was a pretty good little actress, I gotta say, and a looker like her? She could have made it big. With actresses, it's all about looks."

"Yeah, I've heard that," Gabriella said. "So you guys hang out, or what?"

"Not really. I mean, sometimes a cup of coffee after class, but that was it."

"So when you had coffee, what'd you talk about?"

"You know, what was going on in acting class, how we ended up in New York, stuff like that. Most actors like talking about themselves, but not Leslie. Like, once, I told her about my kid brother dying of measles when he was six. It's rare, but it happens. Anyway, I got kind of emotional telling her, ya know? When I finished, Leslie did open up a little, but I remember thinking it wasn't coming from a personal place. It was more like, 'You told me some personal stuff, here's something about me.' She rattled off a couple of facts—her father left the family, her mother died of a heroin overdose, and something about a half-sister in Russia—but not like she was telling her story, you know? Very detached. She clearly didn't want to talk about it, so I never brought up her personal life after that."

Leslie had told me all of that, except the bit about the Russian half-sister. One of her more colorful lies. Unless it was true.

Todd shifted in his seat and rubbed his face with both hands before continuing. "A few months later, I stopped going to that class, and we lost touch. Then about a year ago she showed up at the store lugging a couple of suitcases."

Gabriella said, "By 'the store' you mean Tiffany's?"

"Yeah, Tiffany's. I was glad to see her and all, but Leslie made it clear she wasn't interested in a reunion for old time's sake. She put her left hand down on the counter so I could get a load of her fancy ring. Then she told me she just left her Russian fiancé for good. She wanted to know how much the ring was worth because she needed cash. So I told her to wait there, and I took the ring in the back and showed it to one of the jewelers, who put his jeweler's loop on. He took a good long look at it, handed it back, and told me the ring was maybe worth half a million."

"Holy mackerel," Gabriella deadpanned. "You tell Leslie?"

"Well, no, not right away," he said. "I just said it's worth a lot and that I knew some wealthy customers who might be interested, and that I'd make a few calls."

That got my attention. "Hold on, Todd. You're telling me Tiffany's management doesn't care if their salespeople do deals on the side?"

"Look, I didn't go back and read the employee handbook, okay? There's a couple of foreign guys, big spenders, and they gave me their numbers and told me if anything interesting comes up, I should call them. I figured it was a private sale, and I was just helping out a friend."

I shook my head.

"Oh, fuck off. It's not easy making ends meet, so I do what I have to do. And you're not exactly honest citizen of the year, snatching me off the street."

"Easy, Todd, nobody's judging you, right Henry?"

I nod. "Right." Asshole.

"Then what happened?"

"I handed her back the ring but offered to store it in the safe for the night while she thought it over. She nodded and gave me the ring, and I gave her a receipt with Polaroid pictures and everything. All on the level. That was when she said she had nowhere to stay, so I told her she could stay on my couch for a couple days while we sorted out the ring stuff."

The cabbie interrupted. "Where you wanna get off, lady? This corner okay?"

"Never mind," Gabriella said. "I just found my earring. Let's head back uptown."

"Hang on," he said before making a sudden left turn onto Twenty-Third.

"So Leslie stayed at your place while you tried to find a buyer for the ring."

"Uh-huh. Back at my place we made a deal. If I found a buyer, I'd take half. She offered ten percent, and I said twenty-five or no deal. After some back and forth, we agreed I'd get twenty percent."

"And you found a buyer?"

"Yeah, I called my clients and said I had a line on a choice piece of jewelry that was selling privately. That always gets everyone excited because they think maybe it's stolen, and they can get a great deal. One of my clients—well, not him exactly, he's a Saudi prince or something and never comes in himself, I deal with his assistant— anyway, the assistant called and said the prince might be interested on account of his daughter's sixteenth birthday's coming up, and he needed a great gift, pronto.

"So I texted him a picture and a letter of authenticity from the jeweler. He got back to me with an offer an hour later. Three-fifty. I called Leslie to get her approval before I closed, and she said, 'Three fifty? That all?' and I laughed. She thought I meant three hundred fifty dollars. Leslie's one of the smartest people I know, but she could be a ditz sometimes."

"You got that right," I said.

Gabriella ignored me. "So the ring's sold to a guy halfway around the world, you're flush, and Leslie has the scratch she needs to get her own place. That when she left?"

Todd rolled his eyes. "You'd think, right? I kept dropping hints, but four, five days later she was still crashing on my couch like she was never gonna leave. I'd come home, she'd ask me what's for dinner. I'd been working all day. You'd think she'd offer to make me dinner. And what was she doing all day? She's not the museum type. I didn't want to confront her, because, ya know, if you piss off Leslie it's hell to pay, so I told her I had company coming in a few days, and she had to find another place to stay. I could tell she wasn't happy because she didn't say anything, just started to pack up. I said, 'Hey, you need to stay one more night, it's okay, but she got pouty like she does, you probably know, right, so I let her pack. By the time she was ready to leave it was like nine o'clock, pitch black outside, and raining buckets. So then I insisted she stay the night. But she just picked up her suitcases and took off. Not even a thank you."

"So she left that night, in the pouring rain. Where'd she go?"

Todd shrugged. "Beats me."

I grunted. "She showed up at my place, dripping wet. Asked if she could stay. Told me she wasn't wearing her ring because she threw it at Boris when she left."

The cab pulled up to my apartment building, and the cabbie reached for the meter. "Hold on, cabbie," Gabriella said.

"Jesus, lady, I'm getting dizzy up here."

Gabriella ignored the cabbie. "Todd, can we drop you somewhere?"

"The Museum of Natural History. I'll walk from there." The cab pulled away from the curb.

"One more thing," said Gabriella. "Leslie. We need to find her before the bad guys do. Now, please, for her sake, tell us where she is."

Todd looked at his hands. "I can't. I promised." Everyone stayed quiet for a while, Gabriella biding her time, Todd maybe hoping she wouldn't push too hard for Leslie's whereabouts, and me keeping my lip buttoned as instructed.

Finally, Todd said, "I know you want to help Leslie. I don't know why I believe you, but I do. It's just that I can't be involved with this anymore."

For a minute Gabriella said nothing. I thought maybe she was deciding whether to do the phone-out-the-window thing again, or maybe she wanted me to take over the questioning. But then she said, "Todd, you don't want to be involved, you won't be involved.

But I'm pretty sure she got in touch with you recently and asked you for help. We need to know why she came looking for you again, and we need to find Leslie. You already admitted you know where she is."

Gabriella waited, but Todd folded his arms, dropped his chin to his chest, knitted his eyebrows, and thrust out his lower lip. Like a three-year-old refusing to eat broccoli.

"Okay, Todd, we'll do it your way. Henry, please get Detective Creminelli on the phone. The number is 212-54 …"

"Oh my god, wait," Todd said sitting up, "I swear I didn't know the ring was stolen! Leslie told me it was an engagement ring that she had every right to keep, and I believed her."

Gabriella shrugged. "Maybe the judge will believe you, but then again … You want to take that chance?"

Todd looked down at his hands and shook his head.

"Then tell us when she contacted you and where she is now. Put this shitshow behind you."

"Okay," he said, so softly that both Gabriella and I leaned in to make sure we'd hear what came next. "You're right, Leslie contacted me a couple weeks ago. She said that her ex-boyfriend, the Russian guy, accused her of stealing the ring and wanted it back. He threatened her, so she needed a place to stay where Boris couldn't find her. And she wanted me to help her get the ring back."

"Get it back? How?"

"She wanted to buy it back from the Saudi. I told her she was crazy, it would never work, and no way was I getting involved with that. But I wanted to get her off the phone, so I gave her the number."

"And what about a place to stay? Are you hiding her in your place?"

"What?" he scoffed. "No way! I told her she'd have to find somewhere else to stay, that I didn't want her pissed off Russian ex-boyfriend coming to my apartment. That's when she started crying. Why does crying always sound more pathetic over the phone? Anyway, I said I'd see what I could do."

"And did you?"

"Yeah, I called a friend of mine. She told me her roommate moved out, and she was having a tough time paying the rent by herself. She said Leslie could stay with her until she found a new roommate if she'd pay her share of the rent."

Gabriella and I waited.

"She's a friend from Tiffany's—we work together. She lives in an apartment building called The Luxe on Hudson Street. I've never been there, I don't know the address, but her name's Melissa Shen. She goes by Missy."

Missy! If only I'd just mentioned Leslie's name when I was talking to Missy a few hours earlier, Gabriella and I might have been hearing all this from Leslie instead of Todd.

"Thanks, Todd, you did the right thing," Gabriella said. Then she handed Todd his phone.

The cab pulled up to the curb in front of the museum, and Gabriella let Todd out. "Wait." Todd grabbed the door before she could close it. "No cops, right?"

"We promise," Gabriella said.

"Scout's honor," I added.

"Go fuck yourself, Henry," he said and slammed the door.

CHAPTER 22

Gabriella's backseat interrogation of Todd cleared up plenty, like how the tub of scalding hot water I was in started with Leslie's big fat lie. She'd told me she was so angry when she left Boris that she'd thrown her engagement ring at him. I had no reason to disbelieve her until Aiden's lawyer girlfriend suggested Leslie might have kept the ring and hocked it. Then, during my kidnapping, Boris insisted Leslie had taken the ring and scoffed when I implied he'd misplaced it. Finally, Todd confirmed she'd had it with her when she'd gone to Tiffany's, and that he'd helped her sell it to a Saudi prince. Yeah, Leslie had lied. Shamelessly. Effectively. Tragically.

She'd also lied to me about coming directly to my apartment after leaving Boris. Turns out Leslie went straight to Todd's and crashed on his couch for a week while he arranged to sell the ring. That explained Boris's confusion when I told him Leslie showed up drenched at my apartment at the end of July. He remembered her leaving during a dry spell—it hadn't rained in weeks, he said—and he also recalled hearing a July 4th fireworks display when she walked out. It was a small discrepancy, but the fact that the dates didn't line up had left me wondering what Leslie had done during the missing week. Todd's story cleaned up the timetable.

But the part of Todd's story I found incredible was the part about Leslie wanting to buy back the ring. When she'd shown up at my office asking for money, I'd assumed she wanted it to pay Boris off. But Boris didn't want money, he wanted his ring. Did she actually believe she could buy it back from the Saudi prince?

And what if she tried to buy it back and failed? Would she tell Boris the whole story, that she'd taken the ring and sold it out from under him, and hope that he let bygones be bygones for old time's sake? Boris wasn't the forgiving type—he was more likely to kill her than forgive her. No, Leslie would know better than to level with him. She'd find a way to wriggle out of this. Maybe she'd concoct a story that made me the brains of the operation, say that selling the ring was my idea, that I somehow forced her into it. Maybe she'd already told him something like that, which is why Boris suspected Leslie and I were in it together.

One thing I knew for sure—Leslie would do whatever she had to in order to survive, including setting me up. Even though I still had feelings for her, it was becoming clearer to me every day that she was molded from the same dirty lump of clay as Boris.

But Leslie was no match for Gabriella. Aiden's PI came equipped with the balls required to go up against Boris and his lackeys, and, if need be, Leslie. Up until then, I felt like I'd been rooting around a pitch-black basement full of snakes. Then Gabriella showed up with a flaming torch, and while the snakes hadn't scattered, at least I could see. Now all I had to do was avoid getting bitten and follow Gabriella and her torch to safety.

I was about to ask her how we might approach Leslie when she doused the torch. "That's it for me," she said. "We found Leslie, so my work is done, and I'm outta here. Been nice knowing you, Hank." She leaned forward. "Cabbie, Grand Central Station."

"Wait, you're leaving me?" I said, my throat constricting with fear. "But we haven't found Leslie yet. I mean, what if she's not at Missy's? What do I do then? C'mon Gabriella, you've gotta finish this."

Gabriella checked her watch and then shook her head. "Sorry, Hank. I got a six-year-old at home, and the babysitter turns into a pumpkin at eleven."

"You have a kid?"

"What, you don't think I'm capable of being a mother? Fuck you!"

I held up my palms to calm her. "No, of course you're … I'm sure you're a wonderful mother. I'm just surprised. I didn't picture you married with children is all."

She looked away and crossed her arms. "Who said anything about married? And by the way, Hank, this is all in the 'None of Your Damn Business' file."

"You're right, and I apologize." I stopped to consider how much Gabriella had accomplished over the previous several hours. She came with skills, street smarts, and experience, and knew how to use a gun. She called me an amateur, and while it stung at the time, she was telling me for my own good. This was the highest stakes game I'd ever played. Keeping her involved might mean the difference between life and death.

Gabriella was right—she owed me nothing. Aiden had asked Gabriella to help me locate Leslie and, assuming she was at Missy's, mission accomplished. What came next would involve facing off with Boris, and unless I had the ring, that could be anything from a severe beating to a couple of lethal gunshots. If I had any hope of surviving this, I needed Gabriella's help. I had to find a way to keep her in the game. Maybe Aiden could convince her to continue, but I didn't have that kind of time. I needed Gabriella now.

"C'mon, Gabriella. Aren't you a little curious about whether Leslie's really there?"

"Honestly?" Gabriella scoffed. "I'm more curious about whether my kid got to bed on time."

I started to panic. "But you can't—"

"Look, if I thought it was a good idea for me to be by your side when you first see Leslie, I'd be there. But my professional opinion is that you shouldn't talk to Leslie with me in tow."

I thought about that for a few seconds before deciding I didn't like it. "Remember when you told me this is your turf, not mine? What if I'm walking into a trap? Then how would you feel?"

"Surprised," Gabriella replied. "Hank, I don't know you well, but I suspect you're a guy who plays the odds. You don't really think this is a trap, do you?"

I shook my head.

"If Leslie's there, and I hope she is, the best thing for you to do is talk to her. Alone. Get her to tell you everything she's been up to since the moment she left your office. Taking me with you won't help and might even backfire. Leslie could clam up, because who am I to her? Nobody. And assuming she's up to something shady, she's not going to unload in front of a stranger."

Gabriella was right, and I knew it. But I still wanted her there, if only to keep her trained private eye out for any trouble my amateur eye might miss. "Okay," I said. "I go in alone. But could you do me one last favor? Wait outside Leslie's apartment door—in case there's trouble."

"Waste of time."

"I need you on this, Gabriella."

That got a chuckle. "Well, well. I seem to remember someone telling me to fuck off over the phone this morning. We've come a long way since then, haven't we?"

I nodded. "We have."

Her eyes stayed on me. "I don't know, Henry …" she began. Then she bit her lower lip. Maybe that helped her think better. Maybe her lip needed scratching. Maybe it was just a cute habit. "Tell you what," she said, her lip none the worse for wear. "I'll go with you and wait outside the building for fifteen minutes. That'll give you enough time to size up the situation."

"But how will you know I'm safe?"

"Right before you go into the apartment, call me. When I answer, shove the phone in your pocket. That way I can hear what's going on. I'll listen for a while, and when I'm sure it's not a trap and you're doing okay, I'll head home."

Clearly, this was the best I could do, but I needed a shred of hope that she was still in my corner. "What if something comes up tomorrow, and I need your help?"

"You got my phone number. But I'm not making any promises."

The cab barreled down the West Side Highway on the way to Missy's apartment. We'd been with this cab and driver so long he almost seemed part of the team. He must have overheard some of what we were saying, but even if he pieced together what was going on, I couldn't imagine anything he could do with the information other than telling his cab driver pals over a couple of beers. To him, I was nobody—just another guy in the back of his cab.

Sometimes being nobody, unrecognized and forgettable, leaves me feeling calm and at peace. Kind of how I imagine feeling during the out-of-body experience you're supposed to have just before you die. Witnessing yourself crumpled and unmoving on your deathbed while floating above your body sounds scary, but the way I see it, a guy has to achieve a certain level of tranquility to hover over his dying self without totally freaking out.

Being calm in the face of death. It almost sounded appealing.

***

I glanced at the meter. So far, I'd spent one hundred forty-nine dollars tooling around Manhattan. No complaints—it was money well spent—but the meter wasn't done with me yet.

We took the Fourteenth Street exit toward Hudson and passed through the heart of the meatpacking district. Not much of the old meatpacking going on here anymore. Now the street was lined with swanky downtown bars and chichi restaurants. Inside these joints, the music was loud and the air damp. The clientele was rich and good-looking. Fashion models towered over the crowd, their beauty taunting the less fortunate. Everyone packed so close together they had to hold their drinks over their heads to move around. Not my scene. Not anymore.

We were getting close to Leslie's apartment building. Part of me ached to get this search over and done with so we could get on with whatever came next. Another part of me wanted Leslie not to be there. Maybe I was afraid of seeing her, standing near her, being close enough for her scent—lemon and peppermint with a hint of rum—to overwhelm me. Maybe I wasn't ready for that. Maybe I'd never be ready.

There was also the question of how Leslie would react to seeing me. Would she welcome me as the hero who stopped at nothing to find his ex-wife and pull her out of this mess? She could just as easily tell me to get lost before I had the chance to say I only wanted to help, to offer protection, moral support, and even financial assistance if that was what she wanted. Or she could pull out a Russian Makarov pistol and shoot me. As I thought about that in the back of the cab, the driver dodged and weaved his way through the West Village. When we passed Bank Street, I thought of an old girlfriend who'd lived in an apartment on the corner, a dump of a place in those days. Now it was worth millions.

Gabriella sat quietly beside me, her thumbs flying as she punched letters, words, and sentences into her phone.

Ever since she told me about her kid, I wondered why she'd chosen to be a PI. Wasn't she afraid that something might happen to her? Knowing that Gabriella wasn't alone made me think twice about keeping her on board for the second, and likely more dangerous, part of my adventure. I was still fighting with myself over that one when the cab pulled over to the curb. We'd reached the Luxe.

I paid the fare and then some. The cabbie noted my generosity, thanked me, then said, "Hey Hank—good luck with everything." He reached over his shoulder and offered me his business card. I saw that his name was Carlos. "Take it," he said. "You never know."

Gabriella and I were getting out of the cab when my phone coughed up a text message. It was Emma.

Call me asap. I found something interesting.

CHAPTER 23

I stood at the curb on Hudson Street with my phone out, wondering if "interesting" meant I should put off seeing Leslie. I glanced up and saw Gabriella waiting outside the building entrance. If I stopped now to learn what Emma had found, I ran the risk of pissing off Gabriella.

I decided to text Emma but keep it brief.

Interesting?

Maybe. You said you'd check in with me

Call u later?

Later?? Twenty minutes or next week??!! 😜

Sorry. client stuff, on the clock, couldn't interrupt. Call you in a couple hours?

I'll be out

On a date? Tell Mr. Right something came up

MS Right, a college girlfriend. We'll be at The Naked Hand Bar til 11. Meet me there.

Okay, see you later

I hustled to join Gabriella, who was by now waiting at the foot of the building, her arms crossed, smirking. "Whadja do—stop for ice cream?"

"Sort of," I replied, thinking of Emma in her tennis whites. "Had to return a text, but I'm here now."

"Yeah, so is the doorman."

I hadn't counted on a doorman. "Oh. Shit." I stood there looking at the entrance. "We need to create a diversion, so he'll leave his post."

"A diversion?" Gabriella said, laughing and shaking her head. "Sometimes you amaze me, Hank, but not in a good way. Forget the diversion. Just go in and tell them you're Missy's friend, Todd Whatshisname.

"Winger."

"Yeah, you're Todd Winger, and you're there to see Missy. That should do it. I'll wait here."

I nodded and started to walk away when Gabriella said, "Hey, call me on your cell so we're connected. Remember?"

I dialed her number, and she answered and said, over the phone and to my face, "Hello? Who is this?" and cracked up at her own joke. When she stopped laughing, she said, "I'll listen in on you guys for fifteen minutes and then send a text when I leave. Okay?"

I nodded.

The lobby was modern but not spacious. An Ikea-looking couch and a glass table with a vase full of fresh-cut flowers filled the space. The mailroom was visible through an entryway located next to the elevators. All of it was neat and tidy. The doorman was half standing, half sitting on a stool, and when I approached, he stood up.

"Hi," I said. "Name's Winger, Todd Winger. Here to see Missy Shen."

"You just missed her," the doorman replied. "Ms. Shen left two minutes ago."

I looked at the doorman. He looked at me. Now what? "Really? I was sure she said we'd meet at her apartment. The three of us. Missy and her new roommate." I wasn't sure if Leslie was using her real name. "Can you please try the apartment? Her roommate knows me."

The doorman picked up the intercom phone, ran his index finger down the phone list in front of him, then punched three numbers into the keypad. When someone answered, he said, "I have a Mr. Winger here. He was looking for Ms. Shen … Yes, I told him she was out, but … Yes. Todd Winger … Okay, I'll send him up."

He put the receiver down and said, "Apartment 8C."

I looked back to where I'd left Gabriella, hoping to get a thumbs up or some other sign of encouragement and camaraderie but she was out of eyeshot. Across the lobby, the elevator door opened. I quickly thanked the doorman and double-timed it over there, calling out, "Hold the elevator, please," to a pleasant-looking old man with a dachshund on a leash entering the elevator. The man obliged by putting his arm in front of the closing doors.

"Thanks," I said as I stepped inside. "Nice dog."

The old man looked down at the dog, then back at me. "She's a pain in my ass."

We rode the elevator according to the unwritten rules of elevator etiquette—move to the rear, face front, and no talking while the elevator was on the move. Even the dog faced front, although she started whimpering as we passed the fourth floor. Maybe she had a doggy friend there, or maybe she was just nervous. Like me. The man and his dog got off at six. "Take care, now," I offered. He replied with, "Have a nice evening." The dog replied with a yip and a low growl that was cut off by the closing doors. At least the dog wasn't trying to bullshit me.

The elevator dinged at the eighth floor, and the doors opened. I took my phone out of my pocket. "You there, Gabriella?"

"I'm here. Where are you?"

"Eighth floor walking toward the apartment," I answered. "Making sure we're still connected."

"We're connected. Now put your damn phone back in your pocket."

I did as she said and started down the hall toward the apartment. The door was ajar, but I knocked anyway—three sharp knuckle taps.

A woman's muffled voice said, "Come in. I left it open."

I walked in without a reply and closed the door behind me.

"Hi Todd," she called out cheerfully.

Given the situation, I would have expected Leslie to be keeping a watchful eye out for trouble, but her relaxed tone of voice, not to mention the unlocked door, said otherwise.

"Make yourself at home. I'm just mixing us a couple of gin and tonics. I know you're a bourbon man, but Beefeater's all we've got."

I stood at the door, listening to the freezer door close and then ice cubes going into one glass, then the other, followed by the fizz of tonic water.

"Anyway," she continued, "it's hot as hell in here, even with the AC on. Nothing like a G and T to beat the heat." She stepped into the living room holding the two tall glasses, each sporting a wedge of lime.

"Hello Leslie," I said nonchalantly.

She stopped and stared at me for a second. I'm familiar with that moment when you're expecting something, and it turns out to be something else. Like reaching for your milk and grabbing your orange juice by mistake—you're so surprised you spit out the juice. That's the moment Leslie was caught in.

She dropped both glasses at the same time, leaving her standing there empty-handed with her eyes opened wide and her mouth not far behind. The glasses, the gin, the tonic, and the limes all seemed to fall in slow motion.

"Henry," she said at precisely the same time the glasses shattered on the stone floor.

Leslie was wearing short shorts and a sleeveless blue T-shirt, and unfortunately for her, she was barefoot.

"Hold it," I said, putting both hands out in front of me. "Don't move. You don't want to cut your feet on glass shards. Where's your broom?"

She stood stock still, her eyes not straying from mine, not even to evaluate the carnage at her feet. "What the fuck are you doing here, Henry?"

"Right now, I'm looking for a broom and some towels. Where are they?"

"Kitchen," she said. "Broom's in the tall cabinet next to the oven. Towels, too."

I stepped around the glass into the kitchen, collected the broom, the towels, and a dustpan, rushed back to Leslie, dropped the towels on the floor, and swept the broken glass into the dustpan. Then I dropped to my hands and knees to mop up. When I was sure there was no glass left, I started to dry her feet.

"Don't touch me," she said and backed away.

I looked up at her. "You're welcome." I threw the wet towels aside and stood up.

She walked over to the couch. I'd been there ten minutes, and we hadn't even started getting into it. I didn't want to lose my nerve, partly because I knew Gabriella was listening.

Leslie sat down, pulled a cigarette from behind her ear and stuck it in the corner of her mouth. She didn't light it, just let it dangle. "Fuck," she said as she snatched the cigarette from her lips and tossed it on the table. "Missy says I can't smoke in here."

"Thought you quit smoking," I said.

She crossed her arms. "Yeah, well, just one more thing you thought you knew about me that turned out to be wrong."

Neither of us spoke for a minute. Leslie sat there, brooding, looking around the room, everywhere but at me. I didn't take my eyes off her.

Finally she said, "What's the matter with you? Stop staring at me."

I looked away, saying nothing. My phone vibrated with a text. It had been about fifteen minutes, so I assumed it was Gabriella's sayonara.

Then Leslie barked, "How did you find me?

"Friend of a friend told me you might be here."

"How much do you know about what's going on?"

"I know that you're in trouble, and you're hiding out here. Hiding from Boris. That about the size of it?"

She nodded. "I'm hiding, but obviously, I'm not doing such a great job. Because if you found me, Boris won't be far behind. He's smarter than you."

"Better looking, too," I said. "You should've stayed with him and skipped me altogether."

She grunted. "Well, you're here. I assume you didn't come looking for me to settle a bet. So what do you want?"

"To help."

I started toward her, but she put out her hands. "You wanna sit, sit over there," she said, pointing to a green faux-leather wing chair.

I did as I was told.

"You missed your chance, Henry, remember? When I was at your office a few days ago? I told you I was in trouble and needed money, and that you'd be in trouble, too, if I didn't get it."

"You can't blame me for not believing you. Nobody would buy a crackpot story like that," I said. "Especially coming from you. But when I went home that night and found my apartment had been broken into and searched, I thought it might be connected to you. Then I got kidnapped by Boris. He laid out the situation for me in his charming Russian-inflected Oxford English and made it my responsibility to find you. And deliver a message."

"What message?"

"That returning your engagement ring was the only way for you and me to stay healthy." I didn't mention that Boris also threatened to blackmail me.

"Well, well. You finally get the picture," she said, leaning forward. "Either Boris gets his stinking ring back, or we both end up standing at the end of a pier in twin buckets of freshly poured concrete, while some rat bastard he hired sits in his car smoking a joint and waiting for the cement to set."

"You can't swim," I said. "The cement would be wasted on you."

"Hysterical," she deadpanned, then leaned forward and eyed the cigarette she'd tossed on the coffee table. Finally, she reached for it and lit up with a disposable lighter she pulled from her pocket. "Missy can go fuck herself if she doesn't like it," she mumbled before inhaling deeply with her eyes closed and her head tilted back. She exhaled, blowing the smoke my way. "So we're in this together? Is that what you think?"

I nodded, ignoring the smoke. "Yeah. Just like old times. For better or worse, richer or poorer, 'til death …'"

"Don't, Henry." She took another drag on her cigarette, then looked around for a place to put the ashes. Finding nothing suitable, she flicked the ash on the couch and rubbed it in with the heel of her hand. The couch was gray tweed, and the ashes almost disappeared. Lucky for Missy.

"Well, here's a news flash," she said, her eyes narrowed against the smoke. "We're not working together, and I have no intention of teaming up with you. That ship sailed when you threw me out of your office. You're on your own now, and so am I. Boris knows where to find you, but he didn't know I was here until you showed up. I have to assume he's tracking your every move. Which means I need a new place to hide. Thanks a lot for your help, Henry. Thanks a fucking lot."

My fingers dug deep into the soft arms of my chair. "No, thank you a fucking lot for dragging me into your little crime of the century." I looked away from her in disgust, then back at her, trying to keep from exploding. "When you walked out on me, and we got divorced, I swore I'd never get involved with anyone like you again. The women I dated after our divorce were saccharine, goody-two-shoes, boring as hell, and incapable of hurting my feelings, and that's what I needed after our mess of a marriage." What I didn't mention was that I never found anyone, probably because I wanted someone more like Leslie. "I thought I was done with you, yet here you are once again ruining my life. And this time you've outdone yourself—because of you, we could both end up dead. It's been a swell couple of days for me, lemme tell you. So, again, thank you a fucking lot."

"Whaddya want, an apology? You want me to say sorry for getting you into this? Well I am sorry. Sorry I got me into this, and sorry you couldn't find it in yourself to keep me out of danger. For chrissakes, Henry …"

I cut her off. "And about your run-and-hide strategy," I said with a snort, "Do you seriously think you could just stay hidden from Boris forever? Nobody's that clever or that lucky. Not even you."

"Really? Watch me. With a couple thousand miles between us and some fancy plastic surgery, he'll never find me."

"Maybe, but he'd never stop searching either. And by the way, doll, neither would I, because you're my only way out. I've heard from clients that life on the run is not much of a life. Looking over your shoulder, jumping at shadows, keeping your distance from strangers. After a while the paranoia wears you down. One guy told me it was a relief to finally get caught. So let's me and you find a way out of this that's neat, clean, and foolproof."

Leslie sat quietly smoking and rubbing ashes into the couch. I wondered how long she could do that before the ash stain showed. Finally she said, "I sold the ring for three fifty. There's two fifty left, and the Saudi'll sell the ring back to me for five hundred. So that would require you getting me a quarter million dollars."

I did a quick mental calculation. "I can do that."

"But will you?"

"On one condition," I said. "You promise to level with me. I can't hand you all that money without knowing everything that's happened to you starting with the day you left Boris. I want the whole sordid story, and I want it straight."

As soon as the words left my lips, I knew it would never happen. Sure, she'd tell me a story alright, just like she always did. Half of it might be true, but the other half would be nothing but hooey. Usually, I'd have a tough time figuring out which half was which, but this time, I'd gotten a partial briefing from both Boris and Todd. All Leslie had to do was fill in some of the blanks. And so far, nobody had answered one question to my satisfaction. Why didn't Boris go after the ring at the time Leslie left? Why now?

Leslie smirked. "Okay, Henry. Where do you want me to start?"

"Start with the day you left Boris for good. Don't leave anything out. And keep going until I tell you to stop."

Leslie sat up straight on the edge of the couch. She reached for a throw pillow and placed it on her lap, spent a moment smoothing the fabric, then held it to her stomach as if it were a favorite teddy bear. I sat on the edge of my chair without the emotional comfort of a stuffed pillow on my lap, ready to hear every word. Leslie sighed the sigh of the put-upon ex-wife, then started in on the story. How she'd left Boris after he'd cheated on her with his imported Russian doll named Tanya. How she'd immediately contacted Todd because he worked at Tiffany's, and she needed to have the ring professionally appraised. And how they'd sold the ring to a Saudi buyer for a bundle. It all added up, but I was still hazy on the whole Tanya thing. Why would Boris bring someone into his home like that? Seemed kind of random.

When she got to the part about showing up at my place, I interrupted her. "Let's jump ahead," I suggested, "to when Boris tells you he wants his ring back."

She smiled. "Really? I'm coming to the best part, you know, us meeting and getting married and all."

"By 'and all,' you mean leaving me and filing for divorce? That part I remember. So … Boris contacts you how?"

"Typical Boris," she said, shaking her head. "Couldn't even ask me for the damn ring back himself. He sent his errand boy."

"Go on."

"So a couple weeks ago, I'm leaving my apartment and heading to the park for a run when I feel someone come up behind me. Before I could turn around there's a handkerchief over my face and I pass out so fast I didn't even have time to scream. When I wake up, I'm lying on the back seat of a car. It's just me and the driver. I scramble to sit up, and the driver says, 'Relax, I'm not gonna hurt you.'"

"Weaselly guy," I asked, "with a big honker and a face like an old shoe, name of Leo?"

"Yeah," she said laughing bitterly, "that describes him. Leo the weasel. Anyway, he says, real threatening-like, 'Boris wants his ring back, so hand it over.' I say I don't know anything about any ring, and I wiggle my fingers in his face to show him I'm not wearing one, hoping that would settle it. Then he calls me a lying little bitch and tells me either I give the ring back by the following Tuesday or else. Or else what, I say, you gonna come and beat me up? He tells me that he wouldn't have to because Boris said …" she hesitated.

"What?"

"Boris said he'd kill me himself." She shivered and hugged her security pillow to her chest. "That's when I knew it was real. Because that's exactly what Boris would say, and that's what he would do, too." Her cigarette was all but done. "Shit, I gotta get rid of this," she said and walked into the kitchen.

I thought of asking what happened next, but I figured she needed some time to collect herself, so I kept quiet.

After a minute, she sat back on the couch, returned the pillow to her lap, and continued her story. "I didn't have much time," she said, "so I had to hustle. I figured my best shot was to try and buy the ring back from the guy who bought it. I contacted him and, amazingly, was able to cut a deal. Said the ring happened to be in a safe deposit box at a Manhattan bank, and his secretary could hand me the key as soon as I wired the funds. But then you wouldn't give me the money I needed, so I ran."

We sat in silence. Leslie seemed shaken by her own story. Nothing she'd said hinted at why Boris suddenly wanted his ring back. Boris told me it was none of my business. Todd probably didn't care. Was Leslie as clueless as me?

"One more thing," I said to bring Leslie back to the conversation. "Why didn't Boris come looking for the ring when you first left him?"

Leslie shrugged. "No idea. I assumed he didn't care about me, and he didn't care about the ring. Like we were just a couple of cheap baubles he'd picked up along the way."

"Cheap? You sold the ring for three hundred and fifty thousand dollars, and you offered to buy it back for half a million."

Leslie shrugged. "Maybe he didn't know what it was worth. Maybe business went south on him, and he needs to raise cash. Maybe he wants to give it to his new girlfriend to wear around like he wanted me to do. What's the difference? Boris wants the ring, and I don't have it."

I couldn't shake the feeling that I was watching a play where I had only the vaguest notion of what was going on. The actors on stage were all big as life, but I couldn't make sense of the dialogue. All I knew was at the center of it, or maybe hidden in some darkened corner of the stage, was Boris's damn ring—a ring with a story to tell. I suspected I had a long way to go until the third act when all would be revealed. If I lived to see it.

"Okay," Leslie said, sinking back into the couch, tossing the pillow aside, and tucking her legs under her, "I told you the story like you asked. So now you're gonna help me, right? If you give me the money, we can finish this once and for all."

I weighed my options. I could assume everything Leslie had told me was a fairy tale and walk away, but there was the small matter of Boris—that part couldn't have been more real, since he'd threatened me face to face. Or I could give Leslie the money and hope that she would use it to buy the ring back from the Saudi, knowing there was the possibility that she'd head for some Venezuelan beach and spend my money on discos and daiquiris. But I was offering her a lifeline— why wouldn't she take it and, as she said, finish this once and for all?

I had the money, and although it would wipe out my savings, I'd make do.

"You'll get your money," I said, "and it sure as shit better put an end to this ring business." I stood up to leave. "And count me out of any further dealings with Boris. The guy's dangerous. I'll give you the money, but you're on your own after that."

She sat there with a look on her face that was somewhere between astonishment and disbelief. "You're giving me the money? All of it? Two hundred fifty thousand?"

"Yeah, and I hope I live to regret it." I started toward the door.

"Wait," Leslie said. "I didn't tell you where you should wire the money. I'll write the account number down. It'll just take a second." She disappeared into the hallway leading to the bedrooms. A minute later she came out and handed me a yellow piece of paper.

Leslie's handwriting was notoriously bad, so I glanced at it to make sure it was legible. I looked up. "Why does this account number seem familiar?"

Leslie looked away. "What? I don't know. What's familiar about it?"

Instead of answering, I glared at her, but that didn't force a confession, so I accused her point-blank. "Isn't this a joint account we had when we were married? The one we decided to close?"

Leslie looked down, and I could see red spots forming on her cheeks. "I guess I forgot to close it. There wasn't much in there, remember?"

Having a fight about this now seemed pointless. I just shook my head in amazement and opened the door to leave. As I did, Leslie said, "Henry."

I stopped and turned around. Leslie crossed her arms and gave me a half-hearted smile. She looked more like a scared little girl than the tough gal I'd fallen for so many years ago. If I didn't know better, I would have felt sorry for her.

"Thank you, Henry."

The sincere expression of gratitude coming from Leslie made me feel like a sucker.

"Right." I slammed the door on my way out.

CHAPTER 24

I stood on the sidewalk, not sure which way to go, wondering about what I'd heard from Leslie. The more I thought about it, the more I realized she hadn't added much if anything. Since there was nobody else I could question, I had to assume that was all the information I'd get.

Putting the pieces together was as frustrating as repairing a broken vase. Say you've got a vase you treasure—like the one my grandmother gave me—that gets smashed. You put the pieces in a box, and the next rainy day you get out the glue. When you run out of pieces, you assume you're done. After the glue dries, you place it on the shelf, take a step back, and have a look. That's when you notice the cracks, so you turn it a little to get a more satisfying view, but now you see there's a big piece missing. You turn it back around and go about your business, but you can't stop thinking about it— the missing piece bothers you. You think about it once or twice a day, then once or twice an hour. You start crawling around on your hands and knees in the room where the vase fell. Then you start searching the rest of the house, which of course makes no sense at all, but you're desperate. Either you find that missing piece, or the vase will never hold water. You know it's out there somewhere, and it's driving you nuts.

That missing piece had to be somewhere. I swore to myself I'd find it.

A glance at my watch told me it was early enough that Emma might still be at the bar with her girlfriend. If not, I'd head back to our apartment building and knock on her door. I dropped into the Fourteenth Street subway station and took the L train across town, where I caught the uptown local.

Twenty minutes later my train pulled into the Eighty-Sixth Street station with a squeal. As the doors opened, we were all politely reminded by the imaginary trainman's prerecorded voice to "Please let the passengers off the train first." Left unsaid was "… Otherwise, you might trample someone." You have to admire the New York City transit system hoping against hope that they could inject a measure of common courtesy into the hordes of subway riders, many of whom cared little for the welfare of their fellow traveler. Sure enough, just as I'd witnessed a thousand times before, some idiot came charging in as soon as the doors parted and shoved me out of the way. "Hey," I shouted. "Please let the passengers off the train first, asshole."

Asshole didn't even turn around.

A young woman standing next to me, who was also clipped by the guy, shot me a smile. "Nice try," she said.

I smiled back. "Just doing my best to keep New Yorkers from falling victim to their worst instincts."

"A few million more guys like you, we might have a fighting chance," she said. "But thanks for trying." Then she fast-walked across the platform, hoisting her purse above her head to avoid snagging it on the exit turnstile. The woman, her smile, her thank you, lifted my spirits. It was that kind of brief but satisfying encounter with strangers that made me love living in Manhattan. Whoever she was, her story was like mine and everyone else's—mostly unremarkable but dotted here and there with romance, heartbreak, mystery, adventure, joy, and loneliness. My hunch, and it was just a hunch mind you, was that she lived without the threat of Russian mob violence shadowing her. Must be nice, I thought, trying to remember my life before Friday, before Leslie and her cursed engagement ring. Before Boris, and Leo and Tanya. Before being kidnapped. Before Todd and Missy and Gabriella.

And Emma.

I bounded up the stairs and headed south on Lexington to Eighty-Fourth, where she told me she'd be having a drink with her college girlfriend. The Naked Hand Bar was a favorite of the twenty-somethings who lived four to a room on the Upper East Side. Most of these kids hadn't been out of college very long, and their jobs were just jobs at this point, having not yet hardened into careers. On Saturday nights the place was packed, noisy, and reeked of beer, testosterone, and cheap perfume. The excitement often spilled out onto the sidewalk, where first-time inebriates could be seen puking their guts out. I never went near the place on Saturday night, but this being Sunday, and this being Emma, I couldn't wait.

The bar was about three-quarters full and quiet enough to talk without screaming. I scanned the crowd. Emma must have spotted me first because she had her hand in the air. She and her girlfriend were sitting at a four-top. I smiled and waved back and worked my way toward them. On closer inspection, it turned out the girlfriend was a guy. Emma said something to him and gestured in my direction. The guy turned around. It was Aiden.

I stopped short, like a mime hitting an imaginary glass wall. What the hell was Aiden doing there? Emma and Aiden had had a scrappy divorce, and there was plenty of bitterness on his part. So how in the hell could anyone explain what I was looking at? As much as I wanted to be with Emma, seeing her with Aiden ruined everything. And if there was an explanation for how her "college girlfriend" had become Aiden, well, I didn't want to hear it. Taking a step back, I bumped into a waitress carrying a tray full of empty beer bottles. Even though I turned around and helped steady her tray, my muttered apology was no match for her high-pitched swearing. I felt so bad I pulled out a twenty and dropped it on her tray. She grudgingly thanked me. After that I found my way out and took off down the street.

The door to the bar opened behind me. "Henry!" Emma shouted. "Henry, for crying out loud, what are you doing?"

"Going home," I called out over my shoulder. "Sorry to interrupt you and your 'girlfriend.'"

I kept walking, but Emma ran and quickly caught up.

"What the hell are you talking about?"

I noticed she wasn't even breathing hard from her short sprint. Must be the tennis. I stopped and faced her. "Did I not just see you drinking with your ex-husband, who also happens to be my best friend? What's his name again? The shock of it fogged my memory."

Emma rolled her eyes. "Since when did the sight of Aiden send you to the moon? Last time I checked, you guys were still best friends."

I glared at her, wondering whether to explain myself or leave it. Should I tell her that despite my growing attraction to her, I was still haunted by my own possibly antiquated code of ethics that put my best friend's ex-wife on the other side of a No Trespassing sign? That, while Emma was technically available, and while Aiden was in a relationship with that lawyer friend of his, all the lights were flashing yellow? And that I had no intention of being a heel? Should I have told her all that?

I opened my mouth, but all I could muster was "Jesus Christ, Emma. Really?"

She replied with a torrent of words. "My girlfriend—who by the way was in the ladies' room when you walked in—was also friends with Aiden in college. That's where we all met. When I got to the bar, she said she hadn't seen Aiden in forever and wouldn't it be fun if he'd meet us for a drink. I didn't really want to, but I couldn't say no. That's why Aiden was there, jackass. Now would you relax and come join us?"

I had so much adrenaline coursing through me relaxation was out of the question, and sitting between Emma and Aiden while they reminisced with her college roommate sounded like some kind of hell. "How about I just meet you back at my apartment? Or yours if you'd rather. I need to know what you found out, and that's not something I want to get into in front of your college pals."

"What I found out?" She put a finger to her lip. "Oh, yeah. About the ring." Then she took a step back and crossed her arms. "Wait. Is that the reason you showed up at the bar? For the information? Sheesh, Henry, you really know how to flatter a girl."

"Of course that's not the only reason," I said, backpedaling like a unicyclist confronted by a grizzly bear. "I came looking for you because, well, because I wanted to see you again."

She uncrossed her arms and looked up at me. "Really?"

"Really. I didn't want to seem too forward, ya know? Aggressive? I mean, even though we've known each other for a while, I feel like this afternoon was the start of something. You know what I'm saying? But just now, when I saw you sitting there with Aiden, it occurred to me that maybe you weren't thinking about it the same way. And maybe you didn't care to see me tonight at all. Maybe you just felt obligated to tell me whatever you found that was 'interesting,' as you put it in your text."

She raised an eyebrow, and I saw the hint of a smile. "Wow. You turned that around nicely. I wanted to see you tonight, about a thousand times more than I wanted to see my college roommate and Aiden. I couldn't wait to see you—that's why I sat facing the door, so I'd catch you walking in. If you came. You sounded so busy when we were texting." She stepped toward me and put her hand on my arm. "Of course you got pissed when you saw me sitting there with Aiden, but can't we just call it a misunderstanding and get on with, you know, whatever you and I were doing?"

"Only if you apologize for calling me a jackass."

"I called you a jackass?" She thought for a second. "Oh yeah, I did. But you were being a jackass."

"Apology accepted," I said.

"I'm sorry I called you a jackass," she said, laughing. Then she took a half step closer, which was as close as she could get, and looked up at me. "Are we friends again?" Before I could answer, she stood on her tiptoes and kissed me softly on the lips. We lingered on that kiss for a while, and by the time it ended we had our arms around each other. "How about now?" she asked, stepping back from the embrace, her eyelids heavy, her lips parted. "Friends?"

I nodded.

"Good." She stepped back, and before turning to go, said, "I'll meet you at your apartment in half an hour."

I watched her slip back into the bar, then walked the three blocks to my apartment, reliving that kiss over and over until I had it memorized for future reference. By the time I got home, the memory was replaying itself, like the hook to a hit song that everyone's been humming. I left the door to my apartment ajar, the way Leslie had when she'd thought it would be Todd walking in. But I knew for certain it would be Emma. I wanted her in my arms so badly that I wasn't about to put a locked door between us.

***

Half an hour later, just before the door swung open hard and banged into my bookcase, I heard Emma call out, "Henry!" Her voice sounded strained, but before I had a chance to consider why that might be, Emma stumbled into the room and landed on the floor, followed by Boris's henchman, Leo.

He smiled as he closed the door behind him. "I found something that I think might belong to you," he said.

Ignoring Leo and his B-movie patter for the moment, I rushed over to Emma and asked if she was okay. She'd barely missed hitting her head on the coffee table. When she didn't answer, I asked again. She nodded meekly and with my help, she got off the floor and moved onto the couch. Then I turned to deal with the scumbag who'd thrown her to the floor. He was leaning on my door, hands in the pockets of his gray sharkskin jacket, looking like he didn't have a care in the world.

"Why, you sonofabitch …" I bounded toward him, intending to land one on his kisser. But he was fast, stepping to the side and pulling a pistol out of his jacket pocket.

"Not so fast, Henry," he said, pointing the gun at me as we stood a couple of feet from each other. "Nobody wants nobody to get hurt."

Emma said softly, "Oh my god, is that a gun?"

"What do you want?" I growled.

"I don't want nothing, Henry. But my boss, he's looking for, what did he call it?" He put the gun barrel to his head, apparently to help him think. I made a move toward him, but the gun snapped back into position, aiming directly at my chest. "Don't," he said, as if the pointed gun wasn't discouragement enough. "Now where was I? Oh yeah, I remember now. Boss says I should get from you a 'progress report.'"

I glared at him. "Fine. Tell Boris I found his ex-girlfriend and convinced her to do the right thing. So I've done what Boris asked, and it's not my problem anymore."

Leo shook his head and pursed his lips like a schoolmarm hearing the wrong answer. "Not good enough."

"You want it in writing? I can do that. Got a pen I could borrow?"

Leo's free hand slapped me hard across my face. "Don't be a wiseass. Next time I'll use my other hand," he said, waving the gun. "And that could leave a mark."

I rubbed my cheek. Emma had cried out when he slapped me. I gave her what I hoped was a reassuring glance, but since I wasn't the one holding the gun and doing the slapping, it probably fell short. I had to end this before Leo got a notion to pistol whip me.

"We've located the 'item,'" I said, making air quotes. "We don't have it. Someone else does, a third party I don't know personally. But they've agreed to return it, and we're arranging to get it back. Boris will have it by Tuesday night, Wednesday the latest."

"Wednesday? Tuesday's the fuckin' deadline, Henry," he said. "Deadline," he repeated, this time with a smirk. "Accent on 'dead.' Got it?"

"I got it. Deadline's Tuesday. I don't need another reminder."

"Maybe you do, maybe you don't, but the boss, he ain't taking no chances. I asked him should I break your finger or something, make a lasting impression, but he said just to rattle your cage a little."

"That shouldn't involve my friends."

"Hey, it's not like I hurt her." Leo's eyes moved toward Emma. I took a step to block his view. He peered around me. "I didn't hurt you, did I, sugar?" Emma glared at him but said nothing. "Good," he said. "I'd never forgive myself."

He continued eyeballing Emma. I stifled an urge to take a swing at him, gun or no gun. Instead, I said, "Are we done here, Leo?"

He nodded. Without looking away from Emma or lowering the gun, he opened the door and backed out. "Take good care, Henry.

You too, sugar." The gun slithered out last. Leo shut the door and was gone.

Numbed by relief, my body went limp, my shoulder hit the doorframe and my head hung down, leaving me staring, dazed, at the floor. My knees felt watery, and if they floated away, I'd collapse, but I willed them to hang on. Emma hadn't moved a muscle since I'd picked her up off the floor and moved her to the couch. She was staring wide-eyed in my direction but somehow not at me.

"Henry," she said softly, "I'd lock the door myself, but seeing that you're right there, you think you could do that for me?"

I stood up straight, ran my fingers through my hair, then turned the lock and threw the deadbolt. It didn't leave me feeling safer. Leo's dark scent, aftershave mixed with cigarette smoke, hung in the air like a malevolent fog. Blood seeped into the corner of my mouth, another souvenir of Leo's visit. I wiped it with the back of my hand.

Emma watched me without a word, her tan gone to white, her breathing shallow. "That's not supposed to happen," she said.

I moved to the couch and sat down next to her, not knowing if she was going to hug me, slug me, or bid me farewell and walk out. I wanted to say something comforting, but nothing came to mind. Instead, I reached for her hand, half expecting her to pull away. Her hand nestled into mine.

"Are you hurt?" I asked.

"No, but I'm kind of cold."

I put my arm around her and pulled her close. She was shaking and looked like she might cry. Seeing her afraid made me angry. If she'd been hurt, it would have been my fault.

"I'm so sorry, Emma," I said.

She pulled out of my embrace enough to speak. "Nothing like this ever happened to me," she said. "The guy came up behind me, gripped my arm, and told me to keep going until I reached your apartment. I had no idea what was happening, but I was afraid, as afraid as I've ever been."

I hugged her close again. "You're safe now." We were quiet for a few seconds, and I noticed her shaking had stopped. "Are you still cold?"

"Not as much. Your body's warm, so that's helping." She leaned her head on my shoulder. Her hair smelled good, like a lemon twist pulled from a martini. "Were you scared? You didn't seem that scared. And I could tell you were trying to keep me safe, the way you helped me to the couch and then lunged at the guy like you were gonna rip his head off."

"That was my plan."

"I know. I know you wanted to protect me." She lowered her eyes. "I like you, Henry. A lot." Then she looked up at me, lips parted. "This is where you say you like me, too."

I said it.

Then she kissed me, and I kissed her back. When the kiss ended, and her eyes opened, she said, "You know, when I was walking home from the bar, I had a much different evening in mind. I thought we would …"

I smiled and she smiled back. Then she started to laugh.

"What's funny?"

"Nothing," she said and then laughed some more. "Oh, I might as well tell you. You know how I chased after you when you left the bar? Well, Aiden saw the whole thing. And I guess I felt a little, I dunno, weird, that he caught us together. I mean, I'm his ex-wife and you're his best friend. As I walked back to the bar, I wondered if there's something a little bit wrong with that. But when I sat down next to Aiden, he asked me if we were sleeping together, and I said yes!" Again she laughed. "Can you believe that? Guess I jumped the gun."

"… so to speak," I added.

She stopped laughing, then pushed me away and stood up. "Henry, did that have anything to do with the case you're working? Please don't tell me that creep was your client."

Up to this point, I hadn't leveled with her, but continuing to lie didn't seem fair given what we'd just been through. "I know I told you I was working a case, but no, he's not my client."

She put her hands on her hips. "You're not involved in something criminal, are you, Henry?"

It was a fair question, but it stung. Before tonight, Emma knew me to be a successful defense attorney. She probably figured me for a stand-up guy who played by the rules and kept his nose clean. Her question made me feel like a two-bit crook covered in dirt and blood. "No, nothing illegal." Not yet anyway, I told myself. "I'm trying to help Leslie. She got herself in hot water, and some of it's splashing on me."

Emma narrowed her eyes. "The Leslie you were married to? That Leslie?" She crossed her arms, took a deep breath, and let it out slowly. "Wow. I gotta say I'm surprised."

"Like my surprise when I saw you with Aiden tonight?"

"I told you what that was. There's nothing between us anymore. We're not even friends."

No way could I match that. Leslie still grabbed me by the libido every time I looked at her. And by the balls every time she looked at me. The best I could offer Emma was lame by comparison. "Until two days ago, I hadn't seen Leslie in years."

She sat back down on the couch. "Yeah, okay, I guess I understand," she said. "Look, if you want to tell me what's going on, fine. If not, that's fine, too. I'm not entirely sure I want to know. But am I right to assume this is about that picture you asked me to check on?"

I nodded.

"Something to do with a stolen ring?"

"Stolen ring? Who said anything about a stolen ring?"

"Nobody, but you said you'd located 'the item.' I thought maybe that was the stolen ring."

"It wasn't stolen," I explained, trying to recall when I'd said anything to Emma about Leslie's ring and coming up blank.

"I'm sorry, what?"

"The ring wasn't stolen. See, Leslie's boyfriend, the guy she lived with before we got married, gave it to her. Then when she left him years ago, she kept it. Now, he suddenly wants his ring back. What made you think the item we were talking about was that ring?"

She tilted her head and looked at me quizzically. "We must be talking about different rings. I meant the one stolen from that Russian Museum, The Armoury Chamber in Moscow—that's where that picture was taken, the one you gave me. Ten years ago there was a break-in at the museum. They stole the Russian Crown Jewels that were on display there. It was quite a haul. Anyway, those were the jewels in your picture. It's all in the article."

"Article?"

"Yeah, I found the article that went with the picture!" She reached into her purse, pulled out a piece of paper, and held it up. "See?" Sure enough, at the top of the page under the headline was the photo that I'd found in Leslie's apartment. "It's a feature story about the jewelry exhibit in Moscow."

"Ten years ago?"

"You're not getting this. There was a heist ten years ago. The jewelry in the exhibit was stolen, but they got most of it back, so they're having another exhibit. That's what made me think the item you were talking about—" She stopped and let out a long sigh. "Why don't I just read you the article?"

"Good idea."

"Okay. My translation might be a little ragged, but here goes."

RUSSIAN CROWN JEWELRY EXHIBIT WILL RETURN TO MUSEUM

The crown jewels once owned by the Czar and Czarina of Russia will be displayed at the Armoury Chamber in an exhibition that opens tomorrow and runs through August 25th. This is the second such exhibition of the jewelry collection. The jewels were first exhibited at the museum ten years ago, but the entire collection was stolen the night before the exhibit closed. Fortunately, the perpetrators were apprehended eight months later and the jewels were recovered.

Included in the storied jewelry collection are several pieces originally designed by Faberge as a gift from Czar Nicholas II to his future wife. "This exquisite jewelry is part of our glorious history," said Dmitri Petroff, head of the museum. "We are proud to offer our patrons the rare opportunity to view the entire collection."

The death of Nicholas and Alexandra's family and the jewelry they left behind began a saga that has yet to reach its conclusion.

It was at the close of World War I that the Czar, his wife, and their five young children were taken from their prison cell to a basement room and brutally murdered by the Bolsheviks. On the day of the massacre, the Czarina was wearing a fortune in jewelry and had hidden more beneath her clothing and her children's clothing. Soldiers discovered the hidden jewelry while burying the royal family.

What followed is the stuff of legend. While many pieces were sold to support the revolution or kept by the government, several pieces were presumed lost or stolen. Others surfaced in the hands of collectors around the world.

In 2005, the jewelry collection was moved to President Putin's dacha at his request.

This is the first exhibition since the jewels' recovery following the heist ten years ago. All of the jewels from the previous exhibition will be on display except for the single piece that is still missing: Czarina Alexandra's engagement ring.

Emma lowered the article. "You see, Alexandra's engagement ring is still missing, so I thought maybe that was the item you were talking about. But Leslie's engagement ring can't be the one stolen from the museum, can it?"

"It's unlikely," I agreed, but then I had a crazy thought. "Wait, when was the article published?"

"July 13th," she said, reading the dateline. "That's, what, like three weeks ago?"

Three weeks ago, a week before Boris started looking for Leslie. Sounded like he got wind of the article and came to the ridiculous conclusion that the ring he gave Leslie was the one stolen from the museum. That's why Boris suddenly wanted his ring back, and why he was willing to kill to get it.

Leslie said, "So, does that help? I mean, now you know what's in the picture?"

"It does, but I think maybe I was following a false lead." No reason to go into the whole thing with Emma. Not yet anyway.

"Like a misdirection?" she asked. "By the bad guys?"

"Something like that," I said. "Things aren't always what they appear to be."

But then again, sometimes they are. What if Boris's conclusion wasn't ridiculous, and Leslie's ring was, in fact, the stolen royal engagement ring? That led to more questions, like how Boris happened to have the ring in the first place, and why he had no idea it was a priceless artifact until a few weeks ago.

And what about that newspaper photo in Leslie's drawer? Where did she get it? Probably not from Boris, because he wouldn't want Leslie to know the ring's true value. Did someone else give it to her, like maybe Leo? Or Tanya, that tough Russian punk who lived with Boris? But why would they do that? Whose side were they on?

And then there was the most important question of all—what the hell do I do now?

"I'm going to pour myself a scotch," I said to Emma. "Can I get you anything?"

"Scotch sounds good," she said. "On the rocks with a splash. And bring the bottle."

"Does that mean you're staying?"

"It means I might want more scotch after I finish the first one," she replied with an inscrutable smile. "Just looking to save you a trip back to the kitchen."

"Kind of you."

"I'm known for my kindness." She sat up, reached back behind her head with both hands, and removed whatever was holding her ponytail in place. Her strawberry blond hair fell loosely around her shoulders. "That feels good. Leaving my hair pulled back too long gives me a headache sometimes." She sat back and leaned her head on the top of the couch. "Of course, the headache could be from getting thrown around."

I stood there watching her. The simple act of undoing her ponytail had me mesmerized. "You look gorgeous with your hair down."

"Do I?"

I went into the kitchen and poured the drinks, Emma's precisely as she'd requested it. I went back to the living room, carrying her drink in one hand and the bottle of scotch in the other. I handed her the drink, placed the bottle on the end table, and went back to the kitchen to get my drink.

She called out, "This is really good scotch, isn't it? Johnny Walker Blue Label? My dad used to drink it on special occasions."

"Yes, it's a very good scotch, and this is a special occasion."

"My first time being held at gunpoint?"

I sat down next to her. "Oh, was that your first time?"

"I take it that wasn't your first time," she said.

"That's right, it wasn't. But for me, every time is like the first time."

She smiled and lowered her eyes. "Are you talking about guns or something else?"

We were both holding our drinks. "Here's to something else." I took a drink and put my glass down. So did Emma. Then we leaned into each other and kissed. This time neither of us pulled away. Emma leaned back a little and pulled at my T-shirt. I broke off the kiss and took my shirt off. She started unbuttoning her blouse. Then we kissed some more. It went on like this until we were naked in each other's arms. I suggested we move to the bedroom. She pulled me closer.

"I like my chances here," she said. So we stayed.

When we'd finished, I started to get up. "We're not done," she said.

Once again, she was right.

CHAPTER 25

My left eye opened first. Everything was blurry, although I could tell it was morning because of all the sunshine splashed around my bedroom. I squeezed my eye shut and then opened it again, and I got a clear look at my digital alarm clock: 8:37. The room was quiet enough to hear Emma snoring softly, but there was nothing to hear. I turned over and put my arm where Emma's beautiful, naked body should have been, but the bed was empty. I called her name in case she was somewhere else in the apartment. More silence. Our lovemaking on the couch had continued until around two in the morning, at which point we agreed that my bedroom was a better place to catch some sleep before morning. Once in bed, Emma had decided to keep the good times rolling. We passed out from exhaustion sometime after four.

I untangled myself from the sheet and walked into the bathroom, where I found Emma's note written in red lipstick on the mirror. "Best first night ever. Except for the gun." I smiled. It was unsigned except for those little x's and o's that people use to show affection. I liked it, all of it, the note, the x's and o's, the red lipstick. I washed my face and walked out of the bathroom without cleaning off the mirror.

I pulled on some boxer shorts and turned on my cell phone, then headed to the kitchen. After grinding the beans and setting up the coffee, I checked my phone. There were two texts. The first was from

Emma, saying she would have stayed but she had an early meeting and she'd call me later. The second was from Nancy, my assistant.

Please call the office—asap.

I rolled my eyes. There was enough going on without the addition of some stupid client crisis. Maybe somebody jumped bail over the weekend, or maybe a client had a particularly bad night in prison. Whoever it was would just have to take a number and have a seat while I cleaned up the Russian mobster mess.

On the other hand, Nancy wasn't born yesterday. She'd been my assistant for four years and at the firm for almost twenty. She was seasoned, smart, and dependable. I'd left her a message over the weekend that I was taking a few days off and wanted to be left alone until Thursday. If she texted again, I'd consider it serious enough to call her.

My cup of coffee had just reached my lips when Nancy's second text flashed. I fortified myself with a sip, put the mug down, and called her.

"Something's wrong," I said. "What is it?"

"Maybe nothing," she answered, "but there's something, um, fishy about this envelope that was on my desk this morning."

"Fishy," I repeated.

"It's a nine by twelve manila envelope, you know the kind with a metal clasp?"

"Uh-huh." So far, I didn't smell fish. "Addressed to you or to me?"

"To you. But it's got 'Personal and Confidential' and 'For Your Eyes Only' written on it on the front and the back. And there's a 'Confidential: Eyes Only' seal pasted over the flap." She hesitated. "There's no return address, but I thought you might know who it's from. Were you expecting something?"

"No, and I don't have any idea who sent it."

Probably nothing, I told myself, or a harmless prank, like an envelope filled with confetti.

Nancy interrupted my thinking. "Should I open it?"

"No, don't bother. Just put it in the top left-hand drawer of my desk and lock my office door."

When I ended the call, I took another sip of my coffee and forgot about the anonymous envelope. After one more sip it started bugging me again. I stood there holding my mug, thinking. My night with Emma had made me forget for a few hours how dangerous and unpredictable my life had become. It would be stupid of me to let my guard down now. Maybe the envelope was nothing, but I couldn't take the chance.

Hurrying to my bedroom, I texted Nancy and told her I'd be dropping by the office in an hour to check my mail. I threw on some khakis and a blue oxford button-down shirt, then grabbed a blazer and shoved a tie in the pocket, just in case. A glance in the mirror told me I could get away without shaving.

On my way out, I spied my almost full coffee mug on the kitchen table. It was lukewarm but still capable of delivering a caffeine fix, so I gulped a mouthful before rushing out.

Walking past my bank reminded me to transfer the money to Leslie. Because the joint account she neglected to close was still listed in both our names, the transfer would happen immediately. The branch manager helped me with the transfer without asking too many embarrassing questions, and after a twenty-minute delay, I caught the next subway downtown.

It was Monday morning, and the city seemed quiet. Maybe some people hadn't made it back from their summer places in the Hamptons, the Jersey Shore, or the Catskills. Or maybe people were just grouchy and didn't want to get out of bed and face the week. Either way, the subway wasn't as mobbed as usual, and I got downtown in fifteen minutes.

I rushed past Nancy's desk without saying good morning, only to find my office door locked. As I'd requested.

"Good morning, Henry," she said to my back.

I turned around. "Yes, good morning." I apologized for my rudeness and took the key dangling from her finger. Then I unlocked my door, closed it behind me, and yanked open my desk drawer.

The envelope was exactly as Nancy had described—addressed to me and clearly meant only for me. I flipped it over, tore off the "eyes only" seal, undid the metal clasp, and ripped open the sealed flap. Inside the envelope were two pages stapled together. The first page was a cover letter. Scanning it I saw no letterhead, no signature, nothing to indicate the source. It was addressed to Neil Davenport, the managing partner.

Dear Mr. Davenport:

I recently came across the attached letter and thought you might find it interesting. You'll note that although it's typed on your law firm's stationery and signed "Henry Gladstone, Attorney at Law," it appears to have been written while Mr. Gladstone was a summer associate at your firm some two years before he graduated from law school.

I can only assume that is not typically allowed by a firm of your size and reputation.

Sincerely,

A Concerned Citizen

I flipped the page, and there was the letter I'd written twelve years ago, the one claiming that I was a lawyer at the firm when I wasn't. I collapsed into my desk chair and carefully reread the cover letter. At the bottom of the page was a cc list with only one name—

mine. This was my copy. By now the original could be sitting on my boss's desk. This was no concerned citizen. It was Boris. First, he sent Leo to muscle me, reminding me I was in physical danger if I didn't comply. And now he was making good on his blackmail threat.

But why did he want to expose me now? That wasn't how blackmail worked. He should be holding it over my head, not kneecapping me with it. Maybe he just enjoyed ruining me. Or maybe it was payback for Leslie's leaving him for me. Still, the timing was odd, and like so much else about the last couple of days, it left me scratching my head.

CHAPTER 26

I checked my watch. Neil Davenport typically arrived at work every morning around ten. I walked around my desk and opened my door. "Nancy, can you please check with Veronica and see if Neil's in?" And then, cloaking it as an afterthought, I added, "Oh, and ask if he also got a manila envelope with all the 'eye's only' stuff on it this morning."

I went back to my desk and considered my options. If Neil had seen the letter, I would have heard from him by now, but he probably wasn't in yet. If the letter was sitting unopened in his inbox, I might be able to intercept it.

It occurred to me that having Nancy ask Veronica about the letter might make her suspicious. I signaled to Nancy.

"Hold on a second, Veronica," she said and put her hand over the phone. "Yes, Henry?"

"If you didn't ask about the envelope yet, skip it."

She looked at me. "Umm …" She took her hand off the phone. "Hey Veronica? Never mind about the envelope. Henry doesn't …" She listened. "Oh, okay, no problem. Thanks. See you later." Nancy hung up. "She checked. It's in his inbox." My face fell. "Henry, how can I fix this?"

"It's okay," I said, "it's not a problem."

I went back into my office, sat down, and took a deep breath to keep the panic at bay.

Maybe I was blowing this out of proportion. After all, I'd been with the firm for almost ten years. And Neil and I had a pretty good relationship. If I told him exactly why I wrote the letter and blamed it on youthful stupidity, maybe he'd smack me around a little, or suggest it would impact my bonus, but would he fire me? Take it up with the other senior managers? Or, worse, say it was a matter for the New York State Bar Association? After all, this wasn't likely to detonate the firm's reputation. Neil would see that, wouldn't he?

I picked up my phone and dialed a woman who'd just left the firm for a job as in-house counsel at a television network. The phone rang three times, then four. I was just about to give up when she answered.

"Angela, hi. It's Henry over at Loveless, Brown. How's the new job?"

"Hey, Henry—nice to hear from you! The job's great, but man, it's a steep learning curve. Hey, listen, I got a meeting in a few minutes. Can't talk now, but I promise I'll call you back."

"Wait! No, I mean, this won't take long. Please? I need your opinion on something."

"Okay, but make it quick."

"Right. So this lawyer friend—you don't know her, she's at another firm—she was a summer associate there a few years ago, and as a favor to someone, she wrote a letter on the firm's stationery. Her letter kind of implied she was an attorney at the firm, even though she was still in law school. A colleague just found out about it, don't ask how, it's crazy. Anyway, my friend's worried that if the managing partners get wind of it, they'll be pissed. You think she's got a problem?

"Wait, now she's working at the same law firm where she wrote the letter as a summer associate?"

"Uh-huh."

"Well, she could be in deep shit. Like if that happened at Loveless, Brown I could see the management committee coming down hard, even if it was a while ago. They don't like that kind of thing. It calls into question the integrity of everyone at the firm. I know of a guy who did something like that and—oh Jesus, I gotta run. Short answer, your friend could end up losing her job, maybe get her law license revoked. I can recommend a solid employment lawyer if she ends up needing it. Good to hear from you, Henry. Hey, let's have lunch. I'll try and talk you into coming to work here—it would be a feather in my cap to lure one of Loveless, Brown's top attorneys."

"Can't wait."

"I'm serious, Henry, you'd love it here, and they'd love you."

"We'll have lunch soon," I promised and hung up.

Angela's expert take on the situation didn't leave much room for interpretation.

I started to panic. I'd thought the whole episode was ancient history, but there I was hustling down the hall to my boss's office to do what I could to keep him from finding out about it. I had no idea how I would be able to remove the evidence with Neil's secretary watching.

Veronica was fiftyish but with her bobbed gray hair and perpetual string of pearls, she looked older. She'd been Neil's assistant and gatekeeper for over twenty years, and the loyalty ran both ways. Everyone at the firm assumed she had Neil's ear in matters great and small. I wasn't sure what my play was with her, but staying calm and casual was a good place to start.

Hi, Veronica," I said, scanning her desk for any sign of the envelope. "Neil in yet?"

"No. He just called and said he wouldn't be in until after lunch. You need to see him?"

"It can wait." I forced a smile and glanced at her inbox. No sign of it there.

She looked at the inbox, then back at me. "This isn't about that manila envelope, is it? Nancy said you were wondering if Neil got one this morning."

"Well, yeah, curious is all."

"Curious." She tilted her head. "Uh-huh." She hesitated for a second, but then went on. "After Nancy called, I thought it might be important, so when Neil checked in a few minutes ago, I mentioned it to him. He said he didn't know where it came from and told me to open it." She hesitated. "Are you okay, Henry? All of a sudden you look kind of pale."

"Really?" I croaked.

She watched me for a few seconds. I told my face to go limp. Not sure my face heard me.

"Anyway," she continued, "I opened it, and there was nothing in it but a blank sheet of paper. Neil said to toss it."

I glanced at the area next to her desk, hoping to see a wastebasket. "And did you?"

Veronica's eyes narrowed. She continued watching me while she reached beneath her desk and lifted her wastebasket. It was full of trash, and right on top sat the manila envelope next to a crumpled sheet of paper. "There they are," she said. "Go ahead, take them."

I did. I had to be sure.

After I pulled the envelope and the paper from the wastebasket she returned it to the floor under her desk. I thanked her, and she replied with the tight smile of an assistant principal who catches you at cheating. No doubt she'd tell Neil about this, but I didn't care.

I turned and beat it back to my desk, uncrumpled the blank piece of paper, then neatly placed it with both envelopes and my copy of the letter in front of me. I reread the incriminating letter before picking it up and tearing it into tiny little pieces. The blank page appeared to be just that, but, playing it safe, I tore that up, too. Even though Victoria told me Neil's envelope was empty, I looked inside to be sure before ripping that apart. Finally, I grabbed my envelope, but before tearing it up I was gripped by paranoia, so I looked inside. I saw what looked like handwriting. How could someone write on the inside of an envelope? I carefully slit open the side with scissors.

```
Come to the warehouse at 357 East 128th Street,
Queens, at 10 p.m., Tuesday night. Bring Leslie
but nobody else. Don't forget the ring. Don't
be late. And most important, don't screw this
up, or your boss gets the letter, and your law
career is over.
—Boris.
```

Now I saw the method in Boris's madness. He proved he had the letter I'd written and was prepared to send it to my boss if both Leslie and I didn't bring the ring tomorrow. I had no intention of personally delivering the ring. I'd given Leslie the money and assumed the rest was up to her. Boris had just made it clear my involvement wasn't over until he said it was.

I cut out the note and folded it several times before shoving it into my wallet.

One thing for sure—the borscht was coming to a boil. If Boris wanted me to bring him the ring, I'd bring him the ring. The problem was, as of that moment, I didn't have it. I texted Leslie. "Boris wants the ring by tomorrow night. Let me know when you have it." I waited for a minute for a response, but there wasn't any. Maybe she was busy wiring the money I'd given her. Nothing to do but go home and wait.

"Nancy," I said as I stopped at her desk on my way to the elevator. "If anyone asks for me, I'm unreachable for the next few days."

"Except for Neil, right?"

I cringed. "Right. Except for Neil."

I took the subway back to my apartment. As soon as I walked in, I smelled the coffee. The two-thirds full mug sat on the counter where I'd left it before dashing out to the office. It was almost eleven o'clock, and my need for coffee was so intense I stuck the mug in the microwave rather than brewing a new pot.

Half an hour later, I was surprised the coffee didn't deliver the energy jolt I expected. I realized (with a yawn followed by a satisfied smile) that last night's activities had probably left me sleep deprived. I fought my eyelids for a few minutes before giving up and lying on the couch. Sleep came, and with it, a dream.

Emma and I were walking through Central Park on a bright spring day. There were blossoms on the trees, kids with balloons, and red and yellow tulips waving in the light breeze. The colors were vivid, like in a 1950's movie musical. She and I held hands, and I thought how lucky I was to be with her. She smiled at me, as if she'd registered my thought, and said, "I'm glad I'm with you, too." Up ahead I noticed a couple walking toward us, but I couldn't quite make them out. They were just about to pass us when I saw that it was Leslie and Boris and they, too, were holding hands. Boris smiled at me. I started to say I was surprised to see them when Leslie screamed and pulled her hand away from Boris, but her hand was gone, like it had been chopped off. Blood was gushing everywhere, and Boris stepped away, so I let go of Emma's hand and rushed over to help. Ripping my shirt off, I wrapped it around her wrist, but the blood kept gushing. I looked back to see if Emma could help, but she was walking away with Boris. I screamed her name. When she turned around her eyes were empty sockets and there was blood streaming down her cheeks. She mouthed, "help me," before disappearing into the bushes with Boris. I started after her, but I couldn't seem to free myself from Leslie's bleeding stump, because the blood had clotted around my hands and held me fast. I begged Leslie to let me go. "Not until you kiss me," she said and leaned in, her face swelling and becoming more distorted the closer she got. When she kissed me, my face felt like it had been hit by a brick.

I awoke, face down on the floor next to the couch.

It wasn't much of a fall, and the rug had softened the impact, but I went to the bathroom mirror to make sure my face still looked like me. Emma's lipstick note on the mirror required me to move around a little to get the full picture. My nose was scraped but not broken. There was a darkening bruise around my left eye that hurt when I touched it. I wasn't bleeding, at least not that I could see. There was a scratch on my left cheek. It seemed the nightmare left me mostly unscathed, at least physically.

From the bathroom I heard my phone beep. It was a text from Emma.

Crazy client, crazy busy. Working late tonight and maybe tomorrow night too.

Catch you when I can. Miss you xoxo 🖤 🖤 🖤

Just as well, I thought, and typed,

Miss you too

Despite my nap, I felt tired for the rest of the day. I spent the afternoon fretting about whether Leslie would get the ring in time and what would happen if she didn't. I checked my phone every few minutes hoping to hear something. At four o'clock, I texted her. Nothing. I even thought about going down to Missy's to find her. Waiting was killing me. I decided to distract myself with an early dinner at a neighborhood Italian joint. Afterwards, I tried watching some television but couldn't concentrate. I poured a glass of whiskey, then knocked back another before finally falling into bed and starting what turned out to be a fitful, unsatisfying night of sleep.

CHAPTER 27

As soon as I woke up, I reached for my phone, hoping there'd be a text from Leslie. Finding none, I dragged myself out of bed, checked myself into the bathroom for a while, then wandered to the kitchen. There was nothing in the fridge that could pass for breakfast, so I considered going across the street to the diner for my usual—one egg on a toasted buttered bialy with a slice of American cheese. Their coffee was always burnt and bitter, but I didn't feel like fussing with the coffee maker. I pulled on the same clothes I'd dropped on the bedroom floor the night before and headed for the diner.

"Hey, Sammy," I said to the doorman as I walked by, "how 'bout a cup a coffee—you take it black, right?"

"That's right, Mr. Gladstone," he replied. "And thanks!"

As soon as I walked outside, someone shouted my name. I turned to see Leslie hustling across First Avenue in a pink sleeveless top, sky-blue workout shorts, and expensive-looking navy-blue high-top sneakers.

"Leslie?" I called back. "What the—"

"Henry, thank goodness I caught you."

"Well, I wasn't going far." I glared at her. "What is it? Something go wrong? I texted you last night, and you never texted back. You see my text? Do you have the ring?"

I waited while she leaned over and put her hands on her knees to catch her breath. When she stood up, she wiped the shine off her forehead with the back of her hand. Sweat stains dotted the front of her top. She looked up at me and said, "I've got it."

She held out her hand, palm down, and wiggled her ring finger. All I saw was a plain silver-colored band until she turned her hand over. There, resting in her palm, was the ring. I figured she'd turned it around on her finger so the thing wouldn't catch anyone's attention.

I cradled her hand in mine and held it steady and bent down for a better look. The stones caught a blast of morning sunlight, and the red ones glowed like embers in a dying fire.

"It's a miracle you got it back," I said. "That Saudi sheik who bought it could have just as easily told you to take a hike."

She shrugged. "He saw an opportunity to double his money. He's probably bragging about it to all his friends."

It was the first time I'd seen the ring since Emma filled me in on its history. If she was right, and I had no reason to doubt her, the ring on Leslie's finger was worn by the czarina a hundred years ago and possibly removed from her bullet-ridden body minutes after she, her husband, and several children looked into the soulless eyes of their executioners and wondered if they were really going to die.

From Stalin, to Putin, to the Russian Museum, to the jewel thieves who pulled off the heist, the ring had found its way to a Russian gangster on Long Island. The moment Boris handed Leslie what she maintained was her engagement ring, it launched a whole new drama. Leslie could turn a clay ashtray into a crisis that had nothing to do with the ashtray and everything to do with Leslie.

That ring had seen a lot of mayhem.

She closed her fingers, leaving me cradling her fist. "Now what?" she asked, smirking. "Do we leave it outside Boris's front door, ring the doorbell, and run? Or maybe get a safe deposit box and mail him the key?" She pulled her hand away, and I smiled at her playfulness now that she'd gotten the ring back.

"Neither, I'm afraid. Boris sent me instructions. Told me to meet him at a warehouse in Queens tonight at ten."

I left out the part about Boris wanting both of us to come.

It didn't take two of us to deliver the ring. Knowing Boris, he wanted us both there for another reason—to teach us a lesson we'd never forget. The lesson might be a tongue-lashing, but I didn't imagine we'd get that lucky. More likely was a beating, the kind that broke bones, loosened teeth, and knocked some sense into us. Or it could be the ultimate lesson, the one delivered by a bullet to the back of the brain. In that case the last person I'd see might be Boris, or Leo. Or maybe a terrified Leslie. It also occurred to me that if things went south, I might be able to make a run for it somehow, and having to look after Leslie's well-being might slow me down.

That's why I would go alone.

Leslie crossed her arms. "I don't like it. He's angry—he might take that out on you."

"You want to go instead? After all, you got us into this."

"Don't be an asshole. It's just … well, I'm worried about you."

I wanted to believe her, but I knew better. I put out my hand. She slid the ring off her finger and placed it on my palm. Then she took a step toward me and, pulling me close, kissed me on the lips, softly. I let her, thinking I could handle it without feeling anything. I ended the kiss before she did. To be safe.

When she turned to go. I grabbed her elbow to stop her. "I'll let you know when it's done. If you don't hear from me by eleven o'clock, call the cops." I pulled out my phone and texted her the address.

Leslie nodded. "Just be careful," she said.

I stood there for a few seconds, watching her walk away until she disappeared around the corner. Then I watched the corner for a few more seconds and wondered if leaving Leslie out of the warehouse delivery was noble or just stupid. Probably both.

I put the ring into the left pocket of my shorts and pushed my index finger through the loop before heading back into my building. In the elevator I reviewed all the possible hiding places, and after rejecting the all-time favorite—sock drawer—and several other possibilities, I decided to put it in a box of frozen peas. Pleased with my choice, I took the elevator back down and crossed the street to the diner.

When I walked in, Nick, the owner, gave me the big hello and took my order at the register. I scanned the place to make sure Leo wasn't lurking. Usually, I sat on a stool and watched them prepare my order in case I had to offer encouragement ("more salt") or make a mid-course correction ("You mind giving that bialy another blast in the toaster?"). However, at that moment, self-preservation seemed more important than the perfect breakfast. I turned my back to the grill so I could keep an eye on the entrance.

"You want cheese on that, right, Mr. Henry?" Nick asked.

"Yeah, and extra butter on the bialy. And two large coffees, one black, one regular."

Nick rang me up.

I crossed the street, handed Sammy his coffee, and hit the elevator call button. When I got to my apartment, I retrieved the ring from the frozen peas, put it on the table in front of me, and started in on my egg sandwich. As I ate, I thought about whether there was something odd in Leslie's showing up unannounced, or if I was just being paranoid. Leslie lied about everything. Her kiss seemed genuine, like she was worried about me, but maybe that was a feint to keep me from seeing what was really going on—the way a magician distracts the audience to pull off his magic trick. What could she be hiding? I couldn't put my finger on it, but something was wrong.

After draining my coffee, I put the paper cup in the bag with the sandwich wrapper and tossed it in the trash. Breakfast was over. Time to get to work.

First, I wrapped the ring in newspaper and put it in a small plastic bag, the kind you put leftovers in. Then I wrapped that in packing tape for no good reason other than it made me feel better. I briefly thought about sewing the package into the lining of a light jacket to be extra safe, but it was too hot to wear a jacket, and I couldn't sew. Instead, I'd put on my tightest pair of jeans and put the package in my front pocket so I could feel it pressing against my leg.

Although Leslie got away with it, I couldn't see carrying a priceless historical artifact on the subway. I'd been pickpocketed on the F Train years ago. Other than a slight jostle as a guy rushed past me and out the subway car door, I'd felt nothing. As I'd explained to a bored subway cop, being pickpocketed was like failing to notice being bitten on the neck by a rabid bat. Both are upsetting, and both leave you with a grudging respect for the predator.

With the subway nixed, I decided to ask Aiden for a ride. I started dialing when I realized we hadn't spoken since he found out that Emma and I were together. Would he be angry? But, I argued to myself, why should Aiden hold that against me? He and Emma had been divorced for years. And wasn't he involved with Debbie, the lawyer I'd met at his apartment?

Then I asked myself how I would feel if I found out Aiden was sleeping with Leslie? I'd be pissed, I admitted. But wouldn't I put that aside if he needed my help?

Without answering that question, I dialed his number.

"Henry," he said when he picked up.

"Hey Aiden." He didn't reply so I forged ahead. "How's it going?"

"About the way you'd expect when you find out your best friend is sleeping with your ex-wife," he said, and hung up.

I redialed only to hear Aiden answer the phone with a peevish, "What now? You want the number of my current girlfriend?"

"Aiden, I …"

"Tell you what, I'll throw in the names and number of all my old flames. How's that sound?"

It sounded unhinged. "I'm sorry, Aiden, I guess I didn't think it through. Maybe I fucked up." Aiden stayed quiet so I kept talking. "I sense this isn't the best time to ask for a favor. I shouldn't have called."

No response.

"You still there?"

"Yeah," he said softly. "I'm here."

Neither of us spoke. I listened to Aiden's breathing, and I suppose he listened to mine.

Finally Aiden said, "Man, I don't even know why I'm so upset about this. It's just, I guess I feel like I have to be. It's just … there's something tawdry about this. I'm definitely over Emma, but when she told me she'd slept with you something inside me, I don't know, I just …" He trailed off.

I thought of telling him how Emma lied when she told him we'd slept together. That wouldn't happen until later that night, not until after Leo dropped by. Maybe Emma was trying to make Aiden jealous, or maybe she wanted to see his reaction. I hadn't thought about it before, but why the hell *did* she tell Aiden that we'd slept together when we hadn't?

The awkward silence continued. Then Aiden changed the subject. "What's the favor? Something to do with Gabriella? We haven't spoken since I asked her to help you find Leslie. Anything happen, or did you tell her to fuck off again?"

I smiled. Maybe the storm had blown over, at least for the moment. "You were right about Gabriella. She's been a great help. Thank you."

"She find Leslie?"

"She did that, and more." I quickly brought Aiden up to date, mentioning Emma only in connection with her helping me identify the Russian newspaper photo and leaving out the romance. When I was done, I said, "So, I need a ride to the warehouse tomorrow night. It's not far—somewhere in Queens—357 East 128th Street. But I'm not asking you to come in with me or anything."

"Three-fifty-seven East 128th. Why does that sound familiar? Wait, I know that neighborhood. I once had to go there for a client, but I can't remember why." He got quiet again for a bit. "I don't know, Henry. I still feel bad about the Emma thing. Maybe I need time to process."

"Okay," I said, surprised by his use of the word "process." Aiden wasn't that self-aware, or at least I'd never known him to be. Maybe we don't really know our friends until we do something to hurt them. If the hurt was deep enough, our friendship might never be the same.

This was not the time to try and work it out. Aiden had to process, and I had to deal with Boris.

"Don't worry about it," I said, "I'll get to Queens one way or another."

After we hung up, I sat there staring at the ring package, hoping for inspiration. I could ask one of my other friends, but then I'd have to explain why they were driving me to a warehouse in Queens. There was the car rental place around the corner or the car service I used for the airport, but that meant credit cards and witnesses. I wanted to keep this on the down low. Maybe I'd keep it simple and just take a cab.

After showering, I dressed, put the ring package in my pocket, and, needing something sweet, I grabbed an energy bar. The sell-by date had come and gone, but I unwrapped it anyway. One bite later I picked up the trash can and spit out the mouthful of partly chewed energy bar. That's when I noticed the business card with the picture of a taxicab, the one I got from the cabbie the other night. I extracted the card from the garbage with two fingers and shook off the crud. The cabbie had heard Todd telling the whole sordid story. I wouldn't have to explain anything to him.

I dialed the number on the card.

"Hello?"

"Carlos?"

"Yeah, who's this?"

"It's Hank. From a couple nights ago? I need a ride."

CHAPTER 28

Carlos didn't immediately register who I was. "Long car ride Sunday night? Three of us in the back? Big tip at the end?"

After hesitating a second, he remembered. "Oh, yeah, Hank! Sure, now I remember. Sorry, man, I just didn't think I'd hear from you this fast."

I explained why I was calling, and we quickly negotiated a price. "I can't take you in my cab," he said. "This is strictly off-book. But my brother-in-law's limo is parked in my driveway on account he's on vacation. With his girlfriend."

"Description?"

"Funny you should ask. She's Dominican, which, you know, is mostly okay by me, and she's a looker …"

"No, I meant a description of the limo."

"Oh, right. It's a limo—black, tinted windows, full bar. A limo limo."

"Sounds perfect."

"I'll pick you up at your place at 9 o'clock. That'll give us plenty of time. Shouldn't take us more than twenty-five minutes to get there, depending on the bridge traffic. But Hank?"

"Yes, Carlos?"

"Could be an accident or something. You never know. You wanna be on time, we leave at nine. Got it?"

I said I got it and ended the call.

With my ride arranged, I was feeling pretty good about things. Carlos would pick me up in less than two hours and take me to the warehouse. I'd return the ring to Boris. He'd thank me, I'd get back in the car, and Carlos would drive me home. On the way, I'd call Leslie and tell her everything was fake, she could sleep in her own bed and not worry about a thing from now on. I'd hang up and never see or talk to her again. That might sting a little, but that was where Emma would come in.

A smile came to my lips despite my knowing that my little daydream was just that … a dream. My smile faded to black.

Boris might let bygones be bygones, but that wasn't something I could count on. I'd be walking into this meeting armed with only one thing—the ring. And in less than two hours, I wouldn't even have that. Either my troubles would be over and I'd walk out of there, or they wouldn't. I knew when and where this whole thing would end. I just didn't know how.

***

It was almost 9 o'clock when I left my apartment to wait for Carlos.

The sun had set, but the city shook off darkness like a wool overcoat on a warm day. Streetlights, headlights, restaurants brightly lit from the inside, electronic billboards, stoplights, neon signs buzzing blue and gold, subway stations pushing light up the stairs, a thousand apartments glowing with television sets flickering like candles all swirled into a blazing bonfire the size of Manhattan.

The day's heat lingered, having been jackhammered into the asphalt and cement since dawn. Air conditioners, both the little ones balanced on apartment windowsills and the compressors the size of delivery trucks atop office buildings, strained against the heat with a roar that deepened at night.

I began sweating as soon as I hit the street.

At exactly nine o'clock, a black stretch limo negotiated the corner at York and Eighty-First and headed toward me. When it pulled up to the curb, I bent down to look inside but saw only my reflection in the tinted glass.

Carlos lowered the window. "Evening, Hank."

"Hey Carlos." I looked him over. He'd skipped the standard white shirt, black tie uniform worn by most limo drivers in favor of a T-shirt that aspired to white but looked gray, and red checkered Bermuda shorts. "You didn't tell me it was a stretch limo," I said, looking down the length of the behemoth.

Carlos smiled. "She's a beaut, isn't she? Twenty-nine feet seven inches from headlights to tailpipe."

I took another look because I thought Carlos wanted me to. The car was clean and polished to a spit shine. "Yep, she's a beaut," I parroted and opened the passenger door. When I started to climb into the bucket seat next to him, he waved me off.

"Back seat, Hank. There's a TV back there. You can watch the Mets get slaughtered if you want. And there's booze. Might as well get comfortable."

I did as he said, sliding into one of the many seats in the back. The cavernous interior, black with red and gold trim, was gaudy enough for high school seniors on prom night. The bar was fully stocked, but the booze looked fake sitting in the back of a car. As much as I could have used a shot of bourbon, I didn't reach for anything. Besides, the bottles weren't labeled. For all I knew, what looked like whiskey was apple juice.

"Like it?" Carlos asked.

"Love it," I said. Carlos pulled away from the curb and made a right at the light. I was on my way.

We headed south on Second Avenue, then swung left and headed over the 59th Street Bridge to Queens.

I always thought of Queens as the borough without looks or personality. Brooklyn had The Heights, The Bronx had Yankee Stadium, Staten Island had the Ferry, and Manhattan had, well, Manhattan. But, unfairly, I still thought of Queens solely as the eighteen miles between my apartment and Kennedy Airport. I'd gazed out of taxicab windows at the endless small houses packed tight as teeth along the freeway, doors and windows open in the summer to catch a breeze, then shut tight against the freezing winter. Other than that I seldom gave Queens a second thought.

We crossed the bridge and immediately headed into a part of Queens that was unfamiliar to me. The streets were narrow, and the streetlamps didn't cast much light. Nothing I could see looked like a warehouse. I knocked on the glass that separated me from Carlos. He lowered the partition. "What's up, Hank?"

"Where the hell are we?"

His eyes found mine in his rearview mirror. "Part of Queens called Long Island City. Stupid name—to me, this ain't anywhere near what I think of as Long Island. It's Queens, for chrissakes."

The partition started back up but immediately stopped.

"Hey, Hank, I didn't ask before, but I'm asking now. You expecting some kind of trouble? I can make this car go fast, but tearing around corners at high speed? That's too much even for a professional driver like me."

"Don't worry. There won't be any trouble," I said, crossing my fingers behind my back like a lying first-grader. "I'm just meeting some people here and dropping off a package. Shouldn't take more than fifteen minutes." When I arranged the ride with Carlos, he'd agreed to wait for me. I never mentioned I was meeting with a mobster and his psycho assistant. No reason to scare him. I was scared enough for both of us. "You'll wait for me, right?"

"You want I should wait, I wait. Not like I gotta have the car back by a certain time. Like I said, my brother-in-law owns the car, and he's outta town."

"Just double-checking. Thanks."

"And Hank? If it's cool with you, I'm gonna leave the partition down so we can, you know, communicate easy."

Ten minutes later Carlos came to a stop sign. "We're here," he said, pointing to a squat building across the intersection on the right.

The abandoned warehouse took up the entire block. The building was made of brick, suggesting it had been there for at least seventy-five years. There was a row of large windows near the roof of the building, all dark. A parking lot and loading dock were locked behind a metal fence topped with barbed wire. No cars in the parking lot. No lights.

"Looks like nobody's home," Carlos said.

I checked my watch. "We got a few minutes. Let's circle the block, get the lay of the land."

Carlos went straight through the intersection and drove slowly before reaching the end of the block and turning right. The row of windows continued on the second side of the warehouse. No other distinguishing features. Carlos turned right again. Halfway down the third side was a small parking lot with maybe six spaces—must have been for the warehouse bigshots—in front of a door with a small light over it. It looked like one of those motion-activated lights, and for the moment, it was off.

Just ahead of us on the other side of the street was a fire hydrant, and next to that, an empty stretch of curb. "Park by the fire hydrant," I said. "We can wait there, see if anyone pulls into this lot."

Carlos slowed the car and looked at me in the rearview mirror. "You wanna know what I'm thinking?" he asked, and I nodded. "As a professional driver and all, I'm thinking if they own the place, they might unlock the fence and park at that loading dock in front. I would. It's nighttime, and this ain't the safest neighborhood."

"Good point," I said. "Head for the corner. We can see both the parking lot and the loading dock from there."

When we got to the corner, there was nowhere to pull over. "I'll get out here," I said. "You find somewhere to park. I'll call you when I'm done."

When I got out, I crossed the street and stood under a busted streetlamp where it was dark. My glowing watch dial said five minutes to ten. I leaned against the streetlamp and waited.

A car passed, then another, but neither of them stopped at the warehouse. After ten minutes of standing in one place, I needed something to happen. My feet had swollen in my white leather Nikes. My mouth was as dry as a pound of pink cotton candy. I cursed myself for not taking a bottle of water from the refrigerator in the car, but then I remembered there was nothing in there but tonic water anyway.

"C'mon, Boris," I said aloud. "Let's get this over with."

CHAPTER 29

I'd been waiting on the corner for twenty minutes when a black sedan turned into the parking lot across the street. The driver killed the engine but not the headlights. The motion-activated light above the door popped on, further brightening the parking lot. I identified the car as a late model Chevy sedan like the one I'd been kidnapped in. The driver opened his door and got out. His face was in shadow, but from his silhouette, there was no mistaking Leo. He opened the rear door, and Boris got out. Then I heard a car door slam, and a third person walked around the back of the car to join the others. Must be Tanya, I reasoned, but the third person turned out to be a man, about Boris's height but much heavier. Maybe Boris wanted some extra muscle to help Leo keep the peace. Maybe he was a hit man that Boris kept on hand for meetings like this. Or maybe he was nobody, just some mug along for the ride on a hot summer night to keep Boris company. Yeah, and maybe I was Judy Garland.

Leo pulled out a keyring, unlocked the door, and held it for the others before following them inside. The row of windows at the top of the building lit up. A minute later, Leo came back outside. He looked up and down the street before lighting a cigarette. The match flared, briefly illuminating his face, the mix of light and shadow making him look even more maniacal than usual.

I crossed 128th Street and walked the half block to where Leo was standing in the parking lot. As I approached, his head jerked toward me. He took one step back, dropped his right hand into his

211

jacket pocket, and squinted into the smoke. Then he dropped the cigarette and stubbed it out with the toe of his shoe before pulling out his gun and lazily pointing it in my general direction.

"Leo—sorry if I startled you." I nodded toward the gun. "Is that absolutely necessary?"

He ignored the question, and with the gun still in his hand, he frisked me from top to bottom, lowering himself to a crouch in the process. When he stood up, he took a step back and pointed the gun at me again. Guns scare me, especially when the barrel is inches away from my midsection, but I was determined not to panic in front of Leo. He wasn't my first psychopath. I'd defended clients that were scarier than fuck, but none who'd held a gun on me. I found that chatting amiably and confidently threw them off balance, enough that they listened to what I had to say instead of resorting to anger or, worse, violence. It was a good theory, one that had served me well, and it was at least worth a try with Leo.

"Okay, Leo," I said. "You just patted me down hard enough to tell the freckles from the moles. I'm not armed with so much as a nail clipper. So you can put the gun away?"

"You want me to put the gun away?" He smiled, then pulled his jacket back so I could see his long knife shoved into a sheath next to his belt buckle. "Makes no difference to me, but you gotta decide between getting shot and getting cut. In the unlikely event you don't do like you're told." He raised his eyebrows as if daring me to choose. I said nothing. He laughed and let the jacket fall into place. "Right. Now ... Where is she?"

"Where is she who?"

"Stop being a dick and answer the question."

I smiled. "Leslie? Honestly, I have no idea where she is right now."

"Boris ain't gonna like this. He wanted the both of you here." Leo stood there for a few seconds, not moving, as if he didn't know what to do now that it was just me.

"Don't worry Leo, it's not your fault Leslie's not here. It's mine. I'll square it for you with your boss."

That seemed to confuse Leo even more. He scratched his head with the butt of his gun. "Yeah? Well, he ain't gonna like this, and when he don't like something, he—"

I interrupted. "Spare me the details."

For too long we both stood there, not moving. We must have looked like a poster from an old gangster movie starring a couple of unknowns. Finally, I said, "Leo, you've got the gun, so unless I'm mistaken, what happens next is up to you."

He snorted. Then, keeping his eyes on me, he opened the door to the warehouse and waved me in. I stepped inside but stopped. The night was plenty warm, but inside the warehouse, it was hot enough and damp enough to steam broccoli. On top of that, the smell was like someone had beaten a bunch of cats to death with old bricks. The odor was more dead cat than brick, enough to start me retching.

Leo poked me in the back with his gun. I stumbled forward. When I recovered my balance, I scanned the place looking for Boris. All I saw were a couple dozen piles of bricks sitting on a cement floor. Otherwise the warehouse appeared empty.

Then someone said, "Henry! Welcome!" When I turned around, there was Boris in the corner of the room, sitting in a worn leather club chair. To his right, a standing fan quietly blasted right at him, but even that wasn't enough to tousle his grease-slicked hair. His legs were crossed and his bony shins on full display in khaki shorts and sandals, and he seemed cool despite the tropical rain forest climate.

Sitting next to him, not so comfortably dressed, in dark slacks and a light blue golf shirt soaked in sweat, was the heavy guy. His big ears, droopy eyes, and pudgy face made him look like an old bulldog gone to seed. And like a bulldog, he was pigeon-toed. This guy looked way too soft to be muscle.

The two of them were ten feet from where I was standing. I liked it that way.

"Hello Boris." We locked eyes for a second. "Hey, does anybody else think it's hot in here, or is it just me?"

Boris ignored the wisecrack. "I take it you've come alone."

"Not quite," I said, still eyeing the briefcase. "Leo here was kind enough to escort me in."

Boris smiled. "Ah, yes, I'd forgotten your quick wit." The smile disappeared. "Where is Leslie? Is she meeting us here? I assumed you'd arrive together."

"Leslie's not coming. Is that a problem?"

Boris interlaced his fingers behind his head. "Problem? No, not really. It's just that I was hoping to have you both here. It would have made things easier." He paused, uncrossed his legs, and recrossed them the other way. "That's all."

I didn't like the sound of that.

"What could be easier than handing you the ring?" I asked.

"You're right. Nothing could be easier," Boris said with a cold smile. "But I was hoping to thank you both in person, have a little celebration. I've got a magnum of Piper-Heidsieck on ice in the car. I'd hate to waste it on Leo. What do you say, a final toast before parting?"

"Thank you, but, like Leslie, I'll have to take a raincheck." So far, the bulldog hadn't said anything, not so much as a yip or a bark. It bothered me. "So who's your new friend?"

"My new friend?" Boris followed my gaze. "Of course, you mean Ivan! Where are my manners? Henry, I'd like you to meet Ivan Groskovich."

The man smiled at the mention of his name. "Very nice for to meet with you."

"Charmed," I replied.

"Ivan is a friend of mine, and he's come all the way from Moscow for this meeting. We're lucky to have him here."

"Yeah? Why's that?"

"Because Ivan is one of the most gifted jewelers in the world, isn't that right Ivan?

"Yes, is right. I am … gifted?" Ivan looked at Boris, who clarified in Russian. Ivan smiled. "Yes, gifted. Thank you."

"He's here to make sure that the ring is, what do you call it here in America? Oh yes—the real McCoy."

"You don't trust yourself to recognize your own ring?"

"I'm not taking any chances. The ring is worth a fortune, something I didn't know when I won it in a card game. I knew it was stolen, but I thought the guy had just robbed a Moscow jewelry store. I recently found out I was mistaken."

So Boris knew it was stolen from the museum.

"Do you know what this ring is, who it belonged to?" he asked. "There are collectors who would pay a fortune to have this ring in a display case behind a false wall in their mansion."

Collectors. Of course there would be wealthy art collectors and history fanatics who couldn't care less that they were buying a stolen artifact; people who would be easy to find if you had the kind of connections Boris had.

"Fascinating," I said, feigning lack of interest. "Now can we please get on with this before I burst into flames from the heat?"

Boris laughed. "You Americans, you always want to get right to the business." He uncrossed his legs and leaned forward. "I'm assuming you have the ring with you?"

I nodded.

"Splendid." He turned and said something in Russian to Ivan, who responded by standing up. Boris turned back to me. "Please give the ring to Ivan."

I reached into my pocket but paused. "When I hand over the ring, can you do me a favor and tell Leo to stow the piece?"

Boris seemed to consider it for a moment before saying, "Let's wait until Ivan examines the ring. Then we'll see." Ivan walked toward me and extended his hand for the ring. I resisted the urge to shake and say, "Good dog. Now roll over." Instead I extracted the package containing the ring from my pocket and placed it in his hand. He turned it over a few times then began muttering to himself.

"It's inside the package," I explained.

Boris translated and his jeweler turned to me and said something in Russian.

I took a guess and replied, "You're welcome."

Ivan returned to his seat next to Boris.

There was tape around the package, and Ivan had trouble getting it off. Boris watched him struggle for half a minute before looking up. "Leo, if you've got a knife please lend it to Ivan."

Leo smiled, and in one seamless motion pulled back his jacket, drew the knife, and threw it at Ivan's head. The knife spun a few times, then flew over Ivan's shoulder and stuck in the wall next to his ear. Ivan let out a yelp.

Boris clapped his hands. "Very good Leo! You've been practicing." He reached over to retrieve the knife, took the package from Ivan, then roughly slashed it open. He handed the ring to Ivan, who held it up to one of the ceiling lights, commenting in Russian to Boris as he examined it. Boris shot me a glance and said something else to Ivan, who proceeded to open his briefcase and take out a jeweler's loop and a laptop. First, he spent a few minutes with his laptop. Then he placed the loop in his eye to get a close look at the ring, then looked back at the laptop. After going back and forth several times, he put the laptop on the floor and opened his briefcase again. It must have held a lamp because Ivan's face lit up. Boris, watching Ivan work, leaned over to get a better look.

I couldn't see what was going on and was getting antsy. My legs were getting tired, so I squatted, but Leo told me to stand up, so I did, slowly enough to feel some stretch in my legs.

Ivan closed the briefcase, turned to Boris, and began to speak. Even though it was in Russian, I got the impression he was explaining something complex, because he went on for some time. Again Boris shot me a glance. I didn't know what to make of it, so I remained stone-faced. When Ivan finished his explanation, or whatever it was, Boris put his hand out, and Ivan handed him the ring. Boris looked at it, and as he did, his eyes narrowed. He stood up, shoved the ring into his pocket, and directed a command in Russian to Leo. I didn't have to wait long for the translation.

"On your knees," Leo said as he poked me in the back with the gun.

"What? You just told me to stand up. Now you want me …"

"You heard him," Boris said. "Get down on your knees."

I got down on my knees, then looked up. "What the fuck, Boris?"

"Before I answer that, let me ask you a question. What the fuck, Henry?"

I didn't know what to make of that. And I didn't know why I was on my knees, or why Leo was pointing the gun directly at my head. But putting two and two together, I sensed something was amiss. Seriously amiss.

I glanced to my right at the gun barrel, then back at Boris. My bladder was weakening faster than I was, and I had to concentrate to keep from wetting my pants. There'd be plenty of time for that later, especially if I was shot dead.

"Okay Boris, let me guess. There's something wrong with the ring."

"What, with this ring?" He pulled it out of his pocket and looked at it again. "No, it's a perfectly good ring. Nothing wrong with it. Except—it's not my ring. I'll say this for it, though." He held the ring up and stared at it. "It looks a lot like my ring. In fact, if it weren't for Ivan, I'd probably have walked out of here feeling like a million bucks because I'd just gotten my stolen property back." He stopped talking but kept his eyes locked on mine. His chin dropped slightly, and his eyebrows moved toward each other. He glared at me for the longest time. "Did you really think I was that stupid? My ring is worth a fortune. Ivan tells me this one's full of second-rate stones and isn't even a very good copy. He estimates this ring's probably worth maybe $5,000, if that."

Boris stopped talking again and glared some more. "I'm very, very disappointed, Henry. I thought better of you. I did." He grunted and looked away, then back at me, crossing his arms as he did so. "What did you expect would happen when I found out it was a fake? You must have known I'd come looking for you again. But," he said with a wave of his hand, "you've saved me the trouble of tracking you down. Because here you are."

There I was. A few days earlier, Leslie was in my office begging me for help. When she said my life was in danger, I'd laughed. "You'll believe me," she'd said, "when you're staring down the barrel of a gun wondering if you'll hear the shot that kills you." I wasn't staring down the barrel of the gun. Leo had it aimed at my temple. But as predictions go, hers turned out to be pretty good.

CHAPTER 30

Kneeling on the cement floor of the warehouse with a gun pressed to my head, I couldn't put my finger on what went wrong. All I'd done was give Leslie money to buy back the ring. Sure, the Saudi prince could have scammed her, taken her money in exchange for a phony ring, except why would a billionaire go criminal for what must have been chump change to him? It made no sense.

But what if Leslie never actually got the ring back from the Saudi? What if she'd had a fake made and handed it to me with a grateful smile and a kiss on the lips, all the while knowing Boris would likely kill me when he found out? What if she disappeared, having taken me for the quarter million dollars I'd given her? That and the cash she originally scored from selling the ring would give her more than enough for plastic surgery and a one-way ticket out of the country.

Sonofabitch!

"Wait. Boris. I swear to you I thought the ring was real. Leslie handed it to me this afternoon." I was talking so fast I was just barely keeping up with myself. "See, a few years ago she sold it to a Saudi prince, but she managed to buy it back from him. At least that's what she told me."

Boris shrugged.

"Look, Boris," I shouted, "Leslie not only sent me here with a fake ring, she stole my money. Money I gave her to buy it back. And she set me up in the process. That lying bitch stuck it to both of us!"

The words stung as they left my lips. I knew Leslie was a liar, capable of stealing a man's heart and his money in the time it took him to look her up and down. But I never thought of her as a stone-cold killer.

"I can't believe she did that," I said, trying not to panic and wondering how to get out of this alive and in one piece.

Leo spoke Russian to Boris, who replied by putting his palm up, telling Leo to wait.

"Okay, Henry. Let's say you're telling the truth, and I'm not saying I believe you are, but for the sake of discussion."

"I am telling you the truth."

"Then we're back to square one. I need to find Leslie. And since you admit seeing her a few hours ago when she gave you the ring, you must have some idea where she is."

Again I shook my head. "She didn't say where she was going. By now she could be anywhere." I glanced at the gun in Leo's hand. "Please believe me. I want to find Leslie as much as you. I want my fucking money back. You want your fucking ring back. So why not let me go, and we can look for her together."

Boris laughed. "I'm not letting you go, Henry. And you know why?" He leaned forward and his eyes went cold. "Because I think you and Leslie are in this together—I have since the day I heard she went to your office. Even if she'd already made a plan and gotten the fake, she still needed your money to make it all work. My bet is she offered to cut you in, and you went for it. Big mistake. Maybe she double-crossed you like you say, maybe she didn't. Either way, you got some balls, handing me a counterfeit, thinking you could skip town before I figured out the ring was fake."

"I had nothing to do with—"

Boris cut me off. "I don't believe you," he said. "And I'm getting tired of the bullshit." He slowly dragged his hand down his face.

"Let me make this simple for you, Henry." He paused, and then, with the trace of a smile on his lips, he said, "Either you tell me where Leslie is, or I'll have Leo torture the information out of you." He let that sentence sink in for a few seconds. "Then he'll kill you."

Leo said something in Russian. Boris nodded. Then Leo grabbed my arm above the elbow and muscled me over to where Boris was sitting. He grabbed one of the folding chairs, backed us up about ten feet from Boris, planted the chair, and forced me into the seat. Then he slapped me across the face with the back of his hand so hard I landed face down on the floor. Leo picked up the chair, then kicked me in the side hard enough to crack a rib. "Get up," he said.

I rolled over and started to get up. Moving was painful and taking a full breath impossible. Even so, I wanted to rush Leo, shove his gun down his throat, and pull the trigger. I'd aim at Boris through Leo's skinny neck for good measure. Barring a miracle, the attempt would get me killed for sure. I settled for rubbing my cheek while working my jaw back and forth.

Leo contorted his lips into his killer-clown grin, picked me up by my shirt, and threw me into the chair. "That's just me warming up," he sneered.

Bile rose from my stomach. If I refused to give up Leslie's location, I'd be beaten to death in the next half hour. Or shot. Or knifed. My head fell forward, and my shoulders slumped. For once, I'd run out of things to say.

When I looked up, I noticed Ivan standing and holding his briefcase in front of his mid-section. He looked like he was about to throw up. Boris addressed him in Russian, and Ivan nodded. Then Boris snapped his fingers at Leo, who reached into his jacket pocket, pulled out a set of keys, and tossed them to Ivan, who missed and dropped his briefcase trying to make the catch.

"You'll excuse Ivan," Boris said as he watched Ivan leave the warehouse. "He's not used to this kind of thing, so he'll wait in the car until we're done."

"I'm not used to it either," I said. "Maybe I should wait in the car, too." That got me another backhanded slap, this time on my other cheek. I saw it coming so I braced myself and avoided falling over. When I looked up, there were white spots floating in front of my face. I licked my lips and tasted blood.

"Very amusing, Henry, but I'm not in the mood. It's time for you to tell us where Leslie is. Because," he said, his voice rising, his face turning red, "I want that ring!"

Boris waited a few seconds for me to answer. Then he nodded to Leo, who belted me again, hard enough to start my ears ringing.

"Last chance, Henry. Where's Leslie?"

"You're gonna kill me whether I talk or not."

"Probably."

"That's not much of a negotiation. Let's say I tell you where she's staying. What's in it for me?"

"Well, instead of killing you, I might only rough you up some before letting you go. On the other hand, I might decide to kill you anyway. In that case, a bullet to the back of the head is the best you can hope for. Oh, and a decent burial out on Long Island, if you consider a construction site a suitable final resting place."

That was as close as Boris would come to offering me a lifeline. Even though it was a crummy, frayed, grease-slicked piece of rope, I had to make a grab at it. Giving up the address might save me, but I'd be helping Boris find Leslie. If he killed her, could I live with myself knowing I'd sacrificed Leslie to save my own neck?

I looked Boris in the eye. "Go fuck yourself."

Leo slapped me again, and I saw stars. "Next time, I'll use my fist," he said. "And when my fist gets sore, I'll belt you with my gun."

"Thanks for outlining the program for me," I mumbled.

Everything was blurry, the room was tilting back and forth, and I thought I would pass out at any second. It was not much of a plan, but sleeping through the rest of my beating sounded nice.

Leo made a fist and prepared to clock me, but Boris stopped him. "Leo, that's enough for now. I need to hear what he has to say before he passes out."

Leo dropped his fist and snarled at me before stepping back. He kept his gun aimed at my head and said something in Russian. They started a conversation I assumed had to do with my future, or lack thereof.

I glanced at my watch. Ten minutes to eleven. I'd told Leslie to call the cops if she didn't hear from me by eleven. Of course, I couldn't count on that anymore because she'd double-crossed me. But who knows, maybe there was a spark of good in that black heart of hers. All I could do was try to survive for another twenty minutes and hope for a miracle.

When they finished their conversation, Boris smiled at me. He seemed pleased, like he'd solved a problem. He continued grinning at me for a few more seconds, then leaned forward. "I understand you have a very pretty friend who lives in your building. Leo called her sugar, but her name's Emma, right?" He dropped the grin in favor of a sneer. "I bet she's easier to find than Leslie. Perhaps we should invite Emma to join us."

"You bastard," I hissed, clenching my fists, starting to stand. Leo pushed me back into the seat. "You do what you want with me," I said, "but stay away from her. Emma's got nothing to do with any of this."

Boris shrugged. "Ah, but you leave me no choice, Henry." He held his hand out to Leo. "I'll take the gun, Leo. Go find Emma and bring her here."

Leo winked at me and licked his lips suggestively.

"Wait," I said. Boris had me, and he knew it. "I'll tell you where Leslie is. But you have to promise to leave Emma alone."

"No need to have them both here." Boris said. "Tell me where to find Leslie so Leo can fetch her."

I closed my eyes and pictured Leslie and Emma standing side by side. Two women who had nothing in common except me. Boris was making me choose, but it wasn't much of a choice. The thought of Leo dragging a terrified Emma out of her apartment, his hand over her mouth and his arm around her waist as she struggled, made me sick. Emma was a bystander. Leslie was in this up to her razor-sharp cheekbones. Whether I talked or not, Boris would find Leslie eventually. Emma, I could protect. There wasn't much I could do for Leslie.

"Leslie's staying with a friend," I said, then hesitated, realizing I'd just put another person in jeopardy. Because if Missy was there when Leo came for her, she could end up collateral damage. Or dead. As bad as it felt, I convinced myself that Missy's safety was secondary. "She's in an apartment. Downtown."

"Where downtown?" Boris asked, banging his fist on the chair next to him. "I need the address. Otherwise—" A loud knock cut him off. He looked at the door. "Must be Ivan," he said. "What does he want now?" Boris got up and walked over to the warehouse door.

"Ivan?"

"Da," came the muted reply.

Boris opened the door. Gabriella stood in the doorway, her feet spread apart, shooter's stance, gun aimed at Leo.

"Drop it, asshole!" she shouted.

Boris stood still, but Leo raised his gun. I jumped up and pushed him hard. He still managed to pull the trigger. The bullet missed Gabriella, splintering the doorframe inches from her head. She crouched down, her gun still trained on Leo, but by then, he'd put his arm around my neck and was using me as a shield. Again he aimed at Gabriella, but this time hesitated. He had no shot. Boris body-slammed Gabriella and pinned her to the wall, but she managed to land a knee to his groin. When he doubled over, she smashed the back of his head with her gun. He stumbled, but before he went down, Gabriella grabbed him in a chokehold and put the gun to his head, quickly sliding down the wall and taking a kneeling position behind Boris.

Leo put the barrel of his gun in my ear. "Who the hell are you?" he asked Gabriella, quietly and calmly, like he was chatting over tea. "You a cop?"

"I'm the person holding a gun to your friend's head. That's all you need to know."

Leo tightened his grip around my neck, making it hard for me to breathe. "Looks like we got ourselves a standoff."

"That's true," Gabriella said. "But only until the cops get here, so you might as well put the gun down and let Henry go."

"You're bluffing," Leo said. "You didn't call no cops. Nobody called the cops."

Gabriella said nothing. Leo moved sideways a few feet, dragging me with him. Gabriella shifted position so Boris remained in front of her.

That was when I heard the moan of distant sirens.

Gabriella cocked her head. "You hear that?"

"I don't hear nothing," Leo said.

"You can't hear those sirens? You gotta stop shooting at people. It's making you deaf."

The sirens got louder.

Leo scoffed. "Yeah, now I hear it. Could be fire trucks."

She poked Boris with her gun. "You smell any smoke?" she asked. "I don't."

"Leo," Boris said, his voice straining through Gabriella's chokehold, "that might be the police. If it is, you can't shoot your way out of here."

"That's right, Leo," Gabriella said. "You can't shoot your way out, so you might as well drop the gun."

I felt Leo's grip loosen, allowing me to take a deep breath. Then he moved away from me and put his hands in the air. The gun was dangling from his finger. I couldn't believe he was giving up without a fight.

Gabriella said, "Put the gun on the floor and kick it toward me." Leo bent down and put the gun on the floor. He stood up and kicked it toward her. Gabriella was watching the gun, but I saw Leo flick his jacket out of the way.

"Knife!" I screamed.

Leo had the knife out and in throwing position. Gabriella squeezed off a shot, and the bullet knocked him back before he completed the throw. The knife clattered to the floor. Leo fell backwards. He lay on the floor, feet splayed, blood leaking from his chest. He wasn't moving.

Gabriella let go of Boris and pushed him away from her but kept the gun on him. She waved him to the chairs. "You sit down, asshole, unless you wanna end up like your friend."

The sirens stopped. There was banging on the door. "Police! Open up!"

Gabriella shouted back. "That you, Pete? I'm okay, and everything's secure in here. There's one bad guy down, and I'm holding a gun on the other one. Henry's okay, too. He's gonna open the door and let you in." She nodded to me, and I went over to the door. When I pulled it open, there were two cops with their guns drawn. I instinctively put my hands up.

Gabriella said, "You can holster your weapons, guys."

The first cop looked around before putting his gun away. "You sure you're okay, Gabriella?"

"Yeah, Pete, I'm okay. You okay, Hank?"

"Mostly." My ribcage was sore, and I could still feel Leo's arm around my throat. "I got batted around a little."

"You're still standing," Gabriella pointed out, "It coulda been worse. And you can put your hands down. Nobody's holding a gun on you."

"Oh, yeah, right," I said, feeling like an idiot. I dropped my hands.

Pete pointed at Leo. "What's with that guy?"

"He learned the hard way you don't bring a knife to a gunfight. He's dead or close, but either way, we'd better get an ambulance."

"Called on the way over," he said before turning to his partner. "Andy, put some cuffs on that other guy." Andy spun Boris around and cuffed him. He still seemed unsteady on his feet, maybe from getting kicked in the balls and whacked on the back of the neck by Gabriella. Or maybe from watching her gun down Leo. Still, he shot me a nasty glance as Andy led him out the door. I returned fire without fear, mostly because I assumed that was the last time I'd see Boris.

After watching Boris's exit, Gabriella turned to Pete. "What took you guys so long?"

Pete narrowed his eyes. "I thought we agreed you'd wait for backup before you did anything. What are you, Rambo?"

"Don't bust my balls," she replied with a chuckle. "I was planning on waiting, but then I notice there's some guy sitting in the car, so I drag him out, shake him a little, and ask him what the fuck is going on in the warehouse. He says they're beating the shit out of Henry, so I tell him to stay put and go in. I didn't want to wait." She pointed at me. "He's kinda soft."

"I'm right here, Gabriella," I said, trying my best not to sound soft. "And I coulda held out another few minutes."

"Really, Hank?" Without waiting for me to respond, she said, "Hey Pete, I'll be outside. Hank's coming with me. He looks like he could use a dose of fresh air, too." She reached behind her, tucked her gun in the small of her back, and started toward the door.

"Don't go far," he said. "We'll need statements from the both of you." Pete knelt beside Leo and put his hand on his neck. "Well, this guy's definitely dead."

"Good," I muttered, but I spoke too soon. Leo's death didn't make me feel good at all.

It's not that I felt anything for the crook, what with him beating me and threatening to kill me. Leo chose his life. Violence and the risk of an untimely death came with the job. But violence was not part of my life. I'd scoffed when Aiden said he was scared Leslie would get me into trouble someday, "real trouble" as he'd put it. Maybe Leslie seemed adventurous and even reckless sometimes, but instead of scaring me, she electrified me in a way that nobody else had before. As it turned out, Aiden was right. From the day I met Leslie, violence was just offstage, pacing, waiting for its cue, gleefully anticipating the audience's collective gasp at its dramatic entrance. It had entered, and I'd gasped. But this wasn't a stage play. This was real life, and I'd just seen a man shot dead right in front of me.

Gabriella and I stepped outside. The air felt cool and crisp compared to the jungle heat and humidity I'd endured inside the warehouse. I stopped, closed my eyes, and took a deep breath. New York City had never smelled sweeter.

When I opened my eyes, Gabriella was facing me. She was close enough to kiss me. Instead she put her hand on my left shoulder and shoved me so hard I almost fell over. "Hey!" I shouted. "Whadja do that for?"

"Why didn't you tell me you had a meet-up with these gangsters?"

"I didn't—"

"You walk in there alone, unarmed, nobody watching your back. You got some kind of death wish?"

"Death wish? No, I just thought …"

"You just thought? Doesn't sound like you were thinking at all. Because if you were thinking, you never would have come out here like this. If Aiden hadn't told me where you were, you would have been dead. Worse than dead. Tortured to death and dead."

"Aiden?"

She glared at me. "Yeah, Aiden. Remember him? Your best friend?"

"Aiden called you?"

"Yeah. He told me you'd asked for a ride, but he was pissed at you for something, so he said no. Then he started feeling guilty and tried calling you. When he got no answer, he called me. Lucky for you Aiden remembered the address of the warehouse. Hey, what'd you do to piss him off? Must have been something nasty."

"Maybe it was. I hope he gets over it." Rather than elaborate, I got quiet. "Anyway," I said, changing the subject, "I'm grateful he called you. And I'm glad you showed up when you did. Thanks, Gabriella. You know, for saving me and all."

"Yeah, you're welcome," she said, backing away. I guess I shouldn't have tried to give her a hug.

CHAPTER 31

Gabriella and I stood by one of the police cars and watched the ambulance pull into the lot, siren blaring. Two emergency medical techs, a white man and a Black woman wearing blue uniforms, jumped out of the rig. Moving deliberately, they slid the gurney out and briskly rolled it toward the door. "Hey you guys," Gabriella said. "No need to hurry. The man's dead." They glanced at her but made no attempt to respond or to slow down. Gabriella shrugged, then leaned against the police car, pulled out her phone, and started texting. It reminded me to text Carlos and send him home.

A few minutes later I watched as the EMTs maneuvered the empty gurney out the door. I was surprised Leo wasn't on it.

"Wait, they're just leaving him in there?"

Gabriella looked up from her phone. "When you're dead, you don't go to the hospital, you go to the morgue. The medical examiner will show up eventually and take care of the body."

Not long after the ambulance left, a blue Subaru arrived and a tall Black woman wearing a light-colored pantsuit got out, glanced at us, said nothing, then went into the warehouse. I figured her to be another cop. My watch said quarter to midnight. Things were moving at the speed of a glacier.

At 12:30 the mystery woman emerged from the warehouse, followed by Pete and his partner. She was holding some plastic evidence bags, one with Leo's knife, one with his gun.

"This is Detective Peabody," Pete said. "Detective, you have here Gabriella and Henry. Gabriella's a private dick who used to be on the force. She's good people. Henry I don't vouch for."

I nodded to the detective. "Nice to meet you."

She nodded back. "I'm looking forward to getting to know the both of you. We'll start by having a long talk about what went down here and how one guy ended up dead."

"Gabriella shot him when she saved me," I said, trying to be helpful.

Detective Peabody glared at me for a second, then said, "So I understand. But I'd like to dig into the details, you know, to find out if one or both of you broke any laws. The one I'm thinking of in particular is the law against killing another person." She turned to Pete. "Keep them separated. I'll be at the station in a few minutes." She turned and headed toward her blue Subaru.

Pete told us to put our hands out. "I gotta cuff you guys. Standard procedure. Sorry, Gabriella."

"You arresting us?" I asked.

"No, just standard procedure, like I said. Right now, you're persons of interest."

After Pete cuffed us, I turned to Gabriella, who whispered, "Don't worry. We'll be fine."

"Do I need to call a lawyer?" I whispered back

"Probably not, at least not yet. Stay cool. Answer the detective's questions. Don't fuck with her."

"What does that mean?"

"It means don't lie, at least not about what went down at the warehouse tonight. It'll be your story against mine. And Boris's, come to think of it."

***

They took us to the station in separate squad cars. Gabriella rode with Pete. I said nothing to the cop driving me, preferring to contemplate the situation and Gabriella's advice in silence. The ride took about ten minutes, and both cars arrived at the same time. Gabriella and I were taken inside and led to the desk by our two cop escorts, who, after some preliminaries with the desk sergeant, left to go back on patrol. Another officer in uniform took over without introducing himself. He led us down a hall to the first interrogation room, opened the door, and said, "Ladies first." He held up a small key. Gabriella nodded and offered up her wrists, and he uncuffed her. She rubbed her wrists and went inside. "See you later," I called after her, but the door slammed shut.

We passed the next interrogation room and stopped at the one after that. The cop opened the door and pushed me into the room. When he started to close the door behind me, I said, "Hey, what about my handcuffs?" The cop ignored me and locked the door. The room was just like you see on cop shows—a big one-way mirror next to the door and a table against the wall flanked by two straight-backed metal chairs. I pulled out one of the chairs and angled it to face the door, then sat down and waited.

A few minutes went by before the same cop came back in and took off my cuffs.

About an hour later I had my head on the table and had nearly dozed off when the door opened and Detective Peabody walked in holding a mug. Coffee, by the smell of it.

"No thanks," I said. " I've had mine."

She stopped and furrowed her eyebrows. "Huh?" I pointed to the mug. She looked at it and then back at me. "Oh, the coffee." She took a sip as if to confirm that it was hers and not mine, then set it down on the table along with a file and a small clear plastic bag. She covered the bag with the file, maybe hoping to do a big, "Ta

DA!" later when she showed me the contents, but I could see it was the ring. Then she pulled a digital tape recorder out of her pantsuit pocket and, without turning it on, placed it on the table between us. From her other pantsuit pocket she produced a pen and clicked it open before sitting down, sliding a sheet of paper from the file and starting to write.

The room was quiet except for the ticking second hand of the wall clock and the scratching of her pen against the paper. All that quiet was making me nervous.

"Funny place to keep your pen," I said. "Doesn't it poke you through your pocket when you sit down?"

She looked up at me and rolled her eyes like she couldn't believe I'd said that.

I drummed two fingers lightly on the table and watched her write. The handwriting was small, delicate, and upside down, so I couldn't make it out.

After a minute I gave up trying, stopped the finger drumming, and asked, "Any way I could use the restroom?"

She ignored me.

I shifted uncomfortably in my seat, checked my watch, and compared it to the wall clock. Four minutes apart. I'd been in the room for fifty-five minutes, or maybe fifty-one, depending. Detective Peabody appeared to be in no hurry to start the conversation, so I did. "Couple hours ago, I gave Boris a fancy engagement ring. Is that it?" I asked, pointing to the top of the plastic bag peeking out from under the file.

Her gaze moved to the bag. She picked it up, held it so close to my face I could practically taste the plastic, and jiggled it.

Peering around the bag, I said, "Yeah, that's the ring, alright. Where'd you find it? Boris had it, right?"

Peabody put the bag down and went back to writing. Without looking up, she said, "You talk too much, you know that?"

"It's not the worst thing about me."

"Shut up," she said. After writing for another minute, she finally put her pen down, sat back in her chair, and sighed. "Look," she said, "it's late, and you're tired. You want to go home and clean yourself up, put on your jammies, and get some sleep. I know that. So here's the deal. You tell me the story of how tonight went down, including how you all happened to end up there. If, by some slim chance, it matches up exactly, and I do mean exactly, with the story Gabriella told us, I'll send you home. But if there are discrepancies, well, we'll just have to keep you here until everything becomes crystal clear."

"What did Gabriella say?" I asked, hoping against hope that Detective Peabody was so tired she'd answer me before realizing her blunder.

She snorted. "Nice try, counselor, but I suspect you know how this works."

She took a sip from her coffee mug, then put it down so hard that some of it spilled. We both glanced at the spilled coffee. Neither of us made a move to clean it up.

"So talk to me like you're talking to the priest during confession. And no detail is too small, got it?

I nodded. She turned on the tape recorder, noted the time, who she was, and who she was interviewing. I expected her to ask something to start me off, but she just took another sip of coffee, leaned toward me, and waited for me to talk.

It took me the better part of an hour to tell her everything. Almost everything. I left out the part about Leslie double-crossing me and making off with my money. In fact, I kept Leslie out of the story as best I could, and for the same reason that I'd resisted telling Boris where to find her. Even though Leslie and I were no longer married, I still felt honor bound to protect her. That included not telling the cops anything they could use against her.

I focused on what happened in the warehouse. Peabody asked me a lot of questions, including some she repeated several times. I suppose she wanted to make sure I wasn't lying, or misremembering, or protecting Gabriella by fabricating the story. I caught on to her interrogation MO fast and began keeping my answers short. That way I'd be less likely to contradict myself.

"So," she said, "you went there tonight to give Boris what you thought was his ring. But Leslie gave you a fake, and Boris got mad and had his guy Leo smack you around. By the way, he did a pretty thorough job—your face is a mess. Anyway, before Leo beats you to death, your private dick shows up, and there's some tussling that leads to a Mexican standoff. Leo had a gun to your head, and Gabriella was likewise with Boris. She gets Leo to put down his gun, he goes for his knife, but before he can throw it, she shoots him. Dead."

"Yep."

"Sounds like a ridiculous plan on Leo's part. Bullets go faster than knives."

But it wasn't ridiculous. When Gabriella told Leo to drop his gun, he made a big show of throwing it down and kicking it over. Gabriella had her eye on the floor where the gun was. Maybe Leo thought he'd have time to throw the knife before she saw what was happening. It had been me who'd caught Leo reaching for his knife, not Gabriella. I didn't feel like batting this around with the detective, though, so I kept it to myself.

"So that's it?" she asked.

"That, and the fact that maybe Leo was braver than he was smart."

She looked at me for a few seconds. "So where's the real ring?"

"No idea."

"Maybe Leslie has it. Maybe she gave you a fake and made off with the real one."

That wasn't my theory, but I kept my mouth shut.

She leaned in. "Or maybe you have it."

I shook my head. "I told you I don't know where it is." Then I went into defense attorney mode. "Maybe I gave Boris the real ring, and it just turned out not to be the priceless heirloom he thought it was."

"Maybe," she said. "I'm just asking because I'm curious. You're right, there's no evidence that a ring's been stolen. So far, the Russian guy's not talking, but even if he claims there's a stolen ring out there, who's gonna believe him? Anyway, theft isn't my problem. We got a whole different department for that. I'll tell them what I know, and if they get interested, they'll come looking for you."

She gulped down the rest of her coffee, then put the papers scattered on the table back in the file.

"Are we done?"

"For now, yeah. But Henry?"

"What?"

"Don't take any out-of-town trips in the next few days." With that, she reached for the tape recorder, turned it off, and put it in her pocket. Then she picked up the file, the evidence bag holding the fake ring, and her empty coffee mug, and left the room without a word.

Five minutes later another cop opened the door and told me I was free to go.

CHAPTER 32

I walked into the 103rd Precinct lobby half expecting to see Gabriella there waiting for me, but there was no sign of her. She'd either been let out earlier or was still being held for questioning. I asked the desk sergeant if he knew where she was. "Nope," he replied, leaning forward in his chair, "but tell you what, if you can't find her after forty-eight hours, feel free to file a missing person's report."

Everybody's a comedian.

It was almost one in the morning, and all I wanted was to be home. No sign of any cabs outside the station. Of course not—this was Queens. Empty yellow cabs were hard to come by in Queens, especially at this hour, so I went back in and asked the desk sergeant if he knew of a car company. Instead of the snappy answer I expected, he reached under the desk and produced a business card: Billy's Taxi. "Billy's my cousin on my mother's side, rest her soul." I got it—he was doing Billy and his dead mother a favor, not me.

I took the business card.

Ten minutes later, I climbed into a ten-year-old town car driven by a young Asian-American woman. According to the license tacked on the dashboard, her name was Brooklyn Lee. In her official license picture, she had straight dark hair that hung to her shoulders. From the back seat all I could see was spiky pink hair with a green ribbon on the right side.

"Whoa," she said, eyeing me in her rearview mirror. Then she turned around. Same face as in the picture. "What in the hell happened to you? The cops do that?"

"Do what?"

"Your face. Doesn't it hurt?"

"Um, now that you mention it, yeah, it hurts."

A couple of blocks later, when we stopped at a red light, Brooklyn twisted the rearview mirror my way, turned on the interior light, and told me to have a look. I was a mess. My right eye was swollen but still open. My left eye was bruised. My upper lip looked like a throw pillow. There was blood caked under my left nostril. I wiped it away with the back of my hand but not before squeezing my nose between my thumb and forefinger. It didn't seem broken, but I'm no orthopedic surgeon, so what do I know? The light changed, and Brooklyn adjusted the mirror. I sat back in my seat.

"You wouldn't have any ice, would you, Brooklyn?"

"Ice? Why the fuck would I—wait, hold on a second." She reached for something on the floor. "You're in luck! I forgot I just finished this," she said, holding up a giant paper cup from a fast-food joint. "They sell you this giant tub of soda, and of course, the damn thing's all crushed ice. Maybe two, three slurps, and I'm suckin' air." She gave it a shake and said, "Here, take it."

"Thanks," I said and pressed the cup of ice against my swollen eye. The cold on my face eased the pain a little.

Twenty minutes later Brooklyn dropped me at the front door of my building in Manhattan. The glass door was locked, but I could see Mickey, the overnight doorman, catching some Zs in a lobby chair. I knocked twice. Mickey's eyes snapped open, and he hustled over to the door to let me in. I thanked him, said goodnight, and headed to the elevator.

Before I hit the call button, Mickey told me to wait a second and reached into his pocket. "Here you go, Mr. Gladstone," he said, handing me a small envelope. He noticed my busted-up face and stared for a second but didn't mention it. "Have a good night" is all he said before sliding into his chair to resume his nap.

I punched the elevator call button, then opened the envelope. It was a note from Emma. "Where are you? Miss you! XO Emma." The elevator was still slowly sinking to the lobby, so I texted,

It's been a rotten night. Let's catch up in the morning

When the elevator came, I got in, hit the button for the fourteenth floor, then leaned against the back wall with my eyes closed. A few seconds later the elevator stopped with a ding. I looked up and saw that it wasn't my floor. It was Emma's. The elevator door slid open, and sure enough, there was Emma, barefoot and wearing a beguiling smile but not much else.

She took a couple of steps toward me before she gasped.

"Holy shit, Henry. What—what happened to you? Oh you poor thing."

I said nothing, intending to smile and tell her I was okay, but I had to abort the smile when I felt the pain. I settled for saying, "It looks worse than it is."

When the elevator door opened again, we crossed the hall to my apartment. I fumbled with the lock, so she silently took the key from me, opened the door, and ushered me into my apartment and onto my couch. After turning on a couple of lamps, she went into the bathroom. I heard the medicine cabinet open and a few seconds later "Band-Aids? All you have is Band-Aids?"

I directed her to a first aid kit under the sink.

She came back having found not only the first aid kit but my bathrobe, which she'd put on. "Found it," she said and sat next to me on the couch with one leg tucked under her. In her hand was a wet washcloth. "Now hold still."

I winced every time the cloth touched my face. If it had been anybody but Emma, I might have yelped, too.

After a few minutes of wiping me down and dressing my wounds with the contents of the first aid kit, she sat back to admire her handiwork and smiled. "You clean up nice." I noticed it was kind of a sad smile and I felt bad, knowing the sadness was about me. Then she knelt next to the coffee table and started carefully placing the ointment tube, scissors, gauze, bandages, and tape back in the first aid kit. She closed the box and looked up. "You gonna tell me what happened?"

"Tomorrow morning," I said before standing. "Say, how did you know I was coming up in the elevator?"

She closed the robe around her. "Mickey the doorman. I asked him to buzz me when you came in."

Emma put the first aid kit on the coffee table and stood up. "Okay, let's get you to bed." She led me to the bedroom, sat me down on the mattress, and helped me pull off my T-shirt. It was only then I noticed how sore my body was.

Emma undressed me down to my undershorts and helped me into bed. I closed my eyes as soon as my head hit the pillow. "Stay," I said. She took off the robe, lifted the covers, and climbed in beside me.

The next thing I knew, it was morning. Emma was cuddled up behind me, loosely cradling me with her arm thrown over my side. Her breathing was slow and regular. As much as I wanted to turn over to see her, to mingle my breath with hers while she slept, to run my hand lightly over her hair, doing so would needlessly awaken her. Maybe she wouldn't mind. Maybe I could make it up to her before either of us climbed out of bed. I moved a little to see if my body still ached. It did, but not enough to keep me from Emma. I smiled at the thought, but my lower lip objected, and my smile dissolved in pain. I touched it lightly with my index finger, then winced. Still swollen, it felt like a twenty-pound weight was hanging off my face. That would curtail the kind of passionate kissing Emma and I had already turned into an art form.

As close as she was to me, I wanted to be closer, so I slid myself back a half-inch. That worked. She stirred and moved toward me. Her arm tightened around my chest, and her lips brushed against my neck, but she didn't wake up.

I closed my eyes and enjoyed what some say is the euphoria that comes with surviving a near-death experience. And now, wrapped in Emma's arms, I forgot there was a city outside my window and a world outside the city. I figured most of that was Emma, but some of it had to be the weight lifted from me with Leo gone, Boris in custody, and Leslie on the lam. So what if she double-crossed me and took me for a quarter million dollars? So what if the money wasn't used to buy back Czarina Alexandra's priceless ring? The mortal danger that had been following me around like a rabid rottweiler was no more. And Leslie and I had survived.

My cell phone was on the nightstand. I reached for it and turned it on. There were two texts and two phone messages. I scanned them, hoping one of them was from Gabriella, telling me the cops had let her go and she was fine, but all four were from the office. Something serious was going on.

I removed Emma's hand from my chest, crept out from under the covers, and started to stand up when I felt Emma grabbing the waistband of my shorts. She pulled hard, and I sat back on the bed.

"Where do you think you're going, mister?"

"Nowhere, I guess."

Emma put a firm hand on my shoulder. "You guessed right." She pulled me next to her and kissed my ear, a choice my swollen lower lip appreciated.

Seconds later the phone rang. "Leave it," she whispered. Her lips brushed my ear again, and the ringing faded away.

We stayed in bed for another hour of cuddling before the phone rang again. This time, I picked it up.

"Henry, it's Nancy. Neil called several times looking for you. I think you'd better come in."

Until then I'd forgotten about her phone call. "He say what it's about?"

"No, but he dropped the f-bomb a couple of times. So it sounds serious."

"Thanks, Nancy," I said. "Be there soon."

My alarm clock said 9:43, so I could easily shower, dress, gulp some coffee, and be at the office by eleven. Whatever set my boss ablaze would seem silly compared to what I'd endured last night, not to mention the last few days. After explaining to Emma that I had to go into work for an emergency, I walked into the bathroom and ran the shower, then wondered if I could get away without shaving. I looked in the mirror, and the first thing I saw was what was missing. "Hey, what happened to your lipstick note?"

"It smudged, so I cleaned the mirror," she replied from the bedroom.

"I should've taken a picture when I had the chance."

"I took one. I'll send it to you."

I returned my attention to the mirror and studied my face. Shaving wouldn't have much impact on my appearance. Both eyes were black and blue, and my right eye was buried beneath a pile of swollen flesh. My lower lip had improved a little, but my face still looked like I'd gone six rounds with Mohammed Ali. "Hey, Emma, is there anything we can do to make this mug more presentable? Makeup or something?" I turned toward her so she could see my face.

She sat up in bed, leaned against the headboard, and took a good look. "You could cut two holes in a paper bag and put it over your head."

"Thanks for nothing."

"C'mon, Henry, you're gonna scare the shit out of everyone in the office. Why don't you call in sick like a normal person?"

"I have to go in. My boss wants to see me."

"How are you going to explain your mashed-up face?" Emma said. "And come to think of it, you never told me what happened. If I hadn't seen Leo and his gun the other night, I'd guess that you were in a car accident. But that's probably wrong. You were beat up, right? By the guys who wanted the ring?"

"Yeah, I was," I said. "I don't have time to tell you more about it except that it's over. Leo is—let's just say Leo's out of the picture. And the guy he was working for, Boris? The cops have him."

"What about your ex?" Emma frowned. "She still lurking about?"

"I don't know where she is, and I don't much care. I'm just glad this whole ring fiasco is over and done with." I spat into the sink for emphasis.

"Well, that's good." She paused. "Except it's too bad in a way."

Instead of asking why, I said, "Hold that thought," pushed the plastic curtain aside, and stepped into the shower. It was hotter than I normally liked it in the summertime, but my aching body needed heat. "You mind making us some coffee?" I shouted over the roar of the shower. No answer. Then the curtain slid open.

Emma stood there naked. "Mind if I join you?" she asked and without waiting for an answer climbed into the shower. "Jesus, that water's hot!"

"Sorry, I wasn't expecting company." I put my arms around her and drew her close. As she kissed me, I saw her reach for the soap. I'm not sure exactly what she had in mind, but it was sure to improve my shower experience by 1000 percent. "Emma, honey, I hope you understand," I said as I moved her away from me, "but I do have to get to work."

"This won't take long." She smiled and looked up at me as she ran the bar of soap down my chest and stomach, then past my waist. I grabbed her wrist before she reached the point of no return.

"I'll make it up to you, promise," I said as I removed the soap from her hand and put it back in the soap dish. I lifted her hand to my damaged lips and kissed it.

She got all pouty, said, "Fine," and climbed out of the shower. "I'll just make the coffee." Before I could say anything else, she yanked the curtain closed.

I finished my shower, toweled off, dressed, and followed the coffee aroma to the kitchen. Emma was sitting at the counter with two cups of coffee in front of her. She pushed one toward me. "I don't know how you take it."

"Black is fine, thanks." I took a sip. The coffee was even hotter than the shower. "Maybe I'll add a little milk." I got a carton out of the fridge and poured some milk into my coffee. "Hey, what did you mean when you said it's too bad that the ring thing is over?"

"What I said was, 'It's too bad in a way.'"

"What way?"

"You don't have the ring, do you?"

I shook my head.

"And you don't know who does?"

I shook my head.

"Yeah, as I said, it's too bad. Because it turns out there's a reward."

"A reward? What, for the ring?"

244

"Uh-huh. I turned on a Google alert in case there were updates to the story, and I got one. Turns out the article neglected to mention that the FSB has a team of agents on the case, and they're offering a reward, like a zillion rubles. I did the math. It's just over four million dollars."

"I don't care. In fact, I don't care so much that even if I knew where the damn ring was, I probably wouldn't do anything about it. I'm sick of the whole business. It ended last night, and that's the way I want it."

Emma looked up at me. "I got it. But still, that's something, that they're offering the reward, isn't it?"

"Yeah, it's something. But it's somebody else's something." I took the last gulp of my coffee, then leaned down and kissed her. "Will I see you later? Celebration dinner out somewhere, just the two of us?"

She smiled. "I'll make a reservation."

CHAPTER 33

Half an hour later I walked into my office building and took the elevator to my floor. When I arrived, I was surprised to see my assistant Nancy waiting in the reception area. She walked through the glass doors and met me at the elevator, then put her hand to her mouth. "My god, Henry!" she exclaimed. "What happened to you?"

I'd worked out a cover story on the way over. "Car accident. I was in a taxi that rear-ended a truck. I should have been wearing my seat belt, but …"

"Are you all right?"

"Yeah, I'm fine."

"Well, you look terrible. You probably shouldn't have come to work."

"Not my first choice, but the boss wants to see me, and it sounds urgent."

"That's why I waited in reception," she whispered, taking a step closer to me. "I need to tell you something before you go see Neil."

"Okay," I said. "Talk to me."

"Not here," she whispered. "Your office?"

We stood at the glass doors and waited for Maggie, the receptionist, to buzz us in. "Holy moly!" Maggie exclaimed. "What did you do to your face?"

"He was in a traffic accident, but he's okay," Nancy explained.

"My taxi hit a truck," I clarified, knowing that Maggie would spread the news at twice the speed of light. "It looks worse than it feels."

"Really?" Maggie seemed dubious. "I hope that's true."

Nancy and I left the lobby and headed to my office. I ushered her in and closed the door. Neither of us sat. "Now, what is it?" I asked, arms folded.

She held her hands in front of her, rubbing one with the other as if she had arthritis, which as far as I knew she didn't. "Remember I said that when Neil asked me to find you, he was cursing?"

I nodded.

"Well, Veronica told me that Neil's very, very upset. She thinks it has something to do with another letter that came today in the same manila envelope as the one sent yesterday. You know, no return address, eyes only, that stuff?"

"Oh," I said as unemotionally as I could, despite the dread that was creeping up my legs toward my vital organs. "Did I also get another mystery envelope?"

"No. Nothing like that came for you. I even went down to the mailroom to double check."

That made sense. My copy, complete with a note inside the envelope, arrived the day before.

"Anything else?" I asked.

She shook her head. "No, that's it." She looked down at her hands. "I do hope it's nothing serious. I just thought I'd better—"

"Hey, you did good, Nancy," I said. "Thanks for the heads-up."

When she looked up, I attempted a reassuring smile, and she looked relieved.

"And whatever it is," I said, opening the door for her, "I'll handle it." Before following her out, I grabbed a legal pad and a pencil from my desk.

Fast-walking to Neil's office, the halls were eerily quiet. The carpeting muffled sound, and most of the office doors were closed, adding to the stillness. A couple of partners stood chatting at the far end of the hall. They stopped talking when they saw me. I nodded hello and kept walking. They didn't resume their conversation until I turned the corner toward Neil's office.

It was time to come up with a strategy. My first thought: Lie.

As a kid, lying and blaming others was my go-to defense, and I was surprised when it didn't always work. By the time I was twelve, I understood that a lie usually made things worse. Most people came to that conclusion sooner or later, but the urge to lie lingered in some. It lingered in me.

The closer I got to Neil's office, the more I liked the idea of lying. "Neil, I have no idea who wrote that letter, but it wasn't me. Some creep forged my signature. And when I find that sonofabitch, why I'll …" Yeah, I could make that work.

I was so lost in thought that I almost walked straight into Neil's office unannounced.

"Hold on, Henry," Veronica said, standing up. "Let me tell Neil you're here." She didn't ask about my busted-up face. Maybe she didn't notice. Maybe she didn't care.

Knocking on Neil's door and peeking in, she said, "Neil, Henry's here." She opened the door all the way and stepped aside to let me pass. I heard the door close behind me.

Neil sat at his large polished-walnut desk reading something on his cell phone. A college football star in the eighties, he still had the big beefy look of a linebacker, making him seem too big for his oversized executive office chair. I expected him to invite me to sit down, and when he didn't, I had no choice but to stand a few feet away from his desk with my hands at my sides and wait.

Finally Neil put down his cell phone, opened his desk drawer, and pulled out some papers. "Henry ..." he began. Then he saw my face and interrupted himself. "What in hell happened to you?"

I repeated the car crash story and told him I felt fine. He stared at me for a few more seconds before saying, "Well, I'm glad you're okay."

"Thanks," I said.

He returned his attention to the papers in his hand, then held them up in front of me. "Now, Henry, I hope for your sake this letter to—" he glanced at the letter "—to a Mrs. Dodie McCraney, whoever the fuck she is, is some kind of a lame prank."

A lame prank! Perfect! Why didn't I think of that? All I had to do was say yes, and maybe that would be the end of it. I weighed that against being caught in a lie. "It's not a prank," I said, then stood up as straight as I could. "I wrote it. Pretending to be a lawyer when I was still a summer associate was ... not right."

Neil glared. "It's worse than not right. It's a betrayal of trust. My trust, the firm's trust, our clients' trust." He slammed the letter on the desk.

"You're right. All I can say is I'm sorry." When Neil didn't respond or soften his glare, I said, "Not that this is an excuse, but lots of summer associates make mistakes. Remember that Harvard kid a few years ago? The one who—"

"Of course I remember," he shot back. "The Harvard kid fucked up, and he didn't get an offer." He let me think about that for a few seconds. "And what about this other thing?" he barked, pointing at his desk.

"I'm sorry, the other thing is ... what?"

Instead of answering, Neil picked up the letter and handed it to me. I scanned it and recognized the first part—it was identical to the version I'd seen yesterday. But there was a second part.

I also learned from a former Loveless, Brown &
Cunningham employee that despite becoming aware
that a colleague, David Houston, had sex with
a client in one of your conference rooms, Mr.
Gladstone chose not to report the incident to
protect Mr. Houston.

Uh oh.

Dave Houston and I had joined the firm the same year, and he
sat across the hall from me. A case of mine was due to go to trial,
and I found myself working Christmas Eve. At about eleven, I finally
called it quits. On my way out, I noticed light peeking out from under
the conference room door where we'd had our Christmas champagne
toast that afternoon. I hadn't seen a soul since four o'clock and
assumed nobody else was in the office, but I was wrong. Thinking
I ought to wish whoever it was a Merry Christmas, I opened the
door. There was Dave, lying on the conference table enjoying some
holiday cheer in the arms, and legs, of a mostly naked woman I didn't
recognize. He'd thoughtfully placed a cushion from one of the office
chairs under her ass. Another cushioned her head.

"Sorry," I said, then backed out and closed the conference room
door. I stood there collecting myself for a few seconds. Walking away,
I heard the conference door open behind me and turned around.
Dave was in the process of pulling up his pants.

"Gladstone … wait."

I stopped. "Merry Christmas, Dave."

"Yeah, right. You're not planning to tell anyone about this, are
you?"

"You're lucky it was me and not one of the partners," I said.
"But no, I won't tell. Why ruin everyone's holiday?"

Shortly after New Year's, while walking through the reception
area, I spotted Dave's Christmas friend standing at the reception desk.
She was an attractive blonde woman in her forties, smartly dressed

in black slacks and a white blouse, and wearing a gold necklace and gold hoop earrings. I quickly looked away and kept walking. As I did, I heard Maggie say, "Mr. Houston, your client is here."

Dave had crossed a crimson line by sleeping with a client. That it happened in the office made it worse. Even though the legal code of ethics required me to report it, I didn't. As it turned out, Dave was fired two years later for sleeping with three more clients. The firm tried to keep it quiet, but of course, it was leaked to the press. "Uptight Law Firm Loveless, Brown Finds Love at Last," read one rag's cringeworthy headline. The partners were furious. Because it blew up, I knew that if they discovered I hadn't reported it I'd be in trouble, and I lost a lot of sleep during the brouhaha. While there was no reason for Dave to mention that I'd caught him in the act, I knew from working with criminals that they often feel the need to implicate others, even if it's just to say, "He made me do it," or in this case, "He should have stopped me." Luckily, no one connected me with the Christmas incident at the time.

The only person I'd ever told was Leslie.

We'd just started our relationship, and she was still living on Long Island with Boris. I was so smitten I told her a lot of things I shouldn't have. According to her, she'd told Boris all about me. I guess she really did mean everything.

I looked up from the letter. "I don't know what to say."

"When you think of something," Neil said, leaning back in his chair, "save it for the management committee. I have no choice but to inform them."

"You referring me to the bar?"

"If it was my call, I sure as shit would, but it's up to the management committee." Neil glowered at me for a second before slamming his fists on the desk. "Jesus Christ, Henry, you really fucked up! I don't have to tell you how serious this is. I don't know who wrote this letter or how they got the information, but they're clearly not wishing you a long and prosperous career as a lawyer. And right now, neither am I. You're in deep doo-doo, and it stinks."

He took a deep breath, then slowly exhaled, placed his forearms on the desk, and leaned forward. "You're a good lawyer, better than most in fact, and you've been good for the firm. There probably isn't an attorney in the city who hasn't done something that could have gotten them reprimanded or worse. But you got caught. I'll be sorry to see you go if that's what the management committee decides. But there's nothing I can do."

I nodded and placed the letter on his desk. Neil pushed it away, like an unappetizing dish he'd tried and had enough of.

"Starting now," he said sharply, "you're on unpaid leave. See that your case files get to Michaela Rossi before you leave the office, and let her know if anything's coming up—a deposition or a hearing or what have you."

Michaela Rossi was a good lawyer and a hard worker, but my caseload was probably more than she could handle. I'd tell her I was taking a leave of absence for personal reasons when she asked me what was going on. She'd find out the real reason soon enough. In a couple of hours the entire office, from the mail guys on up, would know I was in deep shit, the kind you don't dig yourself out of without a very big shovel, or in this case, without a powerful friend on the management committee. Last time I checked, though, no shovel and no powerful friend. I was all but finished being a lawyer at Loveless, Brown.

"I'll do the handoff today before I leave the office."

I wanted this to be over, but I remained standing at the desk. Neil looked at me with disgust. Or maybe it was pity. Maybe both. Or maybe I was projecting my feelings about myself onto him. We were quiet for a few seconds, and I wondered if I should thank him, or shake his hand, or just turn around and leave. Instead, I said, "Anything else?"

"Yeah," he snapped. "Close the damn door on your way out."

I returned to my office and spent the rest of the morning assembling my active case files and composing a memo to Michaela. I stopped every so often to consider how I'd gotten myself into this and whether or not I deserved it. I alternated feeling sorry for myself, thinking I was the world's biggest idiot who didn't deserve my career as a lawyer, and blaming Leslie for all my troubles. Leslie. Jesus Christ, I should have known better than to fall for her, to trust her, to marry her. I felt like crying, but like so many men steeped in the American tough-guy tradition, I couldn't.

At around one, Nancy came in and asked if I'd like her to order me a sandwich, but I told her I wasn't hungry. A half hour later, I finished the memo, phoned Michaela, and asked if I could stop by her office and talk to her about an important matter.

"Sure, no problem," she said. She didn't ask why, which could mean only one thing—she'd already heard. Saved me the trouble of lying.

When I got there, I dropped the foot high stack of files on her desk. On top was the memo summarizing relevant information about my current cases, as well as a rundown of my clients' quirks, invaluable information I'd learned the hard way. "It's all here," I said, handing it to her. "The files of every case I'm currently working on. And my memo lays out additional details, so hopefully that's everything you need to take over."

"Oh my god," she said. "There's more here than I expected."

While I watched Michaela slowly flip through the pages, I thought back to when she'd first started at Loveless, Brown. There was some concern among the partners that her Alabama upbringing might have left her a little rough around the edges, so I was assigned to mentor her for six months. We'd gone out for drinks a couple of times after work, but nothing came of it, because by then, Leslie had entered the picture. Not that I didn't find Michaela attractive, with her green eyes, long blonde hair, and a southern drawl that became more pronounced as the evening and the drinking progressed.

She flipped to the last page. "Oh good, your cell number is here. I may have some questions." She smiled and looked up at me. "Or I may want to ask you for a drink or something," she said, her drawl kicking in right on schedule.

"That ship's sailed, Mick. Without us."

"Yeah. I'm still sorry about that." Her smile turned wistful. I started to smile back but grimaced instead.

Michaela suddenly looked concerned. "That hurts, huh? What happened to you?"

I gave it to her straight. "Last night I was kidnapped by a Russian mobster. Luckily, the cops showed up before he beat me to death."

Michaela looked stricken for a second. Then she laughed and told me she'd already heard about my taxi accident from Maggie the receptionist, but she was hoping to get the inside scoop from me. I begged off, saying I was tired, which was the god's honest truth.

With my case files in Michaela's capable hands, I started to walk the forty blocks back to my apartment with my head down and my hands in my pockets. Despite the blistering heat, the Third Avenue sidewalk was jammed with tourists. I paid them no mind. Several times I nicked somebody as I barreled down the sidewalk, but I was moving so fast I didn't know, or care, if I'd pissed them off.

At the corner of Sixty-Fourth, I passed a bar just as someone opened the door. The alcohol smell washed over me. Made me think about stopping for a quick one. Then a rummy staggered out of the bar and slammed into me. I stumbled, regained my balance, shouted, "Fuck off!" and pushed him so hard he fell. A lady screamed. I stopped and turned to see this old guy, shabbily dressed in shorts, sneakers, and a dirty white T-shirt, lying there, not moving. He didn't deserve to get pushed to the sidewalk because I was having a shitty day.

I went to help, but these two big lugs wearing identical Mets baseball caps got there first and lifted him up by his arms.

One of the lugs looked at me and said, "Whadja do that for? Make you feel good pushing around old guys? That your idea of fun?" He took a step toward me.

I backed up and put my palms out. "Sorry. My fault. I didn't mean any harm. The guy's drunk, he walked right into me, and— look, I don't want any trouble." A few people stood nearby, watching.

The other lug grabbed his friend's elbow. "C'mon, Casey, leave it alone. We're late as it is."

Casey pulled his elbow away and got right in my face. "Listen, asshole, how's about you buy this nice old man a drink? Even the score a little."

"Fair enough," I said. With that, Casey took a step back, and I pulled out my wallet. When I handed the old guy a twenty, he thanked me, turned around, and went back into the bar.

Casey, apparently satisfied by this outcome, said, "Try and keep your nose clean, asshole," and walked away with his pal. The onlookers dispersed but not before somebody said, "Fucking yuppies think they own the place."

I hailed a cab.

***

I got home and showered before pouring myself a tall glass of Johnny Walker Blue Label—this too was a special occasion—and flopping onto the couch. Skipping lunch made the scotch work fast, but I decided one glass wasn't enough. I was about to get a refill when the phone buzzed. It was a text from Emma. She'd somehow managed to get a reservation for dinner at eight-thirty at Per Se, one of the best restaurants in the city, to celebrate the end of my ordeal with Boris. How could I tell her the ordeal hadn't ended because Boris had figured out a way to torture me for the rest of my life?

He must have used his one phone call after his arrest to call someone and tell them to deliver the envelope to Neil's office. He could have used his phone call to have me killed. I almost wished he'd done that instead.

I decided to put off my second glass of scotch until dinner. Slurring my words while explaining to Emma how my career had just crashed into the side of a mountain didn't sound like a good idea. Maybe I shouldn't tell her until my fate was decided by the management committee and the NY Bar Association. With four hours to think about it, I lay down on the couch and closed my eyes. Pretty soon, I found myself drifting off to sleep.

It was during that twilight between waking and sleeping that I had a terrible thought: If I got fired and lost my license to practice law, I'd need to live off my savings. But my savings were no longer my savings. Leslie had taken it all.

My eyes popped open and I sat up, fully awake, my heart pounding.

I had to find Leslie. Again.

CHAPTER 34

Gabriella answered on the fourth ring. "I'm assuming you butt-dialed me," she said, "so I'm hanging up."

"Wait!" A few seconds went by. "I need your help."

"What now?"

"I need you to find Leslie. She's …"

"Find Leslie? Didn't we just see this movie? Together? Not much of an ending—you survived, and I'm in trouble with the cops for killing Leo."

"What do the cops want with you? You're a licensed PI carrying a licensed pistol."

Silence.

"Oh shit, Gabriella, tell me you're licensed."

"Of course I'm licensed! But the gun, I took it off a drug dealer years ago when I was a cop. Serial number was filed off, so I figured it was finders keepers." She grunted. "Actually, I knew better, but I liked the gun, a Sig Sauer Automatic, so I kept it. Anyway, the DA is giving me shit."

"Did they charge you last night?"

"No. Pete, my cop friend who came to the warehouse last night, he vouched for me, so I'm pretty sure I'm not going down for murder. But they temporarily revoked my PI license, and they're thinking of charging me with unlawful possession of a firearm. No good deed goes unpunished, am I right?"

"Maybe Aiden can help. I think he's got a friend in the DA's office."

"Already called him. Anyway, I can't work for you, so you'll have to get someone else to find Leslie."

I didn't want anyone else. Gabriella taught me that working alone isn't always the best idea, and I liked her. She was good. She was smart. And she'd saved my life.

"Hey, how come you have to find Leslie again?" she asked. "Boris got arrested, Leo's dead, there's no more threat. You still in love with her or something?"

"No, I'm not still in love with her."

"Yeah, right," she snarked. "If you're not in love with her, why the manhunt?"

"Because." I sighed. "I gave Leslie all my savings. A quarter million dollars. She said she needed the money to buy back the ring, and I believed her."

"So she played you for a quarter million dollars, had you pass a counterfeit ring to Boris, and almost got you killed in the bargain?"

"I guess that's one way to look at it."

"For chrissakes, Hank, that's the only way to look at it!" she shouted into the phone. "And if you're not still in love with her, why the hell would you give her all that dough?"

"I don't love her," I protested, registering the lack of conviction in my voice. "It's … it's complicated."

"Sounds simple to me."

I pulled the phone from my ear and lay down on the couch. Maybe Gabriella was right, I thought. Sure, I'd fallen hard for Leslie when we first met. And when she walked out on me, she broke my heart. For a while, she was a habit I assumed I'd never kick. I hadn't thought about her for a long time, but when she showed up in my office, it was like a reformed junkie running into his former dealer.

Gabriella said, "Hey, you still there?"

I sat up and said, "It doesn't matter whether I'm still in love with her or not. Leslie stole my money, and I need it." I filled her in on how Boris managed to fuck up my career at Loveless, Brown.

When I was finished, Gabriella said, "What a mess."

We sat in silence for a few seconds. Then she said, "I'm sorry for your troubles, Henry. Real sorry. But I'm not the one to help. Besides, I didn't get much sleep last night, what with all the gunplay and cop interrogations and stuff. I'm too tired to look for Leslie today. Or tomorrow, for that matter. Or ever, now that I think about it."

That was when I played my ace. "In my book, you're the only one to help. We're kind of a team, and I want to keep that going. We're both in the same boat—not being able to work for a while, I mean. I don't know about you, but with my savings gone—"

"I'll get by somehow. So will you."

"Yeah. But wouldn't an extra two million dollars make it easier?"

She went silent. I heard her kid in the background, whining that he was missing a birthday party. She shushed him. "Where you gonna get that kind of money?"

"There's a four-million-dollar reward courtesy of the FSB. That's the Russian security agency.

"I know what the FSB is."

"Right. Anyway, when we find Leslie, we find the ring. Either she has it, or she can tell us where it is, or at least where to start looking. Be nice to walk out of the Russian embassy with all those rubles."

She paused. "Why not just ask that chubby actor, whatshisface? Doesn't he know where she sold the ring?"

"Todd? Maybe," I said. "But I'd rather not tip my hand and have Todd muscle in on the reward. We find Leslie, get my money back, and find out where the ring is before she realizes what we're up to."

"It's not a sure thing."

"Worth a try, though." I listened as she shushed her impatient kid again. "You still there?" I asked.

"I'm thinking." There was a long pause. Finally she said, "When was the last time you saw Leslie? Not talked to her on the phone, actually laid eyes on her."

"Yesterday morning. At about ten-thirty. That's when she handed off the ring."

"She's had twenty-four hours to make tracks. She could be soaking up sun on any beach in the world."

"Or she could be buying suntan lotion at the drug store across the street from Missy's apartment. Or at the Russian embassy filling out the reward claim form."

"Maybe. My hunch is she's rabbited by now, but anything's possible with that crazy dame of yours."

"Ex-dame."

"If you say so. Anyway, we should leave now before the trail gets cold."

Neither of us had a better idea where to start, so we made plans to meet outside Missy's building and go up to her apartment together. Missy might know something, or maybe we could pump the doorman for information. Or maybe we'd get lucky, and Leslie would still be there.

Before hanging up, Gabriella said, "You know, Henry, finding Leslie is one thing. Getting her to give back your money and spill the whereabouts of the ring? That could be another story. We may have to threaten her or rough her up. You good with that?"

Twenty-four hours earlier I might have said no, because maybe deep down I did still love her. Since then she'd double-crossed me, stolen my money, and handed me a fake ring knowing it was a one-way ticket to a shallow grave in a vacant lot. I was finally getting the picture, all framed up nice, something I could put on my nightstand as a reminder. I meant no more to Leslie than the cigarette ashes she'd ground into Missy's couch with the heel of her hand.

"Sure," I said. "If playing rough is what it takes, I'm fine with it."

I was tired of being in love with Leslie, the way you get tired of loving your special teddy bear when you're a kid. One day you come to your senses and realize it's nothing but a stuffed toy that's old and ratty and smells like baby drool. That's when you know it's time to put what's left of the teddy bear on a shelf. Or in the trash. For me, Leslie's time had come.

CHAPTER 35

There was no sign of Gabriella when I arrived at the building, so I sat down on a nearby bench to wait.

Despite Emma's best efforts to soothe my wounds, my face was starting to hurt badly enough for me to crave whiskey, but I would have settled for a couple aspirin. The pain was creeping into my head like a scarab beetle working its way up my nasal cavity in the hopes of reaching my brain. Every now and then the beetle would stop, have a look around, back up, nibble around the edges before resuming its journey brainward. Five minutes later, two beetle friends crept into my inner ears and began heading toward each other like they planned to meet mid-brain for a reunion. I noticed a drug store across the street, and a few doors down from that was a bar. The drug store seemed the better choice, only because the bar didn't appear to be open.

Gabriella was heading toward me. "You okay?" she asked as she sat down next to me. "Your face looks like it could be in a butcher's display case next to the ground pork."

"Difference is the ground pork's been put out of its misery."

"Yeah, you're right. Coulda been worse though. Good thing I showed up last night when I did."

"Twenty minutes earlier you might have spared me the facial."

"Really? Last night you were all 'Thank you, Gabriella.' Now you accuse me of dereliction of duty? I had to get my kid to bed."

I smiled at the thought of Gabriella tenderly tucking her kid in one minute and the next minute less tenderly killing the bad guy and saving me. "Ya know, you never told me your kid's name."

"You're on a need-to-know basis when it comes to my private life, remember?"

"Still? After all we've been through together?"

"Yeah, still, and until further notice. We're not foxhole buddies yet."

"Okay, got it." I started to stand up, but Gabriella grabbed my arm, so I sat back down.

"I forgot to tell you. This morning, I got a call from the detective who worked me over last night. Told me they got an anonymous call on the tip line around midnight. The tipster said there was a dead body in the warehouse and gave the address, and that Boris was the doer. Sounds like whoever called was thinking Boris killed you."

"Was the caller male or female?"

"Yeah, I asked. The caller was muffled, but according to the detective, it was a woman, or maybe someone trying to sound like a woman."

"So it could've been Leslie, or Todd, or someone else."

She shrugged. "My money's on Leslie. With you dead and Boris arrested for your murder, she'd have nothing to worry about from either of you. Seems to me she was making sure the cops knew about what went down at the warehouse, even though she got it wrong. The dead body wasn't you."

"Did the detective say if there were any other calls?"

Leslie was supposed to call the cops at eleven if she didn't hear from me. If she called, maybe she was on the level, and Gabriella and I had it wrong.

"Didn't mention any. Maybe I should ask." She stood up. "C'mon. We got work to do."

We walked to the building in silence, which gave me time to think about why Leslie would call the tip line about a dead body, assuming it was her. I decided what Gabriella had said made sense—she wanted to make sure Boris wouldn't come looking for her. What better way to take him out than to finger him for my murder?

When we got to the entrance, I told the doorman we were here to see Missy and Leslie in apartment 11A. He stared at my cut-up face for a few seconds, probably trying to figure out if I was trouble, and if so, how much. He stole a glance at the bat leaning against the wall next to his right hand. When he looked back at me, I pushed through the pain to flash him a smile, the peacekeeping kind. That seemed to do the trick because he picked up the intercom handset, dialed the apartment, and put his hand over the mouthpiece. "Names?" he asked.

"I'm Henry, and this is my girlfriend, Gabriella." He announced us over the intercom and told us we could go up. I asked if it was Leslie who'd answered, and he nodded. I told him to have a nice day. He didn't reciprocate.

We stepped into the elevator, and I turned to Gabriella. "What's our play?"

She considered the question for a second, then said. "We accuse her of fucking you over. She'll deny it, but we keep up the third degree until she breaks."

"That'll never work," I said. "Nobody pulls off a lie like Leslie. And we'd need the doorman's baseball bat to break her."

She looked at me hard. "Don't tempt me."

The elevator doors opened, and we walked down the hall without a word. I knocked on the door. Leslie opened it, and before either of us said anything, she stepped out and hugged me. I didn't hug back, just let my arms hang there. She stepped back into the open doorway and said, "Oh my god, Henry, I thought you were dead!" Then she noticed my face and gasped.

"Yeah, he took quite the beating last night," Gabriella said, elbowing Leslie aside and stepping into the apartment. "Thanks to you."

"Thanks to me? What the—who the hell is this bimbo, Henry?"

"She's a friend," I answered. "Gabriella Lopez."

"Nice to meet you, Gabriella Lopez. Now get the fuck out."

I walked in and pushed the door closed.

"Gabriella stays," I told her. "Siddown. We need to talk."

She put her hands on her hips and glared at me, then at Gabriella, and then back at me. "Fuck you both."

She started to open the door to let us out, but Gabriella grabbed her arm and muscled her away from the door toward the couch.

"Ow," she said, "you're hurting me, you bitch! Henry—"

"Sit your ass down," Gabriella commanded. Leslie tried to twist out of her grip, but she might as well have been trying to slip the jaws of an alligator. After a second, Gabriella pushed her down onto the couch. "Sit down," she said again, standing over Leslie, fists clenched. When Leslie started to get up, Gabriella said, "Don't."

Leslie sat back down and crossed her arms. "What the fuck's this chick's story?" she mumbled.

Gabriella held her threatening pose. "Tell her it's none of her business."

"It's none of your business," I said, pulling up a chair. "But I got another story for you."

Leslie glared at me. "Skip it," she spit.

"Once upon a time, there was a beautiful, conniving woman who stole a ring from a Russian mobster. The mobster demanded she return it, but she'd sold the ring to a Saudi prince and didn't have the money to buy it back. So she asked her ex-husband, who she knew to be a stand-up guy, for money. And he gave it to her."

"Henry, for chrissake, whatever you're doing, stop."

"Almost finished," I said.

She looked away. I wanted to smack her.

"Now, where was I?" I asked myself aloud. "Oh, right. So the standup guy still cared for his ex-wife and didn't want to see her hurt. So he offered to return the ring for her. And that's when it all went to shit, because she'd given him a fake."

She turned her head and looked at me, eyes wide. "What? I didn't …"

"Shut up," I barked. Leslie squirmed but stayed quiet, so I continued. "The Russian got very, very angry, and the standup guy realized that his ex-wife not only scammed him out of his life savings but left him to the mercy of the angry Russian, who proceeded to beat the living shit out of him."

"I swear—"

"And the standup guy was almost killed," I shouted. "But at the last minute he was saved—by his private eye friend. The end."

Leslie turned away and sunk deeper into the couch.

I said, "Pretty good story, don't you think? Wanna hear the epilogue?

"No!"

"Epilogue: The ex-wife is tried, convicted by a jury of her peers, and sentenced to a long prison term."

"Bullshit, Henry," she said. "I didn't steal your money. I used it to buy back the ring! And I didn't fake anything!"

I scoffed. "Oh yeah? The ring was easily identified as counterfeit by Boris's jeweler."

She looked surprise. "Really? The ring was counterfeit?" Her eyes darted from me to Gabriella and back. She looked like a frightened rabbit facing a wolf-pack and coming to the saddest of all conclusions.

We had her.

But, true to form, Leslie didn't give up. Instead, she started talking fast. Fast and desperate. "Wait," she said. "I know what happened. The Saudi kept the real one and gave me a fake. Sonofabitch. It was definitely him. That's the only thing that makes sense."

I shook my head.

"Henry, you have to believe me. Boris is crazy, but I figured once he had the ring, he'd let you go. It had to be the Saudi guy—he sold us a fake ring!"

I couldn't believe she was trying to talk her way out of this. "Why would a Saudi sheik scam you? Like he needs the money? C'mon, precious, you can do better than that."

She held up her hand. "Wait," she said again. "It must have been the go-between. Remember? We didn't deal directly with the Saudi. We never met him, only some guy he told us to deal with. The go-between." She was talking straight at me, as if Gabriella wasn't there. "I thought the guy looked shady from the get-go." She put a hand on my knee. "Maybe you should go look for him. Not sure where he lives, but we met in a hotel lobby."

I removed her hand and turned away from her in disgust. Then I stood up, took out my phone, and began punching in numbers. Leslie looked wide-eyed at the phone. "Who're you calling?"

"The cops. It's over."

Gabriella put her hand on my phone. "Wait a second," she said. "I just thought of something." She looked down at Leslie. "Tell me about how you got the ring back."

"What?" Leslie hesitated. "How do you think I got it back? I found the Saudi, agreed on a price …"

"How'd you contact him?"

"Ya know something? I don't have to answer your questions."
She started to stand up, but Gabriella pushed her back on the couch.

"Yeah, you do. And don't fuck with me."

Leslie looked at me. "Henry, tell your—"

"Answer me!" Gabriella shouted.

She took a moment to glare at Gabriella before answering. "I called him. Well, not him exactly. Like I said, he had this go-between. Todd still had the number."

"So Todd gave you the go-between's phone number, and you called him."

Again Leslie hesitated before answering. "No, it was Todd who contacted him. Todd told me the guy wanted half a million for the ring, twice what he'd paid for it."

"Yeah? And then what?"

"I had to find the money. Luckily Henry came through, otherwise—"

"I know that part." Gabriella shot me a look. "Yeah, I can see Henry being a soft touch." She looked back at Leslie. "So you got the money. Then what?"

"I sent a wire transfer like they asked. Todd got the ring from the go-between and then brought it to me."

"Where'd you wire the money?"

"To the Saudi's Swiss bank account."

"The Saudi sent you the number?"

"No, I got it from Todd."

"Todd gave you the account number." Gabriella looked at me, but I couldn't read her. She said to Leslie, "Okay, I think I got the picture."

Gabriella motioned me away from Leslie and we took a couple steps toward the kitchen.

"Looks like we mighta got this wrong," Gabriella said softly, her head bent close to my ear. "The night we grilled Todd in the cab, he told us he thought Leslie was crazy to try and buy back the ring. Said he walked away after he gave her the contact information and never heard from her again. He said he washed his hands of the whole thing. But Leslie says he arranged everything, including the wire transfer. It's possible Todd could have had the money wired to his own bank account. He took a picture of Leslie's ring when she first brought it to him, remember? It would have been a cinch to hand the photo to one of the Tiffany jewelers and get them to whip up a cheap lookalike." She shook her head. "It's possible that fat fuck lied to us."

"Hey, what are you two talking about?" Leslie called out.

Gabriella ignored her. "Could be Todd took all the money, the whole half million. Then he told your chump of an ex-wife he'd done the deal and gave her the fake ring that she passed on to you. Todd knew Boris was violent. He probably figured Boris would most likely kill the two of you when he found out it was a bogus ring. All Todd had to do was hope you didn't rat him out to Boris before you died. Not a sure thing, but not a bad bet, either."

I nodded. "If you're right, then one of them's lying. So now what?"

She shrugged. "Let's keep her talking. She might know more than she's letting on."

Gabriella turned around and walked back to where Leslie was sitting. Leslie turned her body away.

"Look at me," Gabriella commanded, and Leslie turned her head. "Did it ever occur to you that Todd had you wire the money to his account, not the Saudi's? That maybe he hadn't contacted the Saudi at all?"

"No." Leslie shook her head emphatically. "He would never do that to me."

"Not even for half a million dollars? Honey, I know people who'd kill you for fifty bucks." Gabriella chuckled. "I can't believe a smart-ass like you fell for it."

"Fuck you, I didn't fall for anything," Leslie shouted, then looked at me. "That's not what happened. I would have known if Todd was trying to pull something."

"Oh yeah?" Gabriella shot back. "How?"

Leslie didn't answer. Instead, she went quiet, as if she was digesting everything Gabriella had said. It was a lot to digest, a big meal that didn't go down easy. She bent over and stared at the floor like there was a movie on it. Maybe she was in the movie, and maybe Todd was, too, and maybe it told the story of how she got taken for a ride by someone she thought was her friend. "Well … I guess he could have done it," she said to the movie screen on the floor. "I wonder if he's still in the city." She sat up, looked from Gabriella to me and back. "I could call him."

Gabriella seemed to consider that for a few seconds. "Yeah, what the hell," she said. "Call him. If he answers, which I doubt, make it sound urgent. Maybe get him to meet you somewhere." With the hint of a smile, she added, "And while you're at it, get him to confess."

Leslie looked at me. I nodded my encouragement.

She stood up, pulled out her phone, and, nodding at us like she was now part of the good guys' team, punched in the phone number. It was so quiet I could hear my watch ticking. Leslie mouthed, "It's ringing." She held up two fingers. Then three, then four. Todd wasn't answering. I looked at Gabriella. She shook her head.

Then Leslie stopped counting rings and said, "Todd?… Hi, it's me …" She gave us a thumbs up. "Of course I'm alright, why shouldn't I be?… No, Henry went alone, and I haven't heard from him … Yeah, well I wouldn't put it past Boris to do something like that." She walked toward the window but spoke loud enough for us to hear her. "We have to talk … No not later, now … Where the hell are you anyway?… Okay, I'm taking a cab over right now. Be there in twenty minutes … Fuck 'em, say you have to take a break, it's an emergency." She turned to look at us and nodded her head. "Yeah, an emergency. I'll tell you when I get there."

She hung up. "That motherfucker—he was definitely surprised to hear from me. He thought I went with Henry last night and … oh my god, that motherfucker, he set me up. I could kill him." She tossed her phone on the table. "He's at the theater. Rehearsing. And now he's expecting me. You guys better hurry." She rattled off the theater's address.

I turned toward the door, figuring Gabriella and I would go together, but she stopped me.

"I can handle this, Henry," she whispered. "I want you to stay here with Leslie in case she tries something. She's slippery and there's a good chance she's the one lying."

"Got it," I whispered back. "Text me when you know something."

"Will do."

Then Gabriella bolted out the door to find Todd.

CHAPTER 36

The door slammed shut. Leslie and I looked at each other. At that moment, I didn't know which would surprise me more— learning that Todd took my money and plotted my murder, or that Leslie didn't. Either way, I couldn't shake the feeling that I was still getting played, and that I was in for one more surprise.

I wanted to hear from Gabriella that she'd found Todd and he confessed. And that Leslie, as bad a person as she was, hadn't stolen my money and sent me to the warehouse to die.

I sat down on the couch to wait for Gabriella's text.

Leslie sat next to me. "Now do you believe me when I tell you I didn't do anything wrong?" She put her hand on my knee again, but this time I left it there. "How could I? You convinced me that running was a bad plan because I'd never get Boris off my back. That the only way out was to get him the ring. I even called the cops, at eleven on the dot, like you asked. They told me there were already officers on the scene. It's funny, but in the end I did everything you said."

I nodded, because I didn't feel like talking. Leslie got the message, and the two of us sat there silently, waiting for Gabriella's text. Waiting for all the lies to lift like a 4 a.m. fog.

My phone was on vibrate, and for the next twenty or so minutes, I kept feeling a phantom vibration in my leg—my leg wanted to hear from Gabriella as badly as I did.

Finally, I got the text from Gabriella.

Theater's locked up, nobody's here.

Leslie lied

Also, heard from detective

Analysis proved tip line caller female so could have been Leslie

Definitely not Todd

No other calls regarding warehouse

Leslie had just told me she called the cops at eleven like I'd asked her to. According to the detective, she didn't. I was about to confront her with her lie when my phone buzzed with another text.

Don't say anything until I get there and don't do anything stupid

I shoved my phone in my pocket.

"Gabriella?" Leslie asked.

I nodded.

"What'd she say? She find Todd?"

I didn't answer.

The corners of her mouth dropped, and her eyes widened. "Why are you looking at me like that?"

I stood up. "Gabriella didn't find Todd," I said, trying to hold my temper, "but you knew that. In fact, you knew Todd had nothing to do with this."

"What? What are you saying?"

"Todd's not at the theater."

"Todd lied to me again? I'm calling him back." She got off the couch and reached for her phone, but I grabbed her arm and spun her around to face me.

"You didn't call Todd, you only pretended so you could send us on a wild goose chase, leaving you free to run, isn't that right?"

"Of course not!" she shouted, pulling away from me. "Todd said he was at the theater rehearsing—why wouldn't I believe him?" She pointed to my phone. "Text Gabriella, tell her to try his apartment."

"Stop it!" I fought the urge to slap her.

"Don't look at me like that. You're scaring me," she said.

"Oh, you're scared, are you? That's probably a first. Let's keep this scared thing going until you tell me the truth."

"You've got this all wrong, Henry. I want Todd nailed just as much as you do. Can't you see we're on the same side?"

"Really? I don't think so. You not only lied about calling Todd, you lied about calling the cops at eleven."

"What? No!"

"This whole caper, it was you all along, wasn't it?"

She didn't answer. She didn't have to. Her face told me I was right.

I took another step toward her. Backing away she stumbled but managed not to fall. I glowered at her, daring her to lie some more.

"It's not what you think," she cried. "I didn't want you to get hurt."

"No? Then why'd you drag me into this?"

"I needed money—I went to your office to ask for money. They threatened me, Henry. I was scared. I didn't think they'd go after you."

"What? Bullshit. I seem to recall you saying they would kill me, too. Isn't that what you said?"

"I thought it would convince you to give me the money."

"But when I didn't—"

"That's when I ran—if you hadn't found me none of this would have happened."

"So now it's my fault?"

"You should never have helped me. You should've let me run."

Hearing Leslie say it made me realize what a patsy I'd been. I could have avoided the whole thing if I'd just stayed out of it, not given her any money, not fallen for her in the first place. I was beaten. "Thanks for the advice, but you're too late," I said. My head sagged, and I put my hands over my face for a few seconds. Then I looked up. "Why couldn't you just buy back the ring and be done with it?"

"Because—" She hesitated. "Because the Saudi wouldn't sell—I thought we had a deal but then he ghosted me. His go-between disappeared. I had no choice," she cried. "I had to have a counterfeit made because the Saudi wouldn't sell me the real one."

I looked at her, incredulous. "Wait. The counterfeit ring was you?"

She put her hand over her mouth, as if realizing she'd said too much.

I started shaking with anger. "And you gave me the ring, kissed me goodbye, and sent me off to Boris, knowing he'd kill me as soon as he realized it was fake?" It took me only a few seconds to put it all together. "You knew that when he finished with me, he'd come after you. You needed Boris out of the way, so you called the police tip line and told them I was dead, that Boris did it. You were making sure he'd get arrested for my murder, that he'd end up in prison and not be able to come after you." She shook her head, but I wasn't buying it. "With me dead, Boris in prison, and Todd none the wiser, you were left with all the money, totally in the clear." I pushed her away. "Great plan. I'm curious, how'd you come up with it?"

From behind me a woman said, "Actually, was my plan."

I recognized the voice even before I turned to look, but it made no sense. Standing at the bedroom doorway was Boris's Russian girlfriend, Tanya. And she was holding a gun.

CHAPTER 37

"Hands in air, motherfuck," Tanya said, arms outstretched, both hands on the gun. I raised my hands above my head.

Leslie walked over to Tanya. "Took you long enough," she said.

"You tell me stay out of sight until they leave. You say you get rid of them." She gestured at me with the gun. "This guy still here. What the fuck?"

"He was supposed to leave with that bitch he brought with him."

"They find out truth. Is no good," Tanya said. "Ruin everything."

"Now's not the time for you to lose your shit, Tanya," Leslie said calmly. "We'll leave just as soon as we take care of Henry."

"Take care of me how?" I asked.

"I'm still working on that." Leslie held out her hand. "In the meantime, give me your phone."

I kept one hand raised and got my phone with the other. "I gotta say, I'm surprised to see Tanya here. I assumed you worked your grifts alone. And isn't she in Boris's posse?"

Leslie ignored the question and dropped my phone into a small purse sitting on the coffee table. "Lie on the couch, face down."

When I didn't move, Tanya took a threatening step toward me and gestured to the couch with her gun. As I stepped around the coffee table, I tried to think of some way to separate Tanya from her weapon but couldn't come up with anything. Once again, facing danger, all I could do was stall—and hope Gabriella rescued me again, this time without her gun. I started to lie down with my feet toward the door. Before my head touched the pillow, I sat up and reversed my head and feet. When I started to switch again, Tanya said, "Enough. Face down on couch, or I shoot you now."

"Don't make me lie face down," I pleaded, pointing to my messed-up face. "These cuts and bruises are still fresh." I lay down on my side facing the room. She grunted but let it pass.

My line of sight across the coffee table led directly to Tanya. She was wearing white denim shorts and a Grateful Dead tee shirt. My first thought was she wasn't tan like Leslie. My second was that the coffee table might splinter her shins if it slammed into them with enough force. I glanced up at Tanya's face, then focused on the gun. Any sudden movement, and she might shoot me. I lay still.

As Leslie hurried into the kitchen, she said over her shoulder, "Don't shoot him unless you have to." I heard her opening some drawers and cabinets. "Shit," she said loudly. "I know there's some rope around here somewhere."

I called into the kitchen, "You never answered my question— why is Boris's girlfriend here? Are you guys working with Boris?" Leslie didn't answer. She just kept rooting around the drawers.

Tanya answered. "We work with Boris? Ha! You are so stupid," she said smiling slightly. "Boris is big asshole."

"He certainly has his faults," I said. "Are you guys ripping him off somehow?"

"Gun is from Boris. He taught me to shoot but always is hiding gun. I find it, rip him off." She smiled again. "And bullets. I take bullets, too. But nothing else."

Leslie stepped out of the kitchen. She put her hands on her hips and scanned the apartment. "Where the fuck is that rope?"

I tried again. "Don't tell me that you and Leslie are lovers."

"You are serious?" Tanya snickered and rolled her eyes. "This is favorite American boy fantasy. But we disappoint you. We are not lovers." She smiled and seemed to be enjoying our little game. "You never guess it, not in million years."

That was when it occurred to me—I'd seen that snicker and eye roll combination before. I looked up at Tanya, then Leslie, then back again at Tanya. She was, in fact, a younger, blonde, less striking version of Leslie.

"Ya know, you guys kind of look alike. Maybe you're cousins or something. Is that it?"

Tanya's smile disappeared. I was close.

"Oh my god," I said. "Is Leslie your sister?"

Tanya's eyebrows shot up.

"Impressive, but not quite," Leslie said. "We're half-sisters."

I thought back to the first time I saw Tanya, when she and Leo stopped me on the street near my apartment. Something about her had reminded me of Leslie, but I'd never connected the dots.

"Wait a second," Leslie said. "Missy's always doing her fucking jump roping in here—it's annoying as hell." She opened the coat closet, knelt down, and began rummaging around. "Found it." She stood up holding a yellow braided nylon jump rope with red handles and went into the kitchen. Twenty seconds later she came into the living room with a length of rope in each hand. "Okay, Henry, let's get you bound and gagged up so we can get out of here before that bitch of yours comes back."

"You never mentioned a half-sister," I said. "You told me Tanya was—"

"I lied." Leslie came and stood over me, holding one length of rope and tossing the other behind me. "Truth of it is, we have the same father. When he died, Boris got Tanya out of Moscow and brought her home." She began looping the rope around my wrists. "Everything was hunky dory. Then one day, I caught Boris coming out of Tanya's bedroom, zipping up his fly. That's when I left. Tanya stayed. Claimed it was love." She pulled the ends of the rope tight around my wrist, and I grunted.

"I was stupid teenager," Tanya said.

"You were a child," Leslie snapped. "I shouldn't have left you with that fucking maniac. Hey, what's the best kind of knot for this?"

"If you're asking me, I'd say probably a square knot," I offered, knowing it would be easiest to slip out of.

Tanya launched a big smile. "Was me who knew why Boris wanted ring. For reward—four million American dollars. But Leslie knows where ring is, so we escape from him and get reward," Tanya said. "Then we will be very rich, richer than Boris."

Leslie snorted. "Well, no, but rich enough," she said. "Shit, I don't know how to make a square knot."

"Any knot is okay," Tanya said. "But what about something in mouth to keep this guy from screaming help. Like tennis ball."

I lifted my head off the couch. "Whoa, hold on, that'll break my jaw for sure. How 'bout a scarf," I suggested. "Or a rag, preferably a clean one."

Tanya pulled a kerchief out of her pocket. "Here, my donation to effort." She let it fall on top of me. "What is plan for him after tying up?"

Leslie, still focused on knotting my hands, said, "We knock him out and throw him in the bedroom closet. That'll give us enough time to get away."

"I knock him out with gun," Tanya offered.

"Something heavier would be better." She stopped to think. "I know. There's a big cast iron frying pan under the sink. That ought to do it."

That would more than do it. If they whacked me hard enough, they'd kill me. I started to protest when a sound more like a thud than a knock came from the apartment door. Someone put a key in the lock and turned it. Tanya glanced over her shoulder. Leslie got up and was rushing toward the door when it swung open and almost hit her.

It was Missy.

She walked into the apartment holding a grocery bag in each arm. Tanya swung the gun around. Missy screamed and dropped the bags.

With Tanya distracted, I sat up and used both feet to slam the coffee table into her shins. She let out a howl and fell forward, crashing onto the coffee table. There was a sharp crack followed by the acrid smell of gunpowder.

Tanya grunted as she pushed herself off the coffee table and pointed the gun toward Missy, who was whimpering on the floor. I shook the rope from my wrists before lunging across the table and grabbing Tanya's right leg below the knee with both hands. "Son of bitch!" she shrieked and kicked at my shoulder, but I held on, sliding my hands to her ankle and yanking hard. The gun fired as she fell, and I threw myself at her. She jerked away, rolled over, and tried to stand, but I pulled her back down. Straddling her, I locked onto her wrists and put my full weight into slamming her gun hand against the floor. The gun fired again, but I kept whaling on her hand until she screamed out in pain and let go of the gun. When I reached for it, she shoved me aside and leapt to her feet.

That's when I felt the pain.

Like someone was hammering a white-hot spike into my thigh. I begged whoever it was to stop but they just kept hammering. I tried to stand but nearly fell when my left leg buckled. Blood was seeping through my jeans, and pain was spiraling from the entry wound into my stomach, groin, chest, and a couple of body parts I hadn't thought about in years. I leaned on a chair to keep from falling.

Forcing myself to look up, I spotted Leslie lying on the floor, not moving, eyes closed, hands holding her blood-soaked shirt. There was a puddle of blood on the floor, and it was growing. Kneeling beside her, crying and chanting her name over and over like a mournful prayer, was Tanya. When she saw me watching, Tanya screamed curses at me in some crazy combination of English and Russian. After finishing my tongue-lashing, she bent over and kissed Leslie's cheek before jumping up and running for the door. By the time I pointed the gun, she was gone.

The place was a mess—Missy's grocery bags had exploded on impact. A container of fresh blueberries had burst and hundreds of them dotted the floor. Missy was lying on her back in the middle of the scattered groceries, not moving, staring at the ceiling. She blinked. I asked if she was okay.

"I think so." She sat up and looked around. "Oh my god, you're bleeding," she gasped. "I'm calling 911." Before dialing she said, "You should get a tourniquet on that. I'll get a belt from the bedroom."

The floor started coming at me, but I was determined not to pass out and dropped to my hands and knees.

Leslie's purse lay next to me on the floor, and among the contents that had spilled out was my phone. I picked it up and called Gabriella. She answered on the fourth ring. "It's Henry. Where the fuck are you?" I shouted.

"Jesus, Hank, use your indoor voice. I'm still six blocks away. Be up in a few."

"No," I yelled into the phone. "No, stay down there! There's a blonde girl in a Grateful Dead T-shirt and white shorts coming out of the building any minute now. Grab her." Then I added, "She shot me and Leslie."

"What? You got shot? How bad are you—"

I hung up. Missy was back from the bedroom, holding a belt and reciting her address into the phone. "And please tell the ambulance to hurry," she said. "I already told you. She was shot in the stomach! … Yes, with a gun! … How should I know? A handgun I guess … Okay, thank you." She pulled the phone away from her ear. "On their way."

"They say how long?"

"Five minutes. Hold still while I get this on your leg." She wrapped the belt around my upper thigh and cinched the belt tight. "There, that ought to do it," she said, then looked at my face. "Wait, how do I know you?" Her eyes narrowed for a second. "Oh my god, you're that guy who came into the store asking about Todd! What are you doing here?"

"Right now? Hoping I don't die."

Leslie was only a few feet from me, but even so, dragging myself over to her with a bullet in my thigh was torture.

"Leslie," I said as I got close.

She opened her eyes. "Henry." Her eyelids drooped, then shut completely. Her lips tried to form a smile but didn't quite make it. "Is this how it ends? With you and me on the floor, bleeding to death?" She coughed once. "You didn't shoot Tanya, did you?"

"No. She got away."

Leslie opened her eyes. Her breathing was shallow but steady, her face gray crepe paper. Gently, I lifted one of her hands. A single glance at where the bullet had hit her was all I could take.

She must have seen me grimace. "It's bad, isn't it?"

"Doesn't look that bad to me," I lied. "The ambulance'll be here any minute."

Missy had crouched down next to me, listening.

"Missy," I said sharply, "see if the ambulance is here."

"Um, right, sure thing," she said, getting up. I heard her open the door. "You sure you're okay?"

"Just go," I answered, and she left.

"Henry?" Leslie whispered.

"Yes, I'm here."

"You're not going to turn me in, are you?"

"Don't worry about that now."

"We can blame this whole thing on Boris, then me and you can get the reward. I'm the only one who knows where the ring is. Nobody else'll find that Saudi prince in a million years."

"Sounds good," I said.

"Then we can leave the country, just me and you. Start over. Won't that be grand?"

"I can't wait."

"Hold my hand, will you Henry?" I reached for it and squeezed. She didn't squeeze back.

***

The siren sounded close and far away at the same time. I felt the ambulance round a turn going very fast. There was a guy sitting next to me, taking my pulse. My leg was throbbing. Gabriella was there, too. I tried to sit up, but the guy put a beefy hand on my shoulder, and I lay back. I turned to Gabriella. I tried to ask about Leslie, but nothing came out. The ambulance took another sharp turn, which almost made me puke, but I must have passed out first. When I came to, they were wheeling the gurney through the emergency room. Gabriella was running next to me yelling at someone. I tried to speak to her. She looked down at me. "You're gonna be okay. They're taking you to surgery."

"Call Emma," I mumbled. "Tell her I have to cancel dinner tonight."

"Who's Emma?"

Before I could answer, everything went black.

***

Next time I opened my eyes, the sun was shining through a window. I looked around the hospital room, but there wasn't much to see. The bed next to me was empty. There were flowers on a small table in the corner of the room, and next to it an orange chair that looked barely comfortable. A nurse stood next to me, fussing with the plastic bag dripping fluid into me through a tube attached to my forearm. She was thin, dressed in light green scrubs with a vee neck, and she had skinny arms. Her brown hair was pulled back and plaited, and she looked kind of young. Maybe she wasn't a nurse. Whatever she was doing must not have been going well, because she stepped back, put her hands on her hips, and glared at the contraption.

I tried asking a question to get her attention, but all I could manage was a painful one-syllable rasp. She looked at me and smiled, then said something incomprehensible to me, so I tried to smile back hoping to keep her engaged. It didn't work. She stopped smiling and hurried from the room. I closed my eyes.

When I woke up, Gabriella was sitting in the orange chair. "Look who's back among the living," she said.

"You call this living?" I managed, my voice still straining, and she smiled.

"How do you feel?"

"A little loopy."

"That's the morphine. You got a morphine pump next to you in case you start feeling pain. I'm sure the nurse will explain. I'll get her." She started to stand up.

"Wait. Am I okay?"

"Doc says you're gonna be fine." She sat back down. "They had to operate to stop the bleeding, but the bullet missed the bone. That's a good thing. He says you'll have to use a cane for a few weeks. Big scar but no limp."

"Where am I?"

"New York Presbyterian, the one downtown. It was the closest."

"You manage to find Emma?"

"Yeah. I called Aiden, figured he'd know, what with him being your best friend and all. Turns out she's Aiden's ex. How 'bout that for a coincidence," she said, scolding me with her eyes. "Anyway, she's getting us some coffee. Should be back any second."

I dozed on and off until the door swung open. I opened my eyes in time to see Emma backing into the room holding a cup of coffee in each hand.

She saw me and cried, "You're awake!" She broke into a smile that warmed me inside. "Oh, thank god." She handed a coffee cup to Gabriella, then came to my bedside, put her hand on my arm, and leaned over to kiss my cheek. Her face hovered next to mine for a few seconds. "You okay?"

"Never better."

"I doubt that," she said and smiled. She pulled an empty chair up to the bed.

I looked over at Gabriella. "Tanya?"

"In the wind."

"Boris?"

"Still trying to make bail."

"Leslie?"

She shrugged. "Intensive care's all I know."

I nodded. The three of us were quiet. Gabriella took a sip of her coffee and grimaced. "Even I make better coffee than that," she said, putting down her cup. "Anyway, time to pick up my kid at school, so I'm outta here. I'll come by tomorrow and see how you're doing. Nice meeting you, Emma. You have my number if you need me." She got up and put her hand on the doorknob, hesitated, then turned around and faced me. "I just gotta ask you something. Missy told me

Leslie was conscious before the ambulance came, and she seemed to be telling you something."

"Just that she was sorry. That's all."

Gabriella tilted her head almost imperceptibly. I knew that move. She didn't believe me. Then she shook her head and pushed open the door.

"Wait," I called.

She stopped.

"Thanks."

"For what?"

I remembered what had happened when I'd tried to hug her after she'd shot Leo and saved my life. "For coming by," I said.

She snorted. "Don't mention it."

When the door closed, Emma turned to me and said, "She's a piece of work."

I smiled. "I'm glad you guys met."

"Really? Why?"

"It was time."

"Would have been better meeting her over a cup of coffee instead of over your shot-up leg." She smiled. "Hey, when you get out of here, we need to reschedule our dinner. And by the way, I'm forgiving you for standing me up last night."

"Aren't you an angel."

"Always," she said, and kissed me again.

CHAPTER 38

They had me up and using a walker the next morning. With Emma by my side, we walked around the eighth floor and everyone we passed eyed me with concern. But they nodded their encouragement, and the nursing staff cheered my progress as if I were a toddler taking my first steps.

Outside of my mandatory marching around the floor, nothing much happened the first couple days of my hospital stay. But on day three, Nancy appeared with a bunch of roses. After we talked for ten minutes, she got quiet. "Henry, I have something for you."

She reached into her purse and pulled out an envelope with my name on it. "Neil's assistant dropped it off and said to mail it to you, but I knew you'd want to see it." She handed me the envelope. It had been left unsealed, so I flipped it open and pulled out the single page of firm stationery, addressed to me from the management committee. The letter was short and impersonal. The first sentence said I was fired. The second said they would not be referring me to the New York Bar Association. The third wished me the best of luck. I crumpled up the letter and tossed it toward the small trash can across the room. It went in.

Nancy apparently knew what was in the letter because after I read it, she just sat there quietly staring at her hands. I sensed she didn't know what to say, so I broke the silence. "What happens to you now that I'm out?"

She looked up, and I could see the relief in her eyes. "Oh, I'll be fine," she said, recovering her composure. "They'll put me in the temp pool until something permanent comes up."

After chatting awkwardly for a few minutes, she got quiet again, so I said I was tired even though I wasn't. "Henry ..." she said but didn't finish the sentence. Instead, she leaned over, gave me a hug and said goodbye. As she stood to leave, her eyes watered up. I wished her the best, and I meant it.

On day four, when Gabriella came for her daily visit, I told her I'd been fired, but not why. I also told her I planned to hang out a shingle, but only if I found an investigator who had the goods—someone I'd get along with who was smart, tough, and could get the job done. "Know anyone who fits that description?" I asked, with a grin.

She hesitated. "Well, that's out of nowhere," she said. We looked at each other, me waiting for a definite answer, Gabriella apparently considering my offer—or maybe she was just thinking about her kid. "I know better than to make deals with guys hopped up on morphine. We'll talk when you're out of the hospital." Then she smiled. It wasn't a big smile, but it was enough to give me some hope.

"Hey," she said, voice low. "I didn't want to bring this up in front of Emma, but I'm pretty sure you lied to me the other day about your conversation with Leslie after she was shot. Am I right?" I said nothing. "Thought so. She didn't happen to say anything about the ring or the reward, did she?"

So Gabriella was still interested in the reward. Of course she was. After all, I'd promised her half if she helped me find Leslie. Gabriella had held up her end. I wasn't going to lie to her. "Leslie said she'd tell me where to find the ring if I'd split the reward with her."

"Seriously? She didn't understand she was in a shitload of trouble?"

"No, I think she knew she was in trouble. Why else would she ask for my help?"

"Oh, I get it," Gabriella said, crossing her arms. "Leslie gives you the Saudi, goes to prison, and you deposit her half of the loot in a bank account for her when she gets out." She shook her head.

"That's what Leslie wanted, but it's not what went down. Leslie was trying to play me. Again. She wanted me to lie for her, tell the cops she had nothing to do with what went down—the fake ring, the shooting, my stolen money. She wanted me to point the finger at Boris, concoct a story that he did the shooting, even though it was Tanya. As if anybody'd buy that fairy tale. But she didn't say anything that would lead me to the ring."

"Leslie goes to jail without telling us where the ring is. We don't get the reward. Not my idea of a happy ending." She shook her head. "Hey, what the fuck was Tanya doing there anyway?"

"She's Leslie's half-sister."

"Her half-sister? Didn't you tell me Tanya was Boris's girlfriend, the one he imported from Russia?"

"Well, yes, but she's still her half-sister." I repeated what Leslie had told me—that she'd asked Boris to find her Russian half-sister in Moscow and bring her to Long Island. And how the visit turned into an affair between Tanya and Boris, which is why Leslie left him.

"How in the hell did you ever fall for a crazy dame like Leslie, anyway?"

I shrugged. Even though I knew the story—how we met, our affair, getting together after she left Boris—I couldn't explain how I'd fallen so in love with her that I was blind to who she really was. "She's a survivor," I said. "And I give her some credit for caring about Tanya."

"Both of them are batshit crazy if you ask me."

Later, as she was about to open the door to leave, she stopped. "Shit, Henry, there's gotta be some way we can track down that damn ring."

"I wish there was, Gabriella. That reward was half yours if we found Leslie. Sorry it didn't work out."

Gabriella dropped her head to her chest. A few seconds later, her head popped up, eyes wide. "Todd knows where the Saudi is! He made the original contact, remember? Maybe we can use that to track him down. We'll have to cut Todd in on the reward, but hey, a third of four million dollars is better than nothing. That work for you?"

"Sure. Why not." I doubted Todd knew enough to help. But it kept Gabriella and me together just a little longer. Maybe she'd come around.

***

By day five, I was starting to feel more myself. Even though my leg was still throbbing, the lightning bolts shooting from my knee to my thigh were gone, and I could take a deep breath without wincing. The surgeon came in, unwrapped my bandage, and after several minutes of careful examination pronounced my surgical wound "a thing of beauty, no sign of infection, and healing nicely." When he asked about my pain, I told him it still hurt but the morphine helped.

Shortly after the doctor left there was a knock at the door. I was hoping it would be Emma, but in walked Peabody, the detective who'd grilled me in Queens.

"Why it's Detective Peabody!" I sneered, bracing myself for trouble.

"Hello, Henry." She greeted me like we were old friends. "How's the leg?"

"Lovely of you to ask. My leg's fine."

"Good to hear. I was shot once, took a bullet to the shoulder, so—"

I interrupted. "Enough chitchat. Why are you here? Hold it, I don't want to know. Whatever it is can wait until I'm fully recovered—five or six years from now."

"Funny," she said, sitting down in the orange chair and crossing her legs. "When I heard you got shot, I figured it was connected to the shitshow at the warehouse. So I thought I'd come around and ask you a couple questions."

"Read the statement I gave to the cops. Everything you need to know is in there."

"I read the statement. Sounds like your ex-wife was the center of the storm, but you barely mentioned her to me."

True, I'd kept Leslie out of it during Detective Peabody's interrogation. But in my statement to the cops about what went down at Missy's, I'd given it to them straight. My statement was so clear even the rookie cops would get it: Leslie stole my money and tried to get me killed.

"Leslie wasn't at the warehouse," I said, "and you were focusing on what happened in there."

"Or maybe you were protecting her." She narrowed her eyes. "Were you and Leslie working together?"

I bristled. "That's idiotic and you know it."

"Hey, I'm just trying to piece things together."

My leg started to ache again so I pushed the button and took a hit of morphine. "Let me set you straight, detective. Leslie conned me into giving her all my money. She played me for a sucker. If you don't believe me, you can ask her yourself when she's out of intensive care."

She looked confused for a second, then said, "Um, she's out of intensive care."

291

"She's out?"

"Leslie's, uh—." Her voice dropped almost to a whisper. "She died this morning."

"I'm sorry, what?" I scanned her face for some sign she was lying because she had to be lying. "If you're trying to trick me into talking, that's a pretty fucking cruel way to do it, even for you."

"It's the truth, Henry. Leslie's dead."

I felt my face flush as the shock of it shook my body. Until then I'd assumed if Leslie made it to the hospital alive she'd be okay. Gabriella had said she was in intensive care when I'd asked about her but said nothing about her condition or her prognosis. I'd taken that to mean she was recovering. My eyes watered, and I put my hand over my face, both to hide my tears and to be alone with my grief. I hated Peabody for telling me, and I wanted her to disappear.

My eyes fluttered and closed as the morphine settled in, gently lowering me into a semi-conscious dream. I was standing on a country road. The sun had just set, and it was growing darker. At the end of the road was a woman walking toward me, a wraith lit from behind by a rising orange moon. As she got closer, I saw it was Leslie. She had on the same white chiffon blouse and dark blue pencil skirt she wore that day we went for lunch at the dumpling restaurant. And she was smiling the way she had that day, smiling a smile so subtle you wouldn't know it was there. I spun around, hoping she'd disappear from my sight, but everywhere I turned, there she was. She stopped and stood there on that dark road, hands on hips, and made me look at her one last time.

Detective Peabody stayed quiet. If she was waiting for me to open my eyes, she was in for a long wait. Through the morphine haze I heard her say she was sorry about Leslie. I stayed in my dark place. She waited some more. I heard the door open. "We're not done, Henry," she said. "You and me, we got unfinished business. I'll be in touch."

As I drifted into a deeper sleep, I wondered whether Leslie would still be alive if I hadn't tackled Tanya, if that stray bullet had never been fired. But I guess somebody was bound to end up dead that day. I was just doing everything I could to make sure it wasn't me.

CHAPTER 39

Four days later I was off the opiates, taking ibuprofen for the pain, and anxious to be sprung from the hospital. It wasn't until late afternoon that the doctor showed up to take a last look before discharging me. He explained that I'd need physical therapy for several weeks to fully recover. I shook his hand and thanked him. He nodded to Emma, who'd been listening at the foot of the bed, and left the room.

Emma handed me a shopping bag with my clothes and helped me get dressed. She collected my razor and some other items from my night table and put them in her oversized leather shoulder bag. Even though I was ready to go, the nurse had told us I had to be escorted out of the hospital, so we sat on the bed and waited.

Five minutes later there was a knock at the door and in walked a beefy guy with a beard who introduced himself as "Jack from hospital transport." Jack looked capable of carrying me down the eight flights of stairs without breaking a sweat. Instead, he stepped into the hall and reappeared with a wheelchair. I stood up, put my weight on my new aluminum cane, and took a step. "Thanks," I said, "but I think I can get myself to the elevator."

"Hospital rules," he replied. "You ride the chair."

My cell phone rang. When I saw it was Gabriella calling, I asked Jack to give me a minute, and he stepped back into the hall.

Gabriella was calling with an update. "I told Todd about the reward, and he gave me the Saudi's info right away. I texted, then called, but the guy's phone was disconnected, so I contacted some of my people on the ground …"

"You've got contacts in Saudi Arabia?"

"Yeah, some of my Marine Corps buddies found work there after they finished in Afghanistan. Anyway, they said they'd check it out for me. Turns out the Saudi prince was arrested. Seems he rubbed somebody in the royal family the wrong way."

"That's not good."

"It gets worse. Everything the guy owned was confiscated, probably sold. Or maybe it was all given away as party favors at some royal birthday party. Who knows? No telling where the ring is, but at least we got the name and number of the guy, and we know he's been arrested. You think that's enough intel to get us the reward?"

Unlikely, but I didn't have the heart to say it. Instead I said, "Only one way to find out."

"Okay. I'll wander into the Russian embassy and say I've got a lead on the ring."

I told her to keep me posted.

"Was that Gabriella?" Emma asked, and I nodded. "What'd she want?"

"Nothing," I said, then added, "I'll tell you later."

Jack wheeled me into the lobby, and we waited while Emma hurried ahead to find a taxi. From the look of it, summer still gripped the city. Everyone entering the hospital was shiny with perspiration. Sweat dotted the institutional green scrubs worn by the doctors and nurses returning from their cigarette breaks. Outside, people were moving in slow motion, the humidity making it seem like the sidewalk was at the bottom of a swimming pool. Moms in shorts and tank tops pushed strollers, ferrying toddlers dazed by the heat. Businessmen in suits had their jackets slung over their shoulders.

Smartly dressed women carrying department store shopping bags shaded themselves with brightly colored umbrellas.

Jack steered the wheelchair through the automatic glass doors and out into the heat and humidity, the smell of rotting garbage, and the roar of traffic. Emma was standing on the sidewalk next to the taxicab. She opened the door, and Jack held my arm to make sure I got out of the wheelchair and into the cab without further injury. He handed me the seat belt, wished me luck, and slammed the door shut. I thanked him with a wave and buckled up, happy to be out of the hospital and back in the rapidly beating heart of Manhattan.

The cabby asked where we were going, and I gave my address, or started to. Emma interrupted and gave a different address. I shot her a glance.

She smiled. "I made a six o'clock reservation. We were supposed to have a celebration dinner the night you ended up in the hospital, remember?"

I remembered, but more than anything else, I just wanted to go home. "I'm hardly dressed for dinner," I said.

She checked out my denim shorts, white polo shirt, and the big white bandage on my leg. "You'll be fine."

The cabbie drove uptown on the FDR. The midday sun reflecting off the whitecaps made the East River appear to be throwing off sparks. We took the Sixty-First Street exit, swung north to avoid a stalled garbage truck, and continued crosstown on Sixty-Third until turning left onto Fifth Avenue. Traffic was heavy, and we stopped at every light. I didn't mind—the sights and sounds of the city soothed me. I felt my life sliding back into place, like a misaligned drawer that had been returned to its runners. On my right, acres of trees, grassy fields, bicyclists, kite fliers, hot dog vendors, sunbathers, roller skaters, and little kids with ice cream cones dripping down their arms and onto their sneakers swept by. On my left, stood hundreds of multimillion-dollar apartments stocked with people rich enough, or lucky enough, to wake up to a view of Central Park.

We drove south past the park to Fiftieth, where the cab pulled up to the entrance of the Peninsula Hotel. Emma jumped out of the car, raced around to the other side, and helped me up the steps and into the lobby. She went to the front desk and came back a minute later waving a key card. We took the elevator to the seventh floor and found the room. "It's ours for two nights," she said, beaming as she opened the door. "And this time, I expect your undivided attention."

She'd booked a suite, lavishly appointed, with all the trimmings. I whistled.

"Jesus, Emma, this place must have cost you a fortune."

She grinned. "I do business with the hotel. They gave me a pretty sweet deal. And even if they hadn't, you're worth it."

While Emma ordered room service, I strolled around the suite, checking out the bedroom, the bathroom (jacuzzi, steam shower, bidet), and the view of midtown Manhattan from the living room window. It wasn't home, but maybe it was just what I needed after all.

I walked over to the bar and was pleasantly surprised to find it fully stocked. Emma was still on the phone, so I poured some vodka into a pitcher, filled it with ice, and stirred. Then I located a jar of olives and a couple of martini glasses. When she saw what I was doing, she put her hand over the phone. "Hey, should you be drinking? I mean, after all the painkillers? Maybe it's not such a good idea."

"Nothing about it on my discharge instructions," I lied. "And what's a celebration without a few drinks?"

I filled the martini glasses to the brim and carefully handed one to her. She finished the call, put down the phone, and raised her glass. "Here's to a speedy recovery," she said. We clinked glasses, trying, unsuccessfully, to keep from spilling.

As I drained the martini, I thought about how the last couple of weeks had changed everything. I'd lost my job and most of my life savings. Aiden hadn't visited me in the hospital, so maybe I'd lost my best friend, too. On the other hand, while getting fired stung, it wasn't like I was in love with the job. Maybe lawyering on my own would work out, especially if Gabriella was part of it. And I'd find a way to make ends meet until I got back the money Leslie stole.

But I wasn't getting Leslie back. Nobody was.

From the day we met to the day she left me was only a couple of years, but when Leslie poured herself into my life, I was filled to the brim. Now, there was still some of her inside me, like the tiniest drop of vodka that clung to the bottom of my empty martini glass.

I closed my eyes, raised my glass, and gave a silent toast. Cheers. Here's to my new life.

"Hey," Emma said. "Where'd you go?"

"Sorry." I leaned in for a kiss. "I'm back."

The end.

ACKNOWLEDGMENTS

"The Violence That Finds Us," written by Harry Crews, has haunted me since I first read it in 1984. In the essay, Crews describes a bar fight he had with a stranger. He did not initiate the fight, but confronted with possibly mortal danger, he had to deal with it. As I sat down to write this novel, I knew only two things: my protagonist would be an average guy who would end up in deep trouble through no fault of his own, and he would face, for the first-time, life-threatening violence. How, I wondered, would he react?

I have many people to thank. My writing group, who listened to me read aloud every scene in the book (and many that didn't make it in) over the course of three years: Lisa Mayer, Jessica Rao, Lynn Edelson, Nan Mutnick, Reyna Gentin, Jerry Brody, Marshall Messer, and Ed McCann. Their criticisms, suggestions, and encouragement were inspirational. I consider the leader of the group, Steve Lewis, to be my writing guru. He marked up every page I wrote, and brilliantly.

My editor, Jane Rosenman, who criticized every aspect of the book and forced me to make it better. Her guidance was invaluable. Thanks also to Nina Bodway, my copy editor, who rearranged my commas and so much more.

Thanks to Brian McLendon and Claire Chun at Ulysses Press, who guided me throughout the publishing process; and Keith Riegert, CEO of Ulysses Press, who chose, to my surprise and delight, to publish the book.

Several people read early versions of the novel and assured me that I was on to something good: Maryann C. Bohr, Rina Terry, Abby Livingston, and Larry Bell. Special thanks to my daughter, Thea, for reading several iterations of the novel and applauding them all without reservation; and to my daughter, Julia, for her love and support throughout the writing process. Finally, the biggest thank you goes to my wife, Carrie, who has read nearly every word I've ever written and has never failed to praise me when I deserved praise and gently redirect me when I messed up. She is my first and most important reader, as well as my muse and soulmate.

ABOUT THE AUTHOR

Art Bell is a writer and former television executive known for developing and launching the Comedy Channel (later Comedy Central) while at HBO; and, as president of Court TV, overseeing daily live courtroom coverage and the production of hundreds of hours of original true-crime television series, documentaries, and movies. His memoir *Constant Comedy: How I Started Comedy Central and Lost My Sense of Humor* was a finalist in the 2020 Best Book Awards in both the memoir and business categories. Bell has had short stories, nonfiction, and satire published in several journals, including *Lowestoft Chronicle*, *Aethlon: The Journal of Sports Literature*, *The Ocotillo Review*, *Fiction Southeast*, *Castabout Arts and Literature*, *High Shelf Press*, and *Writers Read*. *What She's Hiding* is his first novel. Bell lives with his wife, Carrie, in Park City, Utah.